THE

Garland Ball

THE
Garland Ball

CONNOR FALLS CHRISTMAS SERIES
BOOK THREE

Robin Maderich

POTTER STREET BOOKS
ZIONSVILLE PA
2025

ISBN: 979-8-9914596-7-9

© 2025 Robin Maderich
All rights reserved.

Printed in the U.S.A.

Cover design by Robin Maderich

Potter Street Books/Robin Maderich Publishing
www.potterstreetbooks.com

"Sometimes the best Christmas present is
remembering what you've already got."
— **Cathy Guisewite**

AUTHOR'S NOTE

Life is full of stressors. We all know this. Sometimes, especially during the holiday season, those stresses are amplified. Amplified when, in all honesty, they shouldn't be. Even so, they happen. Planning and implementing all those things we do to make the holidays special can cause the pressures to build up. Love, hope, friendship, family, and certain welcome surprises are exactly what we need to help us remember the value and joy in this wonderful time of year.

Have a delightful Christmas, everyone. Happy reading!

All the best to you,

Robin Maderich

Chapter One

Cindy thumped the weighty cardboard box in her arms onto the counter, causing the paperwork inside to surge against a corner gap barely held closed by aging tape. She patted the papers back in with ginger movements before smoothing out the label on top. She didn't recognize the writing on it, although she suspected the lovely cursive belonged to the committee's former secretary, Eleanor— Eleanor Barkley, keeper of so many things for so many years. Beginning long before Cindy's time, certainly. When this box had been packed up, stored away, the contents, the reasons for them, hadn't even been on Cindy's radar. At ten years old, she'd been too busy with softball to show any interest in the Garland Ball. Fancy gowns, worries about dates and partners, back then she'd pretty much shunted off such considerations as unimportant, something for old people.

And now here she was, thirty years later, getting ready to dig into a carton filled with aged notes, searching for the secret to the Garland Ball's erstwhile success, as well as the reason it had drifted into non-existence, hoping she could somehow ward off failure. Because now, three decades after, Connor Falls as a community had not only voted to celebrate the antiquated and the defunct by reinstating the gala event but had elected her as chairperson.

Sure, she'd passed certain remarks at the last town meeting. Suggestions, really. Apparently, opening her mouth at all had resulted in the impromptu motion to have her spearhead the committee to bring the ball back to life. She could have declined, but after speaking her mind she felt somewhat responsible, too. After all, her suggestion the Garland Ball could be good for local businesses had carried the day.

Sinking her teeth into her lower lip, Cindy lifted the scissors, turned the shiny tool in her fingers. To be honest, the Garland Ball would be especially good for Cinderella Silks. Cindy had known that, even before this last meeting. Despite her disinterest at an early age in fancy gowns, she'd taken up sewing over softball in the eighth grade and by the time she'd reached high school was making custom clothes for classmates. Cindy had kept up the income-producing practice through college, and upon return to Connor Falls had officially opened shop. Tailor-made clothes—ironically, yes, even fancy gowns—hadn't brought in money hand-over-fist initially, but in time she'd been able to expand and hire assistants to help manufacture her designs. When Gran and Pop closed their dry-cleaning business, Cindy rented the entire building from them, establishing a roomy brick-and-mortar home for Cinderella Silks. And for herself.

Cindy snipped the twine, then positioned the scissors for a jab at the golden-yellow tape, reminding herself one more time it was in her best interest to make this darned ball a success. The shop owners had left the decision rather late, though, bringing it up for final vote at the October meeting. Tentative suggestions had been put forth in the spring. Spring would have been a great time to begin the process. The first week in October, not so much.

Shattering under the blade, brittle tape flaked off in an oddly shiny mess onto the counter. Ten seconds later, what little remained had been stripped away from the box top and Cindy opened the flaps. A musty aroma assaulted her nostrils. She drew back with a grimace. This box would have to be aired out before digging into its contents. Somewhere else, somewhere not in the store. The front door opened while Cindy hurriedly folded the flaps back down.

"Dan," Cindy said to the man entering the store steering a hand truck loaded with boxes. "Hi."

She'd known Dan Hayes since they were kids together. They'd been classmates most years and friends even when they weren't. All of which was now a long time ago. Still, they'd remained friends whose lives crossed with smalltown frequency. She probably knew astonishing little about his adult life considering how close they'd once been. At this moment the most relevant was the fact he owned the thriving printing business down the street. At the recent town meeting, he'd announced he would print the posters for the upcoming Garland Ball at a discount. They all appreciated it, and this was one thing Cindy could check off her to-do list right away.

"You didn't have to deliver them," Cindy said when he wheeled the cart up to the counter. "I could have sent someone or got them myself."

He stepped up close enough to the counter she thought she heard his boot tap the farmhouse table leg. "Not a problem," he responded with a grin. "I needed the fresh air."

She could smell the crisp, autumnal air on his clothes, along with the pleasantly light cologne she'd noticed on him recently. The scent made her think of granny smith apples. Thanking him, she slipped around the counter and lifted the first box, settling it beside the ancient carton. Dan quickly piled the next two on top.

"That one's a bit ripe," he said, pointing to the decrepit container holding Eleanor's notes.

"I have a feeling Eleanor might have stored it in her basement," Cindy said, wrinkling her nose.

Dan laughed, his somewhat unruly brown hair dipping into his eyes. He pushed the strands away before reaching inside his coat and drawing out an envelope with the printshop's logo on it. "No rush on this," he said, handing her the bill.

"No need for you to pay out of your pocket. Catch up with me once those ticket sales start coming in."

Thanking him again, she slid the envelope into her pants pocket. "That reminds me. I need to get to the bank and find out exactly what's needed to open an account for an event of this nature."

"Can't help you there." He took a backward step, dragging the wheeled handcart with him. "You need anything else, though, you just give me a shout."

"I will," she said.

"I mean it."

Cindy smiled. "I know."

She watched him as he continued to back up toward the door, the cart in tow. Several feet shy, he paused, shifting his weight from one foot to the other. His mouth opened. The door did, too. Jasmine marched in, skirting Dan and the cart and balancing two coffee cups in one hand.

"Hey, Dan," Jasmine said, "what's up?"

He pointed at the counter. "Just dropping the posters off."

"Fabulous," Jas enthused, backing up to elbow the door open again. She held it wide. "Now all we have to do is get people to put them up."

He said something to her Cindy didn't quite hear as he departed. Out on the sidewalk, he waved again and trundled the cart away.

Jasmine crossed the carpeted floor at a swift clip in her three-inch heels and deposited both coffee cups on the counter. Her long brown fingers continued to circle one of them as she eyeballed Cindy's hasty box removal. "Whew, that stinks! Is that the stuff from the former ball committee?"

"Former seems like an odd term," Cindy said, holding the box up against her chest, her eyes nearly stinging. The stench would permeate clothes, for sure. She needed to get it someplace else fast. "Former sounds like it was last year or something. But yes, it is. I didn't realize it would stink so bad."

"Where are you going to put that?" Jasmine raised the coffee cup to her lips. "Not anywhere near the merchandise, I hope."

Cindy rolled her eyes. "For now, in the bathroom. I'll take it upstairs later. Shakespeare won't be happy, but maybe I can put an open box of baking soda inside for a bit."

"Are you kidding?" Jasmine shot after her. "You'll probably find Shakespeare rolling in the paperwork like it's catnip."

"Good point," Cindy agreed, moving on. Passing through a storeroom filled with dresses hanging on racks, bolts of fabric and boxes concealing miscellaneous items, she made her way to the bathroom, where she set the carton for the Garland Ball temporarily atop the sink. She made two trips back into the store, returning with the boxes filled with the glossy posters Jasmine had designed. She piled those on the floor and put Eleanor's carton on top. Sometime in the upcoming week, the posters needed to be distributed to shop owners for their windows. It had been agreed they would go up before Halloween to get people thinking about and buying tickets for the ball well in advance, especially since Cindy required an accurate number for the attendees before finalizing, well, nearly everything.

Grabbing the lavender-scented air freshener, she spritzed a lethal dose on Eleanor's carton. With a hand covering her nose, Cindy stared at the haphazardly tucked lid. Her thoughts went for the hundredth time to the monumental tasks still ahead. Realization didn't help her stress level one little bit.

Another stressor? The fact she needed a date.

Cindy backed hastily from the bathroom and shut the door. A date. To guarantee increased ticket sales, raising more funds for a local charity which supplied food to those in need. Made sense. Great cause. And a date could be anyone. Mrs. Gregory had said she'd bring her well-trained French bulldog and put him in a little doggie tux. In reality, it was anticipated folks would be bringing their life partners or a special someone or even just a hopeful or a friend. The ball was supposed to be a somewhat romantic holiday event, after all.

Yeah. Not happening. Not for her. She didn't have her eye on anyone, nor did she have the time to scout out a potential. Any friends she possessed already had their own significant others. Some, like Jasmine, seemed to have a few, which suggested to Cindy maybe they were not so significant. At least, not in the way Cindy viewed the role. Besides, Cindy was way too busy and her free time only promised to dwindle to nothing as the holidays approached. Especially with this whole Garland Ball extravaganza.

Thank goodness for Jasmine. Cindy meant the sentiment with all her heart. In her deepest aggravation-filled moments, she meant it. In her happiest days, she meant it. Jasmine had been her best friend since second grade when a girl behind her at the water fountain tried to take a shining hank of Cindy's nearly black hair from Cindy's head. Jasmine had stepped in. There hadn't been a fight. Jasmine had a way of diffusing everything and everybody, with a smile, a few words, through the vast impact of her physical presence. Yes, even back then.

Before returning out front, Cindy paused to check herself in a nearby mirror, because this was another thing Jas had she didn't. Flair. Sure, Cindy dressed well enough, designed outstanding clothes, but she'd never much cared for making a statement on her own. She preferred the background to the forefront, a place in the shadows near the door rather than center stage. A quiet, semi-invisibility.

Smoothing her short dark hair, patting down the bangs, she made a face at the pale silver strands which had started to infiltrate in the last year or so—and tried hard not to compare her pixie style to the shoulder length tresses Jasmine sported, dark brown curls highlighted with a color that made them look as though they'd been spiraled in honey.

Hearing voices through the open storage room door, Cindy backed up and peeked around the doorjamb. Early afternoon was usually a slow time for business and the mail carrier had already come and gone. Still, Jasmine wasn't alone.

A man stood near her at the counter. Despite Jas's height of five-foot-ten plus the additional boot heels, the man still had nearly half a head on her. From the back his golden-brown hair looked thick and well-cut. Cindy knew straightaway the suit he wore had been tailored for him. This was how her eye worked; her mind, too. She immediately imagined pins and pleats and careful stitching on a likely silk and mohair combination with a scarcely visible herringbone pattern. Not cheap, by any means.

From the back, Cindy didn't recognize him. Despite being a lifelong resident, she didn't know everyone in Connor Falls, naturally. But she thought she knew all of Jas's friends. The way Jasmine leaned a bit toward him with a booted foot tipped up and turned out on its toe seemed a clear indication this man was one. Yet, it could be Jas just liked his looks. She always judged a book by its cover first. Intrigued by the exterior, however, she also took time to make sure the rest of him appealed, even if short term.

Not Cindy's way, the quick judgment for

interest. But perhaps her way engaged caution to the extreme. In fact, these days Cindy took a while to warm up to anyone.

She backed up and returned to the bathroom. Turning on the overhead light, Cindy opened Eleanor's gritty, dented, stinking box again. She had only shuffled a few items around on the top when Jasmine called her name from the storeroom.

"I'm in here," Cindy said.

Jasmine didn't answer. Cindy stepped out and stopped short. She dusted her hands off. "Hi," she said, extending her right one and praying the scent oozing from porous materials stored for years in the damp hadn't permeated her skin.

"Hi," the man responded in an odd tone, giving Cindy's hand a swift look before shaking it. "How have you been?" Not how are you, not nice to meet you, but how have you been. Cindy squinted a bit at him.

"Cin!" cried Jasmine. "You remember Harrison Carter, don't you? Harry?"

Cindy's eyes widened. "Harry?" she echoed, staring. "Harry…from college?" Harry Carter had attended Jasmine's college. Cindy's first meeting with him at Jasmine's twenty-first birthday party in the dorm room came back to her in a flash. He'd changed from that memory, a young man in black jeans and a torn tee shirt, hair down to his shoulders and his musician's edgy, lean build. She remembered, too, falling immediately, hopelessly in fascination with him the second he opened his mouth. The one and only time such a thing had ever happened.

Goodness, she'd been an idiot child, reacting more to hormones, she supposed, than common sense. And not quite a child, but close enough. All the years since had provided some perspective on age and the rest. They'd all changed since then. Yet, he was still him. Cindy could see that now. How had she not recognized him right off? Her face heated. She pumped his hand harder until, embarrassed, she let it go.

"Sorry," she apologized. "How are you? It's been… I don't even want to say how long it's been. What have you been up to? What are you doing here in Connor Falls?" Overwhelmed by her own rambling and his height in the crowded space, Cindy waved them both out the door into the storefront and followed, striding up to the counter and her neglected coffee. She took a swig, set the cup down, watched Harry as he did a turn in his expensive shoes to check out the racks and displays. "Really," Cindy said, a little calmer now the fluster had faded, "what *are* you doing in Connor Falls?"

Okay, still rambling. She drank more coffee.

They exchanged a look, Jasmine and Harry did, one that made Cindy lower the paper cup back to the counter. Jasmine was deliberately, purposefully single. She'd never married, unlike Cindy and her one failed but maintaining-friendly-with-the-ex attempt. Jas sometimes dated for extended periods, but most times not. Cindy's gaze shot down to Harry's hand, checking for a wedding band or the pale, telltale absence. She found none. In that fleeting instant it hit Cindy that Jasmine and an unattached Harry might have become an item and

Jas hadn't mentioned it. Why else would he be in Connor Falls?

Cindy met first Jasmine's gaze, then Harry's. Harry's, with the odd eye, one more green in an otherwise blue iris than the other. If there hadn't been a shadow across his face, the anomaly would have been a dead giveaway the moment she'd looked up at him in the storeroom.

"Jasmine invited me," he said. "I had a conference in Philadelphia so she asked if I could drive up afterward and provide the marketing information I prepared for you."

Marketing? Right. He'd been a business major, after all. Music had been his passion. But marketing information he'd prepared for *her*?

Cindy felt an odd shock. Her first thought was to wonder how much this was going to cost. Her second was to question why Jas had arranged this without prior discussion. Her third flitted around the question whether Harry Carter could be content without his music. Not that it mattered or was any of her concern. That was a long time ago. Besides, he looked far from miserable.

Jasmine clung to his arm, her manicured nails a lovely purple shade against the mostly gray hue of his suit. She grinned at Cindy. Grinned. Yep, Cindy recognized two adults happy with each other. Not impossible. She drew in a breath and released it gently through her nose.

"The marketing information," Cindy said, latching onto the subject, pretending she hadn't almost fallen out of her shoes. "It slipped my mind for a second." Cindy sent a quick but significant glance at Jasmine before meeting Harry's eyes again. "You really didn't have to come out of your way. You could have sent the information. It is great to see you, though."

Harry gave her a crooked smile. "I didn't mind. You used to talk a lot about this town. Seemed worthwhile to stop and see it. And I thought I might take the two of you to dinner to discuss. Do you get a break for dinner?"

"Dinner," Cindy echoed, glancing at Jasmine again. Cindy reminded herself she did rely on Jasmine for the marketing side of things. She figured this meeting made sense. Yet, how odd Jas chose to pursue a new marketing angle without consulting her. They should have talked about it. Jasmine appeared to be keeping mum about a lot. "Are you okay with a late dinner?" Cindy addressed Harry. "Or I could try and get someone in to cover while we're gone."

"After you're closed is fine by me," he answered.

Jasmine released her grip on Harry's arm and clapped her hands together in a single, enthusiastic smack. "Great, so that's settled. We'll grab a bite at the pub. See you later, Harry!" He looked a bit surprised at the abrupt dismissal, yet gave a nod and smiled. Jasmine leaned forward and pressed a loud kiss against his cheek.

"The shop is great," Harry said. He backed toward the door, looking more like the younger man Cindy recalled, moving with the remembered, loose-limbed locomotion. Upon reaching the door he straightened, now clearly a professional in a tailored suit. Until he grinned. "I'm glad you followed your heart, and your talent. I still have that jacket you made me."

With a wave he walked out. Jasmine smiled after him as if he'd been a toddler who'd just said something brilliant and amazing. Cindy, on the other hand, experienced nothing but mortification. She didn't remember making him a jacket, couldn't even bring it to mind, and a jacket was no easy thing to make. Hopefully, he didn't bring it up again during this unlooked-for marketing presentation.

"Well," Cindy said, once he'd disappeared down the sidewalk, presumably heading back to his car. Jasmine pivoted on her heel, catching Cindy's wide-eyed stare.

"What?" Jasmine asked.

One of those too-innocent what's. Cindy shifted her weight forward, leaning an elbow on the counter. "We should have discussed this first."

"We did," Jasmine said.

"No," Cindy stated, "we didn't."

Jasmine cocked her head to one side. "Last month, we were talking about new directions."

"Yes," drawled Cindy, "but a whole marketing plan hadn't been part of that. Besides, nothing was solidified. It was just talk."

Jasmine strode around the counter, easing past Cindy to retrieve her abandoned coffee cup. She took a mouthful and grimaced. "Ice cold," she said. "I'm going to dump this down the sink."

"Jas…"

"I know," Jasmine said, pausing a few feet away. "I'm sorry. I just figured this might give you a little push. What you'd been talking about was great, but I knew you wouldn't follow through without some solid information. Some specific encouragement. You know, so you'd appreciate your ideas are wonderful and can be realized."

Cindy blew out a breath. She surrendered. "It won't hurt to hear what Harry has to say, I guess."

"Not at all. And free food. Bonus." Jasmine chuckled and spun on her heel, striding once more toward the storeroom.

"I didn't realize you two are still friends," Cindy called after her.

Jas looked back, tossing her hair. A smile teased her lips. More than friends, the smile said. Cindy determined to get the truth out of her at some point. Or the general gist, anyway. She had no desire for details.

Jas halted suddenly, turned halfway around. "Our parents have been close since before he and I were in college. You knew that. Didn't you?"

Cindy thought a moment. "Nope. I can't say I recall that information ever passing your lips. I have a feeling you hold these conversations in your head and not with me."

"Really?" Jasmine started walking again, but threw another glance back at Cindy. "Well, now you know," she said.

Cindy frowned, reminding herself the annoying requirement for all shop owners to make a good showing, to attend the ball with a partner to increase revenue, had been Jasmine's brainchild.

"So," Cindy called after her one more time, "is Harry going to be your Prince Charming for the ball?"

"Maybe," Jasmine answered over her shoulder before vanishing into the storeroom. "We'll see," her voice drifted out. "It's still a long way off."

Sure, if one called a couple months a long way off. But things changed. With Jas, they certainly could and did. Not for Cindy. She thoroughly inhabited her reality. Static may as well be her middle name. Cinderella Static Michaels. No ambition beyond the life she had made. No Prince Charming for the ball, either.

Not that she wanted one. Shakespeare would look adorable in a little bow tie.

Chapter Two

Cindy huddled against an early October chill at the shop door and watched Jasmine for another few seconds as her friend strode in a swift, graceful pace toward the pub to meet Harry. Halfway to the corner, Jasmine pivoted on her booted heel, cupped her gloved hands to each side of her mouth, and yelled, "Three is *not* a *crowd*!" A startled couple across the street spun and stared.

Three being a crowd had been Cindy's final argument when Jasmine adamantly refused to accept work as Cindy's reason for staying behind. Jasmine claimed Cindy was exaggerating to avoid marketing talk and, really, she was half right. Cindy did want to avoid marketing talk. Besides, the pub would be loud, too loud for business discussion. Several more excuses for not going continued to chase each other in Cindy's head. But making excuses certainly didn't mean she wasn't overwhelmed by the work staring at her.

"Have fun," Cindy said with one last wave, after which she zipped inside and locked the door. She stood for a moment hugging herself against the unseasonable chill clinging to her thin sweater and thought longingly about the digital thermostat upstairs and the fact her apartment was already warming up to a cozy sixty-eight degrees. Honestly, she did have work to do, tons. Jasmine knew that. She could get whatever information Harry had to offer from him and bring it back. Besides, if Harry and Jasmine were seeing each other, they didn't need Cindy as a third wheel. So, yeah, three would be a crowd.

With only a few small overhead spots on, Cindy stood in the darkened store and watched several people pass in the street outside. Still hugging herself with one arm, she stretched the other out and flipped the lightweight wooden sign on the door from WE ARE OPEN to WE ARE CLOSED.

Closed. Maybe she was, too. A little more closed than the rest of the world. Recently, she felt as though she'd separated herself from…everything. She'd tried blaming her feelings on her impending fortieth—the day after this ridiculous Garland Ball, in fact—although birthdays had never bothered her before. The work piling up didn't help, either.

Once upon a time, she hadn't viewed her occupation as work. More like a labor of love. An enjoyable way to make a living. Jas had been pushing her to expand, stretch beyond personally supervising her creations from start to finish. Broaden her horizons, according to Jasmine, and give herself a break. Cindy didn't want to. She liked the hands-on. Now, she worried the marketing plan Jasmine had kept secret might be devised to push her to take Cinderella Silks in the direction Jasmine envisioned.

And it could be the right one. Cindy didn't want to think about the possibility right now. After the holidays would be plenty soon enough.

Abandoning the mental search for cause and effect, she went over to the counter and gave the receipts another look-through, double-checking purchases and deposits were separated. Two dresses ordered tonight. After open house and more interest in the Garland Ball, there would be a lot more. Cindy made a few notes, then stowed the paperwork away and headed to the back exit.

She let herself out, locked the door, then trotted up the metal steps to her apartment on the second floor. Early on, she'd had plans to enclose the staircase, but those plans had been nipped in the bud upon learning she couldn't due to fire code. Descending icy steps in the wintertime had become her sport, like skiing was for other people. People with a life.

Inside, Cindy leaned her back against the closing door until the latch clicked satisfyingly into place. Despite her mood, the sense of home she found in the two-bedroom apartment settled at once deep and warm into her bones. When she'd first moved into the apartment, she hadn't expected to experience that homey feel. She'd left behind a pleasant house on a side road, which Jeremy, her former husband, still owned. She'd had a garden there, and a patio where they would sit on summer nights and have a drink, or eat a grilled meal. Now, in the summer, Cindy scooted a kitchen chair out onto the clanging landing amid potted geraniums and herbs. Somehow, it was perfect.

For a moment she felt downright good about things. Until she thought about Harry and the strangely forgotten jacket, Jasmine's push to expand, Harry and Jasmine and the marketing plans. Oh, yes, and the Garland Ball.

"Argh," she said out loud, like a cartoon balloon had popped up above her head. She tossed her keys onto the counter, sent them skittering past Eleanor Barkley's less smelly box. The open baking soda carton wedged against the paperwork had done its work, along with the sweet fragrance from the lidless, pumpkin-scented candle she'd plopped on top.

Cindy pivoted toward a familiar meow. Shakespeare leaped from his favorite spot on the windowsill and trotted to her side. She scratched his head right down to the white ruff around his neck, then scooped him up and buried her face against his. "What is wrong with me?" she whispered.

The cat chirped, less a purr than a staccato complaint. Not exactly in indifference to this sad woman who fed, watered, groomed, played with, and spoiled him, but in reminder his nighttime snack came first, cuddles later.

Opening the nearby half-empty package, Cindy made Shakespeare sit before tossing him his dental treat. Annoyed and affronted, he took it and returned to the sill.

She knew she should eat, but she didn't much feel like it. Sticking her head in the refrigerator, Cindy rummaged around and finally settled on leftover mashed potatoes. She opened the lid before placing the container in the microwave because a) that's what one did, and b) she couldn't remember how old they were and wanted to check for mold. Yes, soon to be forty years old and this was how she fed herself.

Tapping a fork against her hip, Cindy watched the digital clock on the microwave flicking through the seconds. At the appropriate time, she hit pause, gave the potatoes a quick stir, and started it again. At the ding, Shakespeare returned, having decided to forgive in the hope he might share the meal.

Cindy ate standing up at the counter, another decidedly bad habit. Breathing through an open mouth because the leftovers had gotten too hot, she stared down into the box filled with all earthly remains to the erstwhile Garland Ball. Thirty years ago, this had been the hot ticket item for the holiday season. According to Mom, people had started planning for the next one right after the night ended. Oh, what Cindy wouldn't have handed over to be granted half that time.

Rinsing the empty container, she left it to soak in the sink, downing a glass of water afterward, pretending that made up for the lousy dinner. Patting Shakespeare once on the head, Cindy carried the box into the living room and pulled all the contents from it, lining up paper stacks across the coffee table. A dozen faded red rubber-bands, stiff with dry-rot, feebly collapsed in their duty. The fact the papers didn't shift at all did not bode well for their condition.

A half hour later, after peeling the papers apart with care, Cindy discovered accounting made up two entire stacks. Not bad, considering the Garland Ball had been a yearly event for at least fifteen years.

Others papers held descriptions regarding accommodations, theme, vendor's names for chairs, tables, tablecloths, tableware, music, many no longer in business. Dan's dad had prepared the signs and tickets back then. The sensible part of Cindy's brain recognized how much help she'd need and would no doubt receive. The overwhelmed part struggled against it.

Cindy threw herself back against the couch cushions. Shakespeare squeaked and darted onto the floor. When Eleanor's daughter-in-law had insisted on giving the box to her, Cindy thought it might hold some helpful, essential knowledge. All she'd found so far seemed to be useless, outdated materials.

Sitting forward again, she pulled more from the box and located at the bottom two well-crushed, manila envelopes. Cindy set them aside, but impulsively picked one back up and curled open a flap from which the glue had dried up eons ago.

The envelope held nothing but ancient invoices and receipts. Very thorough had been Eleanor, marking each in pen at the upper right corner with the date it had been received and paid. Unlike the flimsy paper received at the register these days, where the ink vanished before you'd even got it home, Cindy could still read every detail. The difference in cost between then and now astounded her in an entertaining-horrifying sort of way, but otherwise didn't serve to help at all.

Crossing her arms, she turned to watch Shakespeare chase a yarn ball across the rug. Her thoughts drifted to the pub, to the warm, savory food, fodder for future leftovers, and to an image of Jas and Harry, deep in conversation amidst tinkling glass, soft music, laughter. Chuckling maybe about the old workhorse and how she couldn't bring herself up for air long enough to enjoy one fun night. Cindy took a breath, looked around.

Her apartment could be very quiet, especially when seated on the sofa. From the cushioned comfort, she couldn't hear much. The closed store below only released the occasional hum when the heat came on. The third floor, with its sewing stations and pressing machine empty now, didn't so much as creak. No street sounds reached her, no cars rolling slowly by at Connor Falls' improbable twenty mile an hour posted limit, no footsteps, no muffled talk between people walking the sidewalks.

"Hey, Shakespeare," Cindy said, suddenly needing to hear a voice, even her own. She snatched the ball from him and rolled it, smiling as he threw himself onto the soft sphere like a mighty lion on prey. Normally silence didn't trouble her. Normally the evening solitude was her salvation, easing her away from the demands brought about by day-to-day business. She welcomed it, savored it.

Not so much right now.

Jumping to her feet, Cindy raced for her cell phone and dialed Jas. It wasn't too late for dessert, right? It was never too late for dessert. Following several rings voice mail picked up. Cindy didn't leave a message. She put the phone back on the counter, plugged it in to charge. Before she had the chance to walk away, a text alert sounded: Jasmine.

Sorry, it's noisy here. You okay?

I'm fine, Cindy replied. *How's it going?* She waited a bit to see if Jasmine would respond, then a bit more, her feet shuffling her away from the counter, hand extended behind in case the phone sounded its tinkling bells again. It did. She snatched the phone up, turned it over.

This text had a picture of Jasmine's grinning face, and Harry's, leering over her shoulder, expression comical, mismatched eyes staring straight into the phone's camera lens. *Missing you,* Jasmine had written.

Missing you, too, Cindy texted back.

Cindy clicked off the kitchen light and made her way into the living room, where she reached for the lamp beside the couch, planning to shut that one off too before heading into bed. Her gaze fell on the second envelope. She fought it, but its presence called to her in reminder of duty and diligence. Kicking her shoes off, she curled herself resignedly onto the cushions, turned the envelope over in her hands, and allowed the contents to tumble out. About fifty photographs flapped down onto the well-worn upholstery beside her. The noise escaping her mouth caused Shakespeare to rocket beneath the nearest chair, glaring at her in reproach.

After returning everything else to the decrepit box, Cindy clicked on another lamp and spread the photos in a collage across the coffee table's surface. One by one she picked them up, turned them this way and that in the light, focused on the clothing, the women's clothing specifically, and the indication of many styles gone by the wayside. Dated, yes, but intriguing. Some were making an updated comeback.

Cindy leaned her head against the sofa cushions and stared up at the ceiling. A smile curved her lips. To get the signage printed quickly, the committee had wasted no time coming up with the theme of Mistletoe and Memories for the Garland Ball. Now Cindy had seen these photos, it seemed a fortuitously perfect theme.

Cindy's mind shifted from tired to overdrive. At the open house in a couple weeks, she would offer to design gowns for the ball much like those in the photos. For those interested in the retro styles, anyway. The rest could order from what she had on hand. Cindy had a little time to make one or two examples of the older designs before the open house. The high school girls modeling that evening would show them off.

Grabbing pen and paper from the end table, Cindy jotted down notes with bullet points. Next, she shuffled the photos around again, sorting them into piles similar in content and clear enough to retain clarity if copied and blown up. She pictured each photo centered on black poster board—no need for the expense of frames, after all—and placed in a gallery along the hallway leading into the space rented for the ball, or perhaps on a wall inside. Such an exhibit would be interesting, spark some fun conversation. In advance, she'd display them at the open house.

"What do you think, Shakespeare?"

Cindy glanced under the chair. The cat had fallen asleep on his side, feet crossed. A whisker moved in response to her calling his name again, an eye creaked open and closed. Cindy returned to the task at hand, spacing the desired photos evenly across the table again. She slid the others into the crinkled envelope. Eventually, all photos could be put up on the Garland Ball website Jas was preparing. The people in the photos might be identified.

Suddenly Cindy leaned forward, frowning. She stood up, moved to the table lamp, and brought the photo in her hand closer to the bulb. It couldn't be…but it sure as heck looked like…

"Of course, that's not me," she said out loud.

Cindy flipped the photo over, checking for a date and finding one scrawled in black ink. Intently, she studied the two people caught in a complicated dance move, the one who looked like her, and some guy who looked vaguely familiar. The woman's hairstyle was unnervingly like Cindy's own except for the teased-up bit at the top. Cindy reached up to smooth down the silver-flecked hair on her pate.

It had to be Gran. Everyone said Cindy looked so much like Gran. Cindy had access to many old photos over the years. The resemblance had never struck her as unmistakably as it did in this one. Gran gazed at her good-looking dance partner with animation. Not Pops. He'd passed about twenty years after this photo was taken and must have been present somewhere. This was definitely somebody else, somebody she felt she should know.

Who? Cindy cut a glance at the clock. Way too late for phone calls that wouldn't startle people into thinking the worst. This could wait until another day. A day when she might surprise Gran, catch her off guard, see her face when she viewed the photograph. Cindy stood, stretched, gathered up the photos and carried them to the kitchen, setting them down near the phone so she wouldn't forget to take them downstairs. She spotted a missed text from Jasmine.

Get your butt over here. You know you want to.

The text had been sent an hour and a half ago. Cindy thought about Gran, Gran at about Cindy's age, performing gymnastic dance moves with some hot guy late into the night. With a sigh, Cindy shut off the lights, returned to the living room and threw herself down onto the couch. No need to muss the bed. Instead, she burrowed into the blanket she kept on the sofa for nights like these.

Chapter Three

Cindy yanked open the top right drawer in the converted farmhouse table counter. She flinched guiltily and glanced around the store for Jasmine, even though she hadn't yet arrived, having texted she'd be late. Cindy shoved the drawer shut again, closing it on the marketing paperwork Jasmine had delivered the morning after her dinner with Harry, almost two and a half weeks ago. Cindy hadn't looked at the proposal yet and, oddly, Jasmine hadn't asked.

True to form, Jasmine didn't talk much about Harry either. She rarely chatted about the men in her life when they weren't imminently due in the vicinity. Cindy brought up Harry's name once or twice, but the brevity of Jas's responses kept her from furthering the conversation. Which was fine. Cindy knew better than to ask.

Huffing out a short breath, Cindy pulled open the lefthand drawer, the one she'd meant to open, the one holding Cinderella Silks' extra business cards. Yanking out a stack, she slipped the thin rubber band off and fanned the cards out for easy pick up. In between customers, Cindy continued work on the goodie-bags for the open house. Each pastel pink bag received a folded pamphlet, fabric swatches, a votive candle made locally with the Cinderella Silks glass slipper logo on the wrapper, a business card, and a coupon for the customer's next purchase.

With only a handful to go, the church bells several blocks away finished chiming the noon hour. The front door opened. Cindy looked up from her task. Like a willowy Amazonian warrior, Jasmine stormed toward Cindy across the floor, her expression rather alarming.

"What's up?" Cindy said to her, arching a single brow and unconsciously crumpling the bag beneath her fingers.

Jasmine halted several feet away. She held up her hand, her cell phone grasped firmly in it. "I just had to tell Harry you haven't even looked at the marketing proposal yet."

Cindy set the bag down and smoothed the top "Oh, crap, I'm sorry, Jas. Is there a bill inside? I really should have paid it already."

Jas's gaze flared. "There's no bill inside. I dealt with that."

Cindy turned toward the register, opened the drawer. "Then I owe you. I'll get cash."

"You don't owe me," Jasmine stated flatly. "It's handled."

Cindy pushed the drawer closed, her fingers dropping from the register to her thighs. However the payment had been managed, Jasmine shouldn't be responsible for it. Business obligations were clearly delineated. Although Jasmine had a small ownership percentage in the business in recent years, the majority remained Cindy's, as did the financial commitments. "It's not your debt, Jas. I need to know how much it was so I can pay you back, as well as for a notation in the record book."

Jasmine shoved the phone into her coat pocket. She crossed her arms. "Harry didn't charge anything. He did it as a favor to me. And to you."

"To me?"

"To both of us, yes," Jasmine said. "It's not a full-blown projection. Just enough to give you an idea where you—*we* could go."

New directions. Cindy hadn't been wrong about the reason for the marketing plan. Picking up the discarded bag, Cindy finished filling it while Jasmine stared at her. Finally, Jasmine released a long breath. She came behind the counter, yanked out the stool and sat on it, folding her hands on her lap.

"What's wrong, Cindy?" she asked. "Because something is."

Cindy sucked her lips in between her teeth, releasing air through her nose. She didn't want to argue with Jasmine about this. Not right now. Besides, there was so much more going on in her head. "I don't know," she said.

"But there is," Jas pushed. "I don't think I'm getting that wrong."

Cindy shrugged, dropping the business card into the bag's open mouth. "I just wish you'd discussed this with me before moving forward."

Jas wriggled on the seat, settling herself more comfortably. "This isn't moving forward. And I can't really do that on my own, anyway, can I? Cinderella Silks is your baby. It's just some information for your digestion."

"And I appreciate it," said Cindy.

"Something else is up," Jasmine pressed. "Is it your birthday? Your fortieth? You've never cared about birthdays. People get weirded out by them. But I don't. You don't."

"I don't know," Cindy said again. She reached a finger up as though scratching her cheek, hiding the fact she prodded a tear from an eyelash.

Jasmine stood abruptly. She slapped her palms together. Cindy jumped.

"Okay," Jas said, "when you're ready to talk, my ears are right here on my head waiting. Let's get these bags finished up. I think we're going to have a lull until the open house. People are waiting for it. They want to see the clothes. But we've got a lot to do in the next few days. And the girls will be here later for their final fittings!"

Cindy sighed, trying not to be annoyed. She didn't need to be reminded how busy they were. She was as aware if not more so than Jas of everything hanging over their heads. She barely slept at night because of it. Cindy opened her mouth to say as much, but Jasmine spoke first.

"Oh, those prints are done and ready to be picked up. What a fabulous idea! Did I say that? Those, and the clothes and the overall theme. You're a genius."

Cindy laughed. She couldn't help herself, despite the slightly hysterical note it held. Jasmine looked at her with something akin to pity before hugging her. Cindy kept on laughing, her face buried in Jas's perfume-scented sweater. Regaining control over herself, she pulled away.

"Thanks, Jas," she said. "You know what this genius needs? Fresh air. A little walk. I'll go grab the prints."

"Sounds like a plan." Jasmine turned her attention to the remaining goodie-bags. Cindy gazed a moment at her, grateful again for their longstanding friendship, then she grabbed her purse and headed out.

Halfway down the block, Cindy discovered herself striding at a ridiculous pace. Deliberately, she slowed her stride. Looked around. Nodded at people she passed. Breathed, really breathed. In. Out. Glanced at the shop windows, the prime placement of the posters for the Garland Ball. Abruptly, she stopped on the sidewalk and closed her eyes.

"That could be fun," a voice said nearby. Cindy lifted one eyelid, spotted two younger women, barely in their twenties, eyeballing the nearest poster. Cindy reached into her jacket pocket and pulled out a business card. She handed it to the nearest.

"I'm having an open house at my store," Cindy told them both. "You might want to stop by, check things out."

"Cinderella Silks," said the one with the card in her hand. "Cute name. Where are you located?"

Cindy managed to stop herself sighing. Her stomach sank a little. Maybe she really should be looking over the marketing material. "The other end of this block," she advised them. "Three stores up from the corner. You haven't noticed it?"

"We're not from around here," said the other. "When's the open house?"

Not from around here. Cindy smiled in relief. "This Thursday. Starts at six-thirty. There'll be refreshments, a presentation, goodie-bags, three girls from the high school modeling the clothes."

"Sounds great. Maybe you'll see us," said the first one with what sounded like genuine interest. Cindy pulled out another card and handed it to the second, just in case. They both thanked her and left. Cindy could hear them discussing walking by the store to check it out. She went on her way, mouth still curving.

As she passed From the Hart bakery, Cindy noticed the door stood open. The scent from baked goods drifted out to the sidewalk. Cindy slowed her pace again, breathing in the aroma before sticking her head inside, her hand on the doorjamb. Gina Hart stood in the middle of the floor staring at something behind the counter, fists on her hips and a frown creasing her brow. She spun at Cindy's hello, dark hair swinging.

"Hey!" Gina cried. "Nice to see you out and about. Beautiful day."

Cindy stepped into the store. "Something smells good. Who am I kidding? Everything smells good."

"Want a cookie? It's on the house."

With a short laugh, Cindy patted her stomach. "I better not. But thanks."

"I'll have somebody drop off your order for the open house Thursday morning. Does that work?" Gina turned her head to quickly eyeball whatever had her attention at the counter, then looked back at Cindy. "How's the Ball planning going?"

"It's going," Cindy said. "The website for tickets Jas set up seems to be working well. There have been sales already, and questions."

"A lot of work," said Gina.

Cindy made no comment.

Mouth quirking up to one side, Gina asked, "Got your escort lined up yet?"

"Nope."

Gina snorted, turned back to the counter, cocked her head. "Does that look crooked to you?"

Moving to stand next to Gina, Cindy stared at a sign hanging on the wall. Apparently, Gina had a cupcake special coming up. "A little," Cindy said.

"It keeps moving. I figure someone in the shop next door must be bumping the wall." Gina glanced down at Cindy. "My brother-in-law's brother—I guess that makes him my brother-in-law, too? Not sure how that works. Anyway, he's coming to visit with my sister and her husband the weekend after your open house. Maybe we could all meet up late one evening?"

Cindy's thoughts were still on the crooked sign and the fact it kept moving. "Maybe," she mumbled, and stopped herself. She tipped her head up a little to meet Gina's gaze. "Wait. Are you trying to match me up with him?"

Gina's shoulder lifted and dropped. "With this outdated notion you need a date for the ball—"

"Not my idea," Cindy interrupted. "Jasmine's. But it will help raise more money."

"I know," said Gina. "I was there. And I'm not trying to match you up with anybody. He's fun, though."

"Do you have your escort arranged?" Cindy asked her pointedly. Gina shook her head, chuckling. "There you go, then," Cindy said. "Ready made for you."

"He's my brother-in-law's brother. Seems a bit, I don't know, wrong somehow."

Cindy laughed, hard. "He's not a blood relation," she said. "And I don't need anyone to find me a date. I don't really want one, to be honest. Like old Mrs. Gregory and her dog, I'm thinking I'll bring my cat."

"Your grandmother might be a better choice," said Gina. "At least she makes great conversation and can dance."

Oh boy, Cindy thought, in her younger days she surely could. Her lips parted to tell Gina about the photo, but they were interrupted by a customer coming in.

"I'll see you around, Gina," Cindy said, heading for the door. "I'm supposed to be running errands."

Gina waved her out. "I'll give your number to Selwyn. Tell him to call you sometime between now and when he gets here. Wait!"

Cindy did. Gina returned a moment later, a bakery business card in her hand. She pressed it into

Cindy's. Cindy glanced down at a number scrawled across the back.

"I know you," said Gina. "You won't answer if you don't recognize the number. Put it in your contacts. Who knows, you might hit it off!"

Already on the sidewalk, Cindy flapped her hand in a loose wave as she left. "No," she said quietly when far enough away. "No, no, no." Who had the time for this? Not her. She only realized she was growling under her breath when the mail carrier stepping out from the next store gave her a surprised look.

"You okay?" the woman asked.

Coming to a standstill, Cindy focused on the face before her. "Oh, Brenda! Hi. Yes, I'm fine."

"You're sure about that?" Brenda pressed, amused.

"Absolutely," Cindy answered. "Really. Yes. Just…a busy day."

Brenda didn't appear to believe her, but she nodded and patted Cindy on the shoulder before walking away to continue her rounds. Pivoting on her heel, Cindy hurried to Dan's printshop, silently praying she wouldn't bump into anyone else along the way. Reaching the shop, she hustled inside.

Dan stood behind the counter, mouth stretching into a smile when he spotted her.

"I hear you have another order ready for me," Cindy said, returning the smile.

"I do," Dan answered. "Wait a second, and I'll grab it." He went into a back room, returning in less than a minute. "I'd carry it over for you, but I don't have anyone to cover the store right now. The originals are in an envelope in the box. A new one. On the house. I threw that stinky one away."

Cindy strode over, took the box from him. "I don't mind carrying it. The box isn't heavy. Shoot!"

"What?"

"I forgot the check," Cindy said. She'd rushed out in such a hurry, grabbing the check for the Ball account had slipped her mind.

"No worries. I'll run by for it sometime."

Cindy hiked the box up a little against her body, readjusted her grip. "You shouldn't have to chase your money."

"I know you're good for it. I'm not chasing anything. Besides," he added, "I know where you live."

"Ha, ha," she said, backing toward the exit with a grin. He hurried past and opened the door for her, following her out onto the sidewalk. His longish hair blew about his face in the breeze, causing him to swipe it away with his sleeve. His hand dropped to his side.

"Cindy, I wanted to ask you something," he said. "It's kind of silly, but—"

Cindy waited, fingers curled around the box edge. Inside the store, the phone began to ring. He shooed her on her way.

"No big deal. If I remember, I'll ask when I come by for the check." Despite the ringing phone, he lingered a fraction of a second longer before rushing inside to pick up the call.

Cindy watched the door close behind him. She wondered if his question might have something to do with his kids. He had them for Halloween this year and they'd stopped by the store with him for their treat before the costume parade. The eldest, Rena, had been very interested in the store and Cindy had promised to show her the upstairs workspace sometime. Rena had probably mentioned it to her dad and he was hesitant to ask Cindy at this point. Cindy made a mental note to mention it to him next time, and continued walking, the box tucked up against her chest.

As soon as she grappled her way through Cinderella Silks' door, she set the box on a chair and glanced around the store. The gift bags were all in place on the counter, filled and looking great. No sign of Jas, though.

A second later, Jasmine's voice shouted from the storeroom, "Coming!" As she appeared in the doorway, she skidded to a halt. "Oh. Only you." Her smile took any sting away. "How was your walk? Feeling better?"

"Loads," said Cindy, hoping her sarcasm didn't show. "Gina offered to fix me up with her brother-in-law's brother. She's threatened to give him my number. Or maybe it wasn't a threat," Cindy added in afterthought, remembering the bakery card in her pocket.

Jasmine hurried over to the box and lifted the lid. "What would be wrong with that?"

"I don't need anyone taking pity on me," Cindy said, bending to pull the enlarged prints out. She was pleased to find they'd been placed on a backing. No extra poster board required. "And I don't need to be set up with anybody. Not even for the Garland Ball. I mean, come on already."

"But you told me you're bringing Shakespeare," Jas reminded her, lips twitching.

"Oh, shut up," Cindy responded.

Jasmine grabbed half the load from Cindy's arms. "Are we setting these up now? May as well, right? Rather than waiting until Thursday."

Jasmine had enthusiastically seconded Cindy's idea to put the prints out to get more folks excited for the event and the theme at the open house. Earlier was better. A ledge ran above the store's wainscoting, providing a perfect spot to place the photos for viewing.

"Look, I'm sorry if I'm not myself. I'm just stressed," Cindy said, leaning the photos from her pile neatly against the wall one by one. Jas did the same, moving in the opposite direction. Suddenly, Jasmine squealed.

Cindy plopped the foam-backed pictures onto the nearest table and hurried to her side. "Please don't say it's a mouse. They're cute and all, but they don't have any place in—oh."

Jasmine held the enlargement of Cindy's grandmother and the unknown dance partner up against her sweater.

"Yeah," Cindy said, "it's Gran. I meant to show you but I rushed all the photos to the printer and I forgot. Everyone always said I look a lot like her, and it seems it's true."

"That's just crazy," whispered Jas. "And the guy? Who is he? He's hot."

"Not Pop is all I know," Cindy answered. "Although, I feel like I should know him."

"You mean you haven't asked? Not your gran,

or your mom?"

"Not yet. Mom's coming to the open house and I figured I'd show her the photo then. If Gran comes with her, we'll corner her, you and I, and get the story from the horse's mouth."

Jasmine spun the photo around for another look. "That's amazing. I think she's a little taller than you, though, your gran."

Cindy nodded. "She was. Still is, but not by much."

They laughed together. Not at Gran. They both loved Gran. The laughing was good, however. Cathartic. Setting the enlargement back in place, Jas linked her arm through Cindy's, pulled her close, leaned sideways to press her head against the top of Cindy's.

"We almost had a fight earlier, didn't we?" Jas said quietly.

"Wouldn't be the first."

"But it's been a long time," Jasmine reminded her.

Cindy nodded, feeling her hair catch in Jasmine's. "It has. We've always gotten over any argument."

Jasmine straightened. "We sure have. Still, I'm sorry."

Nodding again, Cindy extracted her arm. "Me, too." She returned to the photo pile and picked them up again, getting back to work. Jasmine did the same. For a minute or two, the only sound was the snick of the foamboard against the wooden trim.

"Um," said Jas, hesitantly. "You might want to look at that marketing proposal sometime soon."

"I will," Cindy said.

"Real soon," said Jas.

Cindy paused, one more photo in her hand, and turned slowly around. "Why?"

Jasmine paused, too, but she kept her eyes on the print she held. A second passed, maybe two. She dropped the enlargement into place and pivoted with a grin. "Harry's coming to the open house."

Another second went by while Cindy grasped what Jasmine had said. "That's fabulous," Cindy stated. She only hoped her expression mirrored her words.

Chapter Four

Thursday morning, Cindy jumped late from her bed after roughly three hours' sleep. Following a record-breaking short shower, struggling damp skin into her clothes, and hastily supplying Shakespeare with his breakfast, Cindy grabbed a granola bar from a cookie jar on the counter and sped downstairs. She managed to unlock the front door only two minutes late, at the precise second a bakery employee appeared with the pastry delivery for the night's festivities. He came in and set everything on the counter for her. Cindy pulled a five-dollar bill from the register, stuffed it in his hand with a big thank you, then carried the box to the storeroom where it was cool and, more importantly for the time being, out-of-sight, out-of-mind. She didn't want to risk the temptation to start sampling.

The tiny bell on the door tinkled lightly. Cindy hurried back out front to find Jasmine coming in.

"Let me hang up my coat and I'll be right

back," Jas said, hustling past. She returned less than a minute later and caught Cindy chewing on a broken nail caused by her careless handling of the register drawer for Carl's tip.

"What are you doing?" Jasmine cried.

"Fixing it," Cindy muttered through her teeth. "I caught it on the cash drawer."

"Stop that! I know you don't bother with manicures, but at least your hands don't have to look like an animal's had its way."

Jasmine retrieved a kit she kept in the lower drawer, opened it on the old farmhouse table counter like a surgeon. In a few seconds, she had Cindy's nail looking reasonably presentable again. She took a few more seconds to inspect the other nine.

"They're fine," Cindy said, yanking her hand away.

Jasmine tsked at her. Cindy smiled begrudgingly.

"Thanks," she said. "At least they all sort of match now. Not like yours, of course. What color is that?"

"Midnight Lust," Jasmine answered.

Cindy shook her head. "Oh, for crying out loud. Really?"

Jasmine laughed. "No. It's 'In the Navy' or something like that. Do you like it?"

"It's a lovely color. It'll match your dress for tonight."

"Yours, too," Jas reminded her. Suddenly, Jas brightened even further, reaching into the pocket in her brown trousers. She pulled out her phone, performed a brief search and, pressing play on a video, turned the screen face out for Cindy to see Harry, wearing a shirt the same blue as Jasmine's nails.

Somehow, the color managed to make the blue in his eyes appear darker, the green anomaly standing out in sharp contrast. Running his hand through his hair in a habit Cindy remembered, he waved with the other.

"Hi, Cindy! Jasmine made me do it. In fact, she bought the shirt. Said wearing it would show solidarity. So, here I am, supporting your evening. Looking forward to seeing you again and getting a closer look at what you two have been up to."

"Isn't that sweet?" Jas cooed, stowing the phone back in her pocket.

"Indeed," said Cindy. She'd never seen this side of Jasmine before. She didn't coo over anyone.

"He looks fabulous, doesn't he?"

"Yep," Cindy admitted. "He certainly does." And he did. Cindy didn't really want to recognize that fact, but it was hard not to. "Don't I remember you telling me way back when he wasn't your type? What—"

"He wasn't," Jasmine answered, cutting her off.

Ah. Cindy had it now, loud and clear. She crossed to the display window, straightening the basket on a small round table next to a not very valuable but charmingly tufted antique dining chair. Pink. A great many things in the store were pink. Pink didn't happen to be Cindy's favorite color, but Jasmine had pointed out the pastel shade made women comfortable, made them feel at ease.

Jasmine had been right, as she was in so many things. Cindy supposed her decision to date the still-looking-fabulous Harrison Carter with his apparent marketing skills was right, too.

"Did Gina's cousin get in touch with you?" Jasmine asked in irritating directness.

"Brother-in-law's brother," Cindy corrected her. "Not cousin."

"Okay, brother-in-law's brother. So, did he?"

Cindy turned the basket again, first one way, then the other, stepped back to study it before answering. "He texted me. Said meeting me this weekend would be delightful."

"Wait," said Jas. "He used those exact words?"

Even with her back turned, Cindy detected Jas's stifled laughter. Cindy had trouble containing her own. "Yep. Exactly. Delightful. I'd say Gina must not have told him about the real me."

Jas appeared at Cindy's elbow. "And your answer?"

Cindy shoved the basket a few inches to the left and turned to face her friend. "How do you answer something like that? I'm not even sure I will be meeting him this weekend. I wasn't planning on it. I just said thank you, and left it there."

"Thank you? Did he respond?"

"He did," said Cindy.

"No."

"Yep. He said, 'I'll be the one with the red flower in my lapel' with a laughing emoji." Turning her back on the table, Cindy returned to the counter, took a long drink from her water glass. Jasmine followed.

"At least he has a sense of humor," Jas said. "Do you have a picture of him I can see?"

"Nope." Cindy's mouth lifted to one side. "I guess I'll recognize him when I spot the guy wearing the red flower. Or the fact he'll be with Gina. If I go."

"You should," Jas insisted. "He could be a great guy."

"I'm not saying he isn't. Like you said, he seems to have a sense of humor. He uses words like 'delightful.' But I really—"

"Need a date for the Garland Ball," Jasmine finished for her.

Cindy shook her head. "That wasn't what I was going to say."

Jasmine harumphed like a Scotsman and hurried over to the tinkling door, where the three high school students they'd been expecting were attempting to get through it as one unit. Following temporary fittings for the three girls, setting up chairs and the refreshment table, running out for the forgotten coffee urn and a million other little things, Cindy only realized the hour had approached for the open house when Jasmine sashayed up to her side with a grin, waving a blue dress on its hanger.

"Hop to it, Cinderella," she said. Jas had already changed into hers, a design in the same color and style, but in a longer length to sweep her calves and better suit her tall frame. Cindy noted Jasmine's make-up was, as always, expertly applied, enhancing her beautiful dark skin and natural good looks, and making her appear as though she wore none.

"How do I look?" Jamine asked with a twirl on her high heels. Wearing them, she stood a foot taller than Cindy. Mutt and Jeff Cindy's mother always called them, even when they were in grade school. Cindy had possessed no idea who her mom was talking about back then, until she pulled up an old newspaper comic strip on the internet. The reference had not exactly been a compliment, although she knew Mom meant it as a joke due to the disparity in their height. At least, Cindy hoped she did.

"Gorgeous, as always," Cindy said.

Customers and guests usually arrived early for these shows. Cindy hurried into the back to change from her oversized sweater and jeans into her own midnight blue dress. Hers was cut to a shorter length, flattering the one thing she still had going for her: her legs. Jas had been pushing for heels for her, too. Her friend was right about what heels did to stance, leg length illusion, back arch, but Cindy always opted for comfort over style when it came to footgear. Besides, she was a klutz. She had no desire to topple during an open house presentation. Or anytime, if she could manage to help it.

Cindy glanced at herself in the mirror, finding her cheeks rosy from all the running around that day. Natural blush, she liked to call it. She thought about Gran in the photo and Gran now. At eighty-one-years old her skin, though wrinkled, remained soft and porcelain and as lovely as fine silk. Since Cindy resembled her gran so much, maybe she could hope for that, too. Fat chance.

The bell over the door rang again. Cindy

hustled back out front.

Jasmine clutched her notes for the evening behind her back in a manicured hand as she greeted the customer who'd come in. A dozen seats had already filled in the few minutes Cindy had spent changing clothes. Several more customers gathered around the refreshment table. Jasmine turned, thumb up. "We'll be great," she said.

"Always," Cindy mouthed back. She could count on Jasmine's poise, her professionalism, her rapport with the customers. Although the business was Cindy's and everyone knew her, Jas's was the social face for Cinderella Silks. Cindy liked the background, the shadows behind the lights.

From the corner of her eye, Cindy saw Harry slip in after the customer before the door fully closed. Jasmine hadn't noticed him, involved now in escorting Margaret Doyle to the refreshment table, where she pointed out the coffee and pastries. Harry hadn't noticed Cindy either. Lifting a brochure from the seat, he slipped into a chair by the window. Cindy stepped back, watching him open the brochure and study the pictures, his face intent. Though much shorter than when they'd first met, his brown hair still possessed that windblown look from younger years, as if he didn't bother doing anything with it except walk outside into a breezy day every morning.

"Nice looking guy," said a voice behind Cindy. "Who is he?"

Cindy glanced at Alice standing next to her, still in her street clothes, and was reminded suddenly that things needed doing, there were girls requiring final pins and tucks to their gowns before Jasmine's introduction got everyone into their seats. "He's way too old for you," Cindy said to the high school junior.

"I can still look," said Alice.

Cindy glanced back at Harry before steering Alice toward the storeroom. He spotted her, waved. Yes, a nice-looking guy who belonged to Cindy's best friend and who nowadays likely had to spend an hour in the bathroom perfecting that windblown style.

The other two girls waited in the storeroom, already in their dresses, admiring each other in the floor-length mirror. Ten-foot-tall Alice shimmied into her dress and Cindy gave each gown last minute temporary tucks. They stood with muted giggles, listening to Jasmine's welcoming speech. "Watch out for pins," Cindy reminded the girls, right as Jasmine gave the cue from the other room for them to head out.

"Walk slowly," Cindy added. "Leave about ten steps between each of you. Remember, twirl once in front of the counter, pause so people can really see the dress, and then head back here for the next change."

"We got it, we got it," Alice called back with a smile.

Cindy had carefully chosen the style the girls would wear based on each one's size and shape. They were great kids, carried themselves well, lovely, and sparkling, and comfortable in their attire. As soon as they disappeared, Cindy hurried to get the next dresses ready. When the girls returned, she yanked out pins, stuck them between her teeth, hurried each girl into a new design, pinned those, herded them out. She noticed Alice liked to strut her stuff, as opposed to the other two with their more sedate gait. Cindy had heard the girl entertained modeling aspirations. Breathless and smiling and oddly proud of them all, Cindy shifted a little closer to the door to eavesdrop on the comments drifting into the backroom as each girl passed the makeshift podium.

So far, so good. Only five more changes, followed by closing comments, yakking it up with the customers, possible orders, one of those delicious looking éclairs she'd had her eye on, and then—

"Well done," someone interrupted her interior monologue.

Someone? Harry.

Thank goodness she had no pins left in her mouth. She would have swallowed them all and then Harry would have had to try to save her. How embarrassing that would have been. For them both.

Harry stood just outside the storeroom door leaning against the wall. Unlike yesterday's suit, tonight he wore dark gray trousers, the crisp midnight blue shirt, and a lighter gray tie. No suit jacket. She supposed it wasn't the official meeting the last one had been. Cindy hadn't had the time to notice what he'd been wearing beneath his open coat when he came into the store this evening, or how he looked in it. She wished she wasn't noticing now. Alice's remark kept coming back to her.

"You have to go," Cindy whispered. "The girls

will be in here any minute and they will be *changing clothes*," she stressed.

Smiling, he nodded and saluted with two fingers against his temple. "See you shortly," he said.

As if Cindy had no control over her eyes, her gaze followed him on his return to the seat in the back row. She jerked her eyes away, back to her narrow view of the podium. Alice with her loping, swinging stride headed right at Cindy. Over the girl's head she spotted Jasmine, her gaze on Cindy's. Cindy couldn't quite read her expression.

"They're loving it," Alice managed to squeal in an undertone as Cindy ran for the rack and the next outfit. Cindy yanked out pins and fit them once again between her teeth, eyeballing Biz entering the storeroom and already shirking her gown from her shoulders. Cheryl came last. In record time, they were re-dressed and heading back out again. Cindy wiped sweat from her forehead with her palm.

One more, one more, Cindy chanted silently each time they came back. Finally, they were done. The girls high-fived her and raced for their street clothes. Cindy straightened her skewed midnight blue dress, slipped her shoes back on, patted her hair into place and pressed her fingers to her heated cheeks. Jasmine called her name.

Cindy walked out, head held ridiculously high, struggling to catch her breath. Walked straight to the counter-turned-podium, squeezed Jasmine's hand, and looked up into her grinning face. Thunderous clapping filled the shop.

Jasmine bent to give her a hug. "We done

good," she said against Cindy's ear. "Now it's your turn to say a few words."

Cindy stepped up beside the podium resting atop the counter. No point in standing behind it. The wooden structure had been built for Jasmine's height, to hold her cards and whatever else she needed. "Hi," she said, and cleared her throat. Jasmine handed her water in a cup, which she gulped down.

"Hi," she said again, "thank you all so very much for coming here tonight. Some of you I know, some of you I don't, but I am grateful to all for attending the open house and for your keen response. As Jasmine pointed out, the gowns presented tonight, as well as many others in your brochures, can be ordered and recreated for you in time for the Garland Ball, if you choose to attend. The theme is Mistletoe and Memories and the throwback designs should be especially fun."

More clapping. Cindy waited for the noise to subside. "And now, I think we should get to the delicious pastries over there." She nodded toward the refreshment table. "I'll put a fresh pot on. Stick around for a bit, feel free to ask any questions. Oh, and the pink fabric swatch with the Cinderella Silks logo on it in your goodie-bag? Not available in a dress, but perfect for cleaning eyeglasses or wiping down your phone."

A few people laughed, while others peeked inside their bags to see what she was talking about. In his seat by the window Harry lifted his hand, thumb up. Cindy nodded at him with a quick smile and ducked away from the podium, heading to check the coffee pot. At the table, she peered through the people moving toward the table or the door or gathering to chat and exchange thoughts about what they'd seen and the photos in the brochure. She wasn't looking for Harry, but her gaze caught his anyway. He started in her direction. Jasmine appeared abruptly beside her, a basket filled with creamers in her hand. It seemed Harry wasn't heading in Cindy's direction, but Jas's.

"Where's your mom?" Jas asked.

Cindy shrugged. "I don't know. I was just looking around for her. She said she was going to bring Gran. I wanted to show them both that picture."

"What picture?"

Jasmine answered Harry before Cindy could. "Cindy found an old photo of her grandmother at one of the Garland Balls. We're dying to know who she was dancing with."

"Not your grandfather, I'm guessing?"

Cindy glanced at Harry, then around once more. "No. I'm pretty sure he was probably in the sidelines, though. I seem to remember he never liked dancing, especially anything as energetic as in that photo."

"And you?" Harry asked.

"Egads, no," Cindy answered him with a laugh. "I'm surprised you don't remember—" she began to add, but caught sight of Jasmine's expression. A strange expression. Another one she couldn't get a handle on, until Jas raised her hand and pointed toward the door.

"Your mom's here."

Cindy whipped toward the door. Lacie Michaels was a replica of Pops rather than Gran. Short like Cindy, but wider in the shoulder, and with Pop's long, narrow face and dark brown eyes. She did have Gran's smile with the dimple on one side. She and Cindy shared that. Mom wasn't smiling now, however. Standing practically on her toes, she maintained a white-knuckled grip on the door with one hand, frantically waving her over with the other. Cindy's heart performed a funny little skip in her chest. She raced to her side.

"Mom, what's wrong?"

"Where is your cell phone?" her mom demanded without preamble.

Cindy jerked a thumb over her shoulder. "I—I don't keep it on me when—"

"Gran's in the hospital."

Cindy's breath whooshed out like she'd been sucker-punched in the stomach. "Where are you parked?" Cindy saw her mother's car as she spoke, double-parked with its flashers on in the street. "Let me get my coat. I'll be right out."

Wordlessly, Lacie released the door and trotted toward the curb. Cindy scurried across the store, grabbed her coat, shoved her cell phone into her purse, ignoring the missed calls and texts, and started back out, wrestling her coat on as she went. At the counter she hesitated, picturing Gran in the photo, a younger Gran, a spryer Gran, and uttered a quick prayer as she grabbed the original photograph and slipped it into her coat pocket.

"Jas," Cindy said, "I'm sorry to leave you with all of this, but Gran's in the hospital."

"Is she okay?" Jasmine shouted, because Cindy hadn't even paused.

"I don't know," Cindy called back. "I don't know anything yet."

So much nonsense ran through her mind right then, things she knew meant nothing, like the orders that might not get taken tonight because it was a job for two people, and the food that would have to be put away, the trash to be taken out. Cindy crossed the sidewalk thinking about Shakespeare meowing for his evening snack and stepped from the curb recalling Jasmine's fingers sinking into Harry's arm as she called out to her. Cindy wrenched open the passenger side door, climbed into the seat. Mom started the car moving before she'd pulled her seatbelt across her body. Cindy thought about all the times her mother had yelled at her when she was a kid for not having her seatbelt fastened. It didn't matter now. None of it did.

Cindy turned her head in her mother's direction, saw her face, pale and discolored in the dashboard lights.

"It'll be all right, Mom," Cindy said.

She sent a fervent wish into the cosmos for that to be true.

Chapter Five

Cindy's grandmother at eighty-one years old was like most women at sixty-five. Or had been. She didn't look so much like that right now.

Cindy sat in her coat on a chair next to the bed, holding Gran's slender, chilled hand. A blood-pressure cuff wrapped around Gran's arm automatically ramped up to take measurements, reflected on the beeping machine nearby. From under the hospital gown sleeve a narrow intravenous tube ran up to a plastic bag filled with clear liquid, which hung from a hook attached to the bed frame. Other things had been velcroed to the bed gate. One might have been a call button for the nurse. The other probably belonged to the television, muted on its shelf near the ceiling. Cindy took as a good sign the fact they weren't in ICU.

"Your mother and her coffee," Gran said.

Cindy jumped a mile. "Gran! How are you feeling?"

"That's where she is, isn't it? Either that, or

she's hunting down the doctor with questions."

Though sleepy, her voice had an edge to it. Cindy hoped cranky Gran might be a good sign, too.

"What happened?" Cindy asked. "Do you remember?"

"Of course, I do. I felt dizzy and I fell."

"Fell?" Cindy tried to keep the shock from her voice, the worry, but Gran caught it. She squeezed Cindy's hand holding hers.

"Fortunately, my neighbor was there. She saw the whole thing. Called the ambulance and rode over with me. She went home though, when they told her I wasn't getting ready to pop off."

"Not funny, Gran," Cindy said.

"No? I thought it was. Anyway, I didn't hit my head, didn't break my hip, didn't break anything, thank goodness. Got a big old bruise on my thigh, though. The doctor doesn't seem too worried about that."

Sometimes doctors didn't worry about big old bruises because more important things in and on your body had their concern. Cindy didn't say this, however. She kept her mouth shut. She'd seen a post somewhere and hadn't forgotten it: *Sometimes my greatest accomplishment is just keeping my mouth shut.* Yep.

The more Gran talked, the stronger she sounded. Cindy wished Mom would get back from wherever she'd gone so she could hear and be reassured. "Have you had any tests run?" Cindy asked, keeping her tone conversational.

"I'm ancient, my dear. Of course, they ran

tests. Blood." Gran held up her other arm, displaying the narrow bandage inside her elbow. "There's an x-ray scheduled, just to be on the safe side. The doctor talked to me a bit, making sure I still had my words straight. He shined a light in my eyes and all that. I reminded him that Bertie—you remember my neighbor, don't you?—had already told him quite clearly that I didn't strike my head."

Cindy bit her tongue again, not mentioning he could have been making an initial check for signs of stroke. But what did she know anyway? It was best to continue keeping her mouth shut.

The blood pressure cuff squeezed down on Gran's arm again. Under pretense of fluffing Gran's pillow with her free hand, Cindy checked the readout. Not bad. Halfway through the busy evening Cindy's might not have been as good as Gran's right now.

"Are you warm enough, Gran?"

"Cinderella Michaels," Gran answered in flat tones, "don't baby me."

Cindy sighed, lowered her hand back into her lap. "Okay." Gran hadn't released her other one, her fingers wrapped around Cindy's. Cindy wondered if she was scared, if she realized she hadn't let go. Gran closed her eyes, settling back into her pillow. Gray eyes like Cindy's. Faded now with age, or was it cataracts? Somewhat cloudy, yet still seeing the world clearly. Cindy studied her face, looking for the shape of her own in the contours. These days, Gran's cropped white hair possessed more flair than Cindy's 'do.

"Stop staring at me," Gran said, her lips

curving. "The doctor should be back soon. You can ask him what he thinks when he gets here. Dehydration was one of the things he said, or perhaps a reaction to my medication. But I'm no spring chicken, Cindy. There could be something else."

Cindy's stomach rolled. Hearing a footstep on the threshold, she whipped her head around. Not the doctor, only Mom bearing two paper cups filled with steaming liquid. She handed one to Cindy. Cindy frowned into the dark brown brew, thanked her, set the cup on the bedside table. Gran released Cindy's hand and reached for it. Mom was quicker, moving the cup to the window sill.

"Not until you're cleared," she said.

"Tyrant," muttered Gran.

"Caring daughter," said Mom.

No matter what the reason Gran had ended up in the ER, she could still hold her own in the verbal sparring with her daughter. Mom sat in the chair on the bed's other side. She sipped her coffee. She appeared much more relaxed than when driving. Cindy figured seeing Gran helped.

"How'd the open house go?" she asked.

"Really well, I think," Cindy said. "Great turnout."

"I'm sorry I missed it." Lacie crossed her legs, exposing the footgear she wore. Cindy had a feeling she did so on purpose.

"Those boots are magnificent, Mom," she said.

Her mother swung a leg up, turning her foot from side to side, grinning smugly. "I know."

Gran snorted, turning her head to covetously

eye the coffee cup beyond her reach on the sill. In the hallway, someone laughed. A slight, electrical hum emanated from the mechanism attached to the pole holding the intravenous bag.

"What's in that?" Cindy asked, nodding toward the unit.

Gran shrugged. "I'm being rehydrated," she said. "Like instant potatoes."

Mom snorted this time. It seemed to be the way they communicated, Gran and Mom, through snorting; amusement, annoyance, concern, in a sound. "By the way," Lacie said, dropping her booted foot back to the floor and addressing Cindy, "who was tall, dark and scrumptious Jasmine was hanging onto when I showed up?"

"Oh, I'm really sorry I missed that," Gran said.

Cindy frowned at them both. Gran because, well, she was eighty-one and lying in a hospital bed, and Mom because—because Cindy hadn't realized her head would even go there, considering her traumatized appearance when she showed up at the shop.

Standing, Cindy snatched the coffee from the window and took a swig. "Ugh. Not even sugar."

"Sorry," Mom said. "So, who was the guy?"

Cindy's brows arched at her persistence. "Somebody Jas went to school with. Harry Carter."

Mom frowned. "Should I remember him? The name sounds familiar."

"Maybe," Cindy said, not wanting to talk about Harry any more. She knew she sounded petulant, like she was back in grade school being grilled about something she didn't want to share. But she had a point to discontinuing the conversation. There were more important matters to discuss here.

Mom cleared her throat. "So, do you have a date yet for the ball?"

Or not, Cindy thought. Her love life, or even date life, should have been relegated to somewhere around basement level. Gran's gaze slid Cindy's way, waiting for her answer, too. Cindy blew out a long breath.

"The whole stipulation about bringing a partner is ridiculous," she said. "I can just pay for two tickets and it'll serve the same purpose. This isn't my high school prom. I'm probably dreading it as much, though."

"Why?" asked Mom, head tipped to one side. "Because you're single?"

Oh, for crying out loud. "No, it's not because I'm single, Mom. And I'm divorced, to be accurate. Did you ever notice when a form asks for your personal status the word divorced is always listed, as if that makes you any less an individual entity than if you'd never gotten married? And if you want to know, I have found myself objecting to the premise that for business owners to attend they have to bring a significant or not so significant other. That's it."

Mom crossed her arms, the coffee cup against her bicep. "Okay."

She didn't mean okay. Of course, she didn't. Cindy knew what she planned to say before her mother opened her mouth again.

"I suppose if you must bring someone," Lacie commented with false nonchalance, "you could always ask Jeremy."

A slow heat crept up Cindy's face. Lacie grinned, maybe hoping to indicate to Cindy she'd been joking, that she hadn't meant it. But she had. Deep down, she had. Cindy knew it. Her mother had never gotten over losing Jeremy as a son-in-law. Cindy sometimes teased that if she could have gotten rid of Cindy and kept him, she would have. Her mom always laughed, but never quite denied it. Jeremy got on well with Cindy's parents, even now, and Cindy had always been happy about the continuing relationship. He didn't need to absent himself from their lives merely because he and she had gone their separate ways. Taking him as her date to the Garland Ball wouldn't happen though. All Mom needed was that glimmer of hope and she'd be announcing to her friends the wonderful news.

Cindy turned to Gran. "What about you, Gran? When we've got you up and about you could be my date."

Gran chortled. "Which one of us gets to wear the tux? I've always wanted to."

"Mom," said Lacie, "be serious."

"I am," she said.

Cindy shook her head, shoved a hand into her pocket while she drank more coffee with the other. A fingernail caught the photograph's edge. With all this talk about the ball, how could she have forgotten?

"Gran," she said, a little too loudly. Gran jumped. Cindy apologized, pulled the photo out. "Look!"

Gran took the photograph from her, turning it toward the awful fluorescent light above her bed. Lacie clambered up from her seat to see what Cindy had given her. Together, mother and daughter squinted at the image, trying without context to figure out what Cindy had handed over. After a moment, Gran's face creased into a deep smile.

"I remember that night," she said.

"Who's that with you?" Mom asked. "Not Dad. Is that George?"

"Of course, it is. What other man would I be dancing with besides your father?" Gran turned to Cindy. "Do you remember him? George Martins? He and I were friends since oh, I don't know, I can't really remember when we weren't." She smiled at the photo again, wistful, sad. Maybe Cindy hadn't done the right thing, bringing the photograph to her. She'd likely lost George, too.

However, Cindy nodded in recall, although Cindy's memory of George was of an older man. She hadn't recognized him in the younger man in the photo. Apparently, neither had Mom. They should have, though. Now that Gran had named him, Cindy absolutely did.

Satisfied, Gran continued. "He lived in town until about fifteen years ago." Gran looked at Cindy. "He and your dad became great friends. Your dad never judged him, even back then. Not that anyone else really knew, but your dad…your dad understood a man should never be condemned for choices of the heart that hurt no one. Last time I saw George was at his wedding ten years ago. He'd moved away by then, of course, to open an art gallery in Philadelphia. He married his longtime boyfriend. It was a lovely wedding."

Cindy felt an odd relief that the expression on Gran's face in the photo hadn't been reserved for a lover, which had been Cindy's stuffed-down worry. "Do you want to keep the picture, Gran? I'll pick up a frame for it."

"I'd like that," she said. "You should take the photo with you when you go, though, and bring it to me later. It could get misplaced here."

Gran continued to sound strong but pensive. Lacie heard it, too, her gaze altering when she looked again at her mother. The doctor came in, startled to find two other women in the tiny space. Cindy and her mom introduced themselves. The ER doctor talked a bit about Gran's condition and advised she would be staying so she could have a few further tests in the morning. He also told them not to worry. His bedside manner was such that Cindy almost believed him.

Lacie handed Cindy her keys. "I'm going to stick around," she said, "at least until your grandmother is in a room. Take the car. You can drop it at the house if you want and Dad will give you a ride home. He'll get me later."

Cindy admitted the sense to her mother's plan. It seemed evident they both didn't have to stay. Cindy retrieved the photo from Gran, already picturing a frame she'd like to place it in, and hugged and kissed both her and Mom. Walking through the noisy emergency room, she fidgeted with the photograph in her pocket, thinking about Gran and George, wondering what he was doing now. Apparently, he hadn't physically been in her grandmother's life in recent years, but did they still keep in touch?

Cindy located her mother's blue sedan, unlocked the vehicle, and climbed into the driver's seat, smelling her mom's perfume in the fabric seats. Sadness settled over her. She stared across the shadowed parking lot and thought about friends. Friends who once meant a lot. Forgotten friends. Like Harry.

Chapter Six

Cindy called Jasmine on her way back to let her know how Gran was doing. Jasmine told her she'd engaged the high school girls to help with cleanup, especially since Cindy had enough to worry about. Entering through the back after parking her car, Cindy walked in on Biz, the petite, athletic blond girl, putting away the broom and dustpan.

"Biz," Cindy said, "thanks so much for staying to help Jasmine."

Biz grinned. "No problem. How's your grandmother?"

"She's been admitted for some tests, but the doctor didn't seem too worried." Cindy took a step toward the storage room door and called out Jasmine's name before turning back to the girl to ask her if she'd had fun with the show.

Before she could, however, Biz informed her Jasmine had left. "She ran out with that hottie somewhere. She said you'd be here any minute."

Cindy paused. How many high school girls

found a forty-year-old man hot? Rumor had it at least two. "Are you all finished?"

"Yep, all done. Come see."

"One sec," said Cindy. "I'll be right out."

Cindy let herself into her tiny office to retrieve the checks she'd written earlier for the girls' modeling gig. She added a twenty-dollar bill to each envelope for the cleaning. After enthusing over the girls' excellent job both modeling and cleaning up from the open house, Cindy handed them their payment with another huge thank you, saw them out the front door and locked it.

Inside her zippered coat, Cindy's hunched shoulders slowly dropped. She turned away to retrieve her purse from the nearby table, preparing to head upstairs to give Shakespeare his long overdue snack. Get out of her dress, too, and into sweats, some comfy slipper-socks. Curl up on the couch and watch a movie with no sad parts.

Someone tapped on the door behind her. She whipped around.

Jasmine's face pressed to the glass, tongue out and eyes crossed, manicured nails starting up a staccato beat over the surface. With her other hand, she signaled for Cindy to hurry.

Cindy yanked open the door. "Where are your keys?"

Jasmine stepped back. "In my purse. Figured there was no reason to dig them out when you were standing right there." She paused at Cindy's expression. "Don't worry. Your Gran's healthier than the two of us together."

"That's what she says." Cindy held the door

wide. "You coming in, or...?"

"Nope," Jasmine announced. "Got your cell? Good. You're coming out." Grasping Cindy's hand with both her own, Jasmine yanked her out onto the sidewalk. "Lock up, girl. We're going to celebrate."

Cindy stuck the key in the door, unable to suppress a tremor of a smile at Jasmine's exuberance. "Celebrate what?" she asked, taking a second to double-check the door had locked.

Jasmine waved her hand. "Silly, we're celebrating *tonight*. I thought it went really well, didn't you?" She tucked Cindy's hand into her elbow and clamped it against her side as if to prevent Cindy running away.

Moving alongside her friend, Cindy's thoughts jumped from worrying about Gran to wondering what she, Jas, and Harry, would be talking about. Not business. Not the marketing plan. She wasn't in the mood and, to be honest, she'd only given the folder a cursory go-through. Of course, as this was a celebration, nothing about business except the open house should come up. Cindy envisioned nodding and smiling and laughing at things Jas and Harry would say that she'd never been privy to or couldn't recall. Her thoughts went to Jeremy, too, and whether Mom would find the opportunity to pass any weighted hints to him about the Garland Ball. She thought next about all the receipts she'd wanted to look at, to gauge how many gowns had sold and how many assistants had to be called in tomorrow. She thought about the photo still in her pocket and Gran's old friend.

"All the moisturizer in the world won't help if

you don't stop letting your forehead crinkle like that."

Cindy glanced up at Jas and around, realized they'd walked nearly three blocks in silence. "What?"

Jas pointed at Cindy's brow. "Stop stressing."

"Sorry," Cindy said. "Cranky, tired, worried." Cindy smiled at Jas to take the edge from her words.

"I know."

Cindy spied The Sitting Duck straight ahead, heard the music and voices as the door opened and closed. The building's late nineteenth-century architecture was beautiful, the windows tall and open to the street on either side. It sat in an unusual setting where two streets narrowed toward each other to meet Main. No one could fault the conversion into a restaurant. Especially not once they'd sampled the food and atmosphere.

"Come on," Jasmine said, clutching Cindy's coat sleeve and pulling her toward the door.

The instant they hit the warmer air inside, air filled with fabulous aroma, Cindy's stomach growled. She clutched her abdomen through her coat. Jasmine laughed.

"See? Good thing I came and got you. You haven't eaten since lunch, I bet."

"No," Cindy admitted, "I haven't. Not even the éclair I had my eye on."

"We're over here," Jasmine said, tossing her lovely curls.

A banner hung over the back room where a party was underway. In fact, it appeared to have overflowed into the bar in the main room, if the jovial shouts between occupants could be any indication. Jasmine led the way past the commotion toward a corner table. Two people sat there. One rose as they approached and the second followed suit, pulling out a chair next to him.

"Jeremy," Cindy said, lowering herself slowly into the seat, surprised and suspicious at finding him with Jasmine and Harry. "Were you talking to Mom by any chance?"

He pushed her chair in. She didn't usually let a man do that, but he'd been shoving chairs in for her for so long it had become habit. "Jasmine told me about Gran," he said, resuming his seat. "How's she doing?"

Cindy waved at Harry, who took orders for drinks and headed over to the bar, Jasmine on his heels. Anticipating what alcohol would do on an empty stomach, Cindy grabbed some pretzels from a bowl on the table and shoved a couple into her mouth, swallowing before telling Jeremy all she knew. He nodded his head in concern.

"You'll keep me posted?"

"Of course," Cindy said.

He smiled, not a broad grin, but something soft and comforting. She and Jeremy as friends had in time become something so much better—so much more—than Jeremy and she as a couple. Some couples were friends, the best of friends, but they hadn't been. Cindy slowed down her pretzel scramble, observing Jeremy from beneath her lashes as he finished off the liquid in his glass before Harry brought back the refill. Jeremy was still dressed from work, white shirt, diamond patterned tie loose around his throat, his suit jacket tossed across the chair at his back. The earring he'd worn when they'd first met and through half their marriage had left a permanent dent in his earlobe. Since he started losing his blond hair, he kept it cut short. Studying him with a dispassionate eye, Cindy realized she liked it.

Abruptly he lifted a hand and waved. Cindy glanced over her shoulder. Someone from the party returned the gesture with a little twist to the wrist and disappeared into the back room.

"Oh," Cindy said, "are you with—"

"The party? Yep. It's a work event. I think they're doing this party now to get away with eliminating our Christmas thing this year. I saw Jasmine when I came out to use the—you know," he said, jerking his head toward the restrooms, "and she told me what had happened with your grandmother. She said you had a great showing for the open house, too. Good job."

"Thanks," Cindy said, pleased. In a sudden lull, she heard Jasmine ordering a sandwich for her and set the pretzels clutched in her hand onto the table, still within reach. "Look, Jeremy, if you should get a call from Mom about, well, about the Garland Ball…"

"Oh, is she selling tickets? I already got

ours."

Cindy sucked down a pretzel crumb, coughed. Ours? Like hers and his? A moment later sanity took over. "Who are you going with?" Honesty compelled her to add, "I heard you and Sheila Bradford went out a few times. Are you taking her?"

He looked a bit sheepish about Sheila, about not mentioning her, and started to apologize. Cindy waved it off.

"She wanted to go." He shrugged, his smile lop-sided, and Cindy realized it was more than just Sheila wanting to go. It was serious, the two of them. Was this why Jeremy hadn't been mentioning much about Sheila to her? Had he thought she'd be upset? If Cindy's mom knew, she'd been keeping it close to the chest, too. But to the contrary, it would please Cindy to no end to see Jeremy happy.

Of course, their friendship as they knew it would be changed, hers and Jeremy's. Cindy let out a breath, sat back. Naturally it would be. Unless she was mistaken, new loves didn't feel too keen about the old ones still being in the picture.

"The Garland Ball is a big deal," Jeremy said. "Corny, old-fashioned, but everyone's looking forward to it. You're doing a bang-up job with that, too."

"Oh," Cindy said, still reeling a bit from the revelation she might soon lose her friendship with her ex, "it doesn't feel that way."

He laughed, caught someone's eye behind her, and stood. "I've got to get back. They'll think I'm anti-social, and you know how that goes over in the workplace."

Harry stepped up to the table, handed him his beer and told him it had been nice to meet him. Jeremy left, but not before kissing Cindy lightly on the cheek. She doubted that would happen again either. It wasn't the same as kissing a great aunt or a sister. Not to Sheila. Not for a while anyway.

With what felt like a wry, crooked smile on her face, Cindy watched Harry resume his seat. He slid her drink across to her. He had bottled water, which he poured into his glass. Following Cindy's gaze, he lifted the glass and tipped it at her.

"I'm driving," he said.

She nodded, brought her own glass to her lips, and took a huge swallow. She hadn't had a drink in ages, wasn't quite sure why she'd ordered one tonight on an empty stomach, but as the alcohol burned its way down to swirl through barely digested pretzel, Cindy nearly gagged.

"You okay?"

"Yes," she managed, "sorry. I probably should have had a soda."

"I can get you one," he offered, starting to get up.

"No, thanks, I'm good. Or will be, once I have a little more food in me. Did I hear Jasmine order me a sandwich?"

"She's waiting on it." He eased himself back into his seat. "So, that was your ex-husband?"

"Yes," Cindy said. There didn't seem anything else to say.

"You're friendly. That's good."

"Yes," she said again. "Are you married?" She hadn't even considered it, having assumed otherwise, seeing how very friendly he and Jas appeared. Maybe it was the wrong thing to ask.

"Once almost. It didn't work out. Long engagement, abrupt severance." He laughed a little in a self-deprecating manner.

"I'm sorry." Cindy took a second, albeit careful, sip from her glass.

"Nothing to be sorry about. Like you and Jeremy, we remained friendly after. Hasn't soured me on the possibility," he added, his gaze shifting to where Jasmine stood at the bar. His eyes came back to Cindy. "One never knows."

Cindy popped another pretzel into her mouth, offered one to Harry, who took it with a smile. A silence that should not have been awkward stretched. This was Harry; Harry with whom she'd spent countless hours in Jas's dorm room and around campus yammering on about aspirations, music, world events, home. Harry had been Cindy's first semi-adult crush. Jeremy had not been on the horizon yet. With the big four-oh in the offing, crushing had become a thing of the past. Cinderella Michaels, successful business owner and now bona-fide adult had moved beyond such silly, gut-wrenching, glorious, life-altering moments, minutes, hours, days.

Cindy glanced at Jasmine, who remained at the bar chatting up the bartender, Cindy's sandwich nowhere in sight. She turned back to Harry, cleared her throat, and offered him another pretzel, which he politely turned down.

"Sorry," she said, apologizing again for no good reason. "I'm starving."

"I'm not," he said, leaning forward to whisper. "I ate two of those éclairs. I'm going to have to get them shipped to my house on a regular basis."

Cindy laughed. "I know! I was looking forward to one all night, but I left before I had the chance."

"If I'd known, I would have stuck one in my pocket for you."

He smiled. The alcohol in Cindy's drink caused her cheeks to flush. She hoped he wouldn't notice, wouldn't think it might be for any other reason. After all, she'd blushed a lot way back when. Not anymore, though. Not without help from the rare glass of whatever the heck this was. She suddenly couldn't remember what she'd asked for. Cranberry and something.

"How's your Gran?" he asked. "Jas said she'll be okay, right?"

"She passed out and fell—nothing broken," she rushed to allay his alarm. "Could have been from dehydration. Gran pushes herself. She's very active."

Harry nodded slowly, studying her, probably gauging how worried she was. His midnight blue shirt rose and fell as he breathed. Cindy looked away, snatched up the last pretzel lying by her hand.

When she looked back up at him, he'd turned his attention to his water glass.

Cindy bit her lip, decided she had a question she wanted answered. "Do you still play guitar?"

His pensive, water-studying expression altered, face crinkling with a wide grin. "In my secret life outside of work, I have a band. We've been together for years now and play small, local venues. It's a great time. I enjoy the heck out of it."

Cindy took another cranberry juice and vodka swig, realizing with a start that half the glass had gone. She felt the liquid hit her stomach, burning its way out into her veins in a wispy, boozy way. "Does your band have a name?" she asked, glancing again at Jasmine. The sandwich had just made its way to the bartender. Jasmine looked back at Cindy and smiled before pointing a finger at Harry. Cindy turned around. Harry leaned forward once more.

"Guess," he said. "Think about the jacket. That pompous, ridiculous thing I asked you to make."

"Wait, wait," Cindy said, thinking hard. "I really don't remember—oh!" She stared at him, eyes widening. A giggle bubbled up. A giggle. She had to be drunk, or somewhere on her way. She tried to compress her lips but they trembled into a full-blown laugh. "Carter—"

"—and the Cool Cats." He nodded in a comical mockery of proud. "Yeah."

By the time Jasmine set Cindy's sandwich down in front of her, Cindy's head was on the table, tears streaming from her eyes. She had a feeling Harry wasn't much better off. Gasping, she lifted her gaze to view Jasmine. Jas looked from her to

Harry and back wearing an expression like an exasperated but amused parent.

"You've both been cut off. Bartender says." Jas showed her teeth in a huge grin.

This was why Cindy loved Jasmine.

This was why Cindy had loved Harry.

Maybe still did. What? That was the booze talking. Even so, she wanted to get up and run, all the way back to her apartment.

Chapter Seven

Cindy high-tailed it into the crisp night shortly after, leaving Jasmine and Harry to enjoy the remaining hours until they made their way, presumably, to Jasmine's house. She realized as she walked that the giddy, youthful adoration Cindy had experienced way back in college did not still churn inside her for a man who belonged to her best friend. It had been a flashing consideration, a memory. Even so, what a day—Gran in the hospital, Jeremy and Sheila, the remembered Harry in her heart. She needed something, anything, to distract herself from emotional mayhem. Well, not anything. Work would do. If she could manage to sleep, she'd get up bright and early and throw herself into it.

Halfway to Cinderella Silks, Cindy received a text. Figuring it might be Jas cajoling her to come back to the tavern, she ignored the tone for a minute, until it occurred to Cindy her mom might be texting an update. She yanked out her phone.

Not Mom. Selwyn.

Cindy squinted at the message, vowing to never drink on an empty stomach again. Maybe not at all. It wasn't as though she ever enjoyed it.

Selwyn's text was a simple one. *Hi, Cindy. Do you want to have dinner tomorrow, just the two of us, before we all get together?*

Cindy stopped dead on the sidewalk. Did she? Not really. Fridays were usually busy and she'd be dragging after work. Obviously, however, she needed to put herself out there. Make herself available to the possibility of new relationships. Or just a date to the Garland Ball that wasn't Gran or Cindy's cat.

Sure, she answered. *It'll have to be late though, after the store has closed. I could meet you somewhere at 8:30.*

Let's make it easy on you, he texted back. *How about lunch instead, or coffee?*

Well, he was considerate. That was a plus. And he also used full words rather than the annoying abbreviations certain people favored, especially those not due to be forty soon.

Thanks, Selwyn. How about the Main Street Café at around noon. They have great bagel sandwiches, too. As you might assume, —a word she had to correct two times—she really could have done with more food in her stomach—*it's on Main Street.*

Sounds good, he replied. *See you then.*

There. She could do this. Cinderella the Brave and Competent. Moving on. Moving forward. But first, sleep.

In bed, Cindy tossed and turned, aggravating Shakespeare, who wanted nothing more than to curl up in his usual place on the blanket undisturbed by any antics. Two in the morning rolled up fairly quickly. Cindy sat up against the headboard and pulled her knees to her chest. She did not keep a television in the bedroom. The temptation when sleepless to watch some middle-of-the-night movie would be too strong. Of course, the living room and its forty-inch flat screen were only fifteen steps away.

After spending a quarter hour watching car lights bar the ceiling as their illumination passed through the blinds, Cindy reached for her phone. Not to call anyone, not at two-fifteen a.m. To follow through on a niggling, underlying consideration that had been with her all night. She typed in George Martins and Philadelphia. She didn't know anything else so started there.

Apparently, George Martins was a common name. Going deeper into the results might bring up older or more obscure information, but that would only encourage her to stay awake. Besides, she didn't really like doing research on her phone if she could help it. The screen was so darned small compared to the nice, big computer monitor. Nevertheless, she kept at it, wondering what compulsive demon drove her to search for her grandmother's friend. Statistically, she possessed certain expectations about what she would find as the most recent information available, and had no desire to share that with Gran. But something about Gran's face in the photo as well as when Cindy spoke to her in the hospital made Cindy want to know.

Gran had been a long time without Pop now, but at the time she'd attended the Garland Ball they were still together. People must have speculated about George and Gran, not understanding George's preference for a companion did not lie with Cindy's grandmother. Gran had clearly been enjoying herself, his company. Cindy wanted to find him for her, no matter how small her chance for success.

She looked, enlarging each entry until her eyes grew weary. Finally, she gave up. Before putting the phone back on the nightstand, Cindy typed another name into the search. She didn't wait for the response. She didn't need to find out more about Harry, his life since college, where he lived now. Turning the phone face down, Cindy wriggled down under the covers, throwing a blanket edge across her face to block the light from outside.

In the morning, the calls began. Customers stopped in as well. Bleary-eyed both, Cindy and Jasmine took their orders or helped them purchase a pre-made dress off the rack. Many needed some tucking or letting-out here and there and the purchasers made appointments to return. Cindy phoned the sewing assistants, arranging for them to come in to get started on the orders. Jas was barely communicative. Harry had gone home and Jas clearly missed him.

During a short breather, Cindy called her mother. Her mom had sent a text bright and early to let Cindy know she was heading back over to the hospital. Cindy hadn't heard anything since. Lacie picked up, sounding rushed.

"Honey, hi. I'm with your Gran right now, waiting for the doctor to come in. I think everything's okay, but I want to see what the doctor says."

"All right," Cindy said. "Will you—you'll let me know? If they're keeping her another day, I'll run over later."

"Okay, sounds good." Lacie hung up. Cindy held the phone out, staring at it. After a few seconds and a frown, she set the cell down on the counter, turning as the light bell announced another customer entering the store.

Around eleven-thirty, Cindy made her way to the third floor to assure everything was in order before the assistants' arrival. Inside the alcove created by two southern-facing windows stood a machine for cutting patterns from Cindy's designs from the computer. The machine was her pride and joy. It made work a lot more efficient, dispensing with the need for physical patterns for each size and the time required to pin them to fabric and hand-cut them with shears. She quickly checked the sewing machines, lighting, thread and pins, the fabric in its wonderful glistening, colorful bolts, preparing to hurry back downstairs.

She didn't, though. Instead, she sat down in a chair by the window, folded her hands together between her knees. Sunlight touched her face through the glass in warm strokes and colored her closed eyelids. The sewing room was the quietest place in the building, far above the street below and the shop. Cindy breathed deeply, summoning up the calm she needed and hoping she wouldn't fall asleep sitting there.

Abruptly, the outer steps clanged. Someone was coming up.

Cindy reached the door right as Jasmine did. Cindy opened it for her. "Hi," she said. "Is something wrong?"

"Nope," said Jas.

"Who's got the store?"

Jasmine waved her long fingers. "Peg. She's here for her afternoon shift."

"But she doesn't come in until twelve," Cindy said.

"It's twelve-o-five," said Jasmine. "I believe you're supposed to be somewhere?"

Cindy looked at her friend in confusion for a split second before uttering, "Crap!"

Jasmine laughed. "You're a terrible first date."

"It's not a date," Cindy shot back at her as she hurried for the steps.

Jasmine followed more slowly, pulling the door shut behind. "What else would you call it?" she yelled down to Cindy.

Not answering, Cindy rushed down the remaining stairs and into the store to retrieve her phone. She texted a quick apology to Selwyn and told him she'd be there in five minutes. Donning her coat but not bothering to zip it up, Cindy waved hello to Peg and raced out the door. She paused for a brief second to check her hair in the window glass. Good enough.

Lunch hour at the Main Street Café was, as usual, a busy one. Cindy glanced around with no idea what face she looked for. At this point, the red flower would have been a big help.

Hearing a male voice calling her name, Cindy spun, searching for the speaker. A man at a rear table stood up, lifted his hand in greeting. Cindy walked in his direction. "Selwyn?"

"Indeed," he said.

"Sorry I'm late. The store's a bit busy and I, well, I forgot."

"Honesty," said the man. "I like that. I think."

Cindy looked him up and down. He stood about seven or eight inches taller than she and was dressed comfortably in jeans and a sweater. He wore his reddish hair short. The light through the windows reflected on his glasses, yet still revealed the direct study of his eyes. Not scary, stare-you-straight-in-the-eyes-until-you-want-to-run-away, but a comfortable gaze in her direction. "How'd you know it was me?" she asked him.

"I could say I spotted you running down the street and then figured it out when you rushed in looking all around, but really, Gina sent me a photo."

"But you did spot me running down the street, didn't you."

"I did," he said.

"I'm a little out of breath," Cindy admitted.

"I can see that. Maybe you want to take a seat."

Cindy slid into the chair closest to the window. He sat down in the one to her left, rather than across, likely to hear her better. The noise level in the café was intense.

"Well," he said, "lunch or just coffee?"

Cindy glanced at her watch. "I really do have to get back soon. How about a bagel and coffee?"

They both ordered when the server came over and then, to fill an awkward silence once she left, Cindy asked him about his work. Selwyn spent the intervening minutes waiting for their bagels and mugs explaining his job, with frequent touches on her hand. She moved her arm a couple times to see what would happen, but he somehow always managed to reach her fingers. So, a touchy-feely guy. To test how far he'd go, Cindy slipped her hand into her lap. He started stroking her upper arm instead.

Fortunately, their food arrived. His hands engaged in eating, he continued to explain what he did for a living. He worked for a small law firm and, following an explanation of the firm's focus, he broke into an entertaining story about a case, leaving all nameless, naturally. Cindy laughed around a mouthful of bagel, covering her lips with her fingers until she managed to chew and swallow.

"What did you do about that?" she asked.

He lowered his bagel back onto the plate. "That wasn't meant to be funny," he said.

Cindy gaped. "Sorry. The way you told it was, though."

Abruptly, he guffawed. "It was meant to be funny. I'm just teasing you."

"Oh." Cindy took a quick swallow from her coffee mug. Realizing she'd forgotten sugar, she grimaced and grabbed a packet, tearing it open and dumping it in. She added another for good measure before stirring the contents a bit too enthusiastically.

"Am I making you nervous?" Selwyn asked with a wink.

Nervous, she thought? No. Somewhat anxious and perhaps a little annoyed with the grabbing at her arm now his hands were free? Sure. Forcing a small smile, she shook her head and drank some more coffee.

"Tell me about what you do," he said. "Gina says you sew clothes."

Cindy set her mug down carefully in the small ring left behind from her recent splashing. She doubted very much Gina had told Selwyn she "sewed clothes." Gina knew how much existed in Cindy's business, and certainly understood how much running any business entailed. More likely, sewing clothes was all Selwyn had taken away from whatever conversation he'd had.

"I don't do that much sewing these days," she said. "I have employees who execute my designs."

"I see," he said. She figured he did when he asked his next question, a question which made it even more obvious he hadn't paid attention to anything Gina might have said. "So, you have your own business?"

"For years, yes. The store is right down the block now. Cinderella Silks is the name, and I design off the rack and custom clothing for women. Before that, I worked from a converted half of the garage. Before that, I worked wherever I could set up space. I started the business, name and all, when I was in high school."

"What a charming story," he said. "See how I did that? Charming? Like Prince?"

Cindy nodded, the smile on her face slightly forced.

"Wait," said Selwyn, perking up, "is Cindy short for Cynthia, or for—"

"Cinderella," Cindy admitted. "Yep. My mother's favorite story. I'm assuming she never read the original."

Selwyn cocked his head to the side, looking unsure about the reference.

"The original fairy tale," Cindy explained. "A bit more sinister than the modern version. A lot bloodier. Body parts removed with sharp instruments to assure big feet fit into tiny glass slippers."

Eyes flying wide, Selwyn leaned toward the table. "What? Are you serious?"

"Definitely. Also, a talking bird warned the prince to check for blood on the track dripping from each false young lady riding behind him on his galloping steed. Don't spread that tale around, though. People might boycott my establishment."

He laughed, as he was meant to, albeit nervously. "I never heard that."

"The old fairy tales were quite gruesome compared to the scoured, contemporary versions."

Selwyn relaxed against the chair back, his grin still tremulous. "You're funny."

"I enjoy old books. Sometimes what I've read comes out in funny ways."

"Ah." He took another bite from his bagel, speaking after he'd swallowed. "I'm not much of a reader."

"Meaning you read nothing, or you're choosy?"

"I like everything short and to the point," he said. "Magazine articles, summaries, the back of a cereal box."

Cindy snorted.

"Don't knock those cereal boxes. They can provide an entertaining minute or so over breakfast."

Cindy laughed, thinking he might be amusing after all, until he reached out one more time to touch her hand and didn't let go. Cindy eased her fingers from beneath his, picked up her bagel with both. She opened her mouth to take another bite. His next words stopped her.

"I think we're pretty well suited, don't you?"

Cindy lowered her bagel back to the plate. "Pardon me?"

"For an actual date? We seem to be getting along. Dinner tomorrow night should be fun." He punched her lightly on the upper arm. "Especially if we can get a couple drinks into you."

Cindy blanched, went a little cold before heat

surged back into her face.

"Now I've made you blush."

"Hardly," said Cindy, looking around for the server. Spotting the girl, she signaled for the bill. The girl came right over.

"Could I have a piece of foil for this?" Cindy indicated her remaining bagel prior to taking the bill and placing it on the table top, away from Selwyn's outstretched hand. "I have it," she said to him. "Relax and finish yours. I've got to get back to sewing clothes."

She hadn't meant to say the last. She didn't want to be petty. She smiled to make it seem she'd been joking. No reason to hurt the guy's feelings, after all. He likely felt as off center as she did. This whole meeting people scenario wasn't always the easiest street to navigate.

"It's a really busy time for us, especially with the Garland Ball coming up," she explained, fishing in her wallet for some singles and finding only one. "Would you mind getting the tip?" she asked, looking up to catch an odd look on his face. Amused, maybe? Annoyed? She couldn't tell. The fact she couldn't tell didn't bode well for future dating attempts with anyone at any time.

"It'll be better tomorrow," he said. "Not so rushed, right?"

Oh, right. Saturday night. Cindy gave a wordless nod. The girl arrived with the foil. Cindy hastily wrapped it around the partially eaten bagel and swallowed half the coffee left in the mug in one gulp. She stood. Selwyn did, too.

"About the Garland Ball," he said. "You, me.

It'll be a great time."

Oh, for goodness' sake, just how much *had* Gina said to her brother-in-law's brother? "We'll talk," Cindy said, backing away and heading for the register. Selwyn followed her over, telling the server as the girl passed him that he was not yet finished and would be right back. He stood close to Cindy as she paid the bill.

"Thanks again for inviting me to coffee," Cindy said, not knowing how else to end the event. She flipped her hand up in a small, hopefully-construed-as-friendly wave and strode toward the door. He followed her outside.

She stopped, turned, took a step away, waited.

"I enjoyed myself," Selwyn said. "I hope I didn't make a bad impression."

"Of course, you didn't," Cindy assured him. She couldn't blame him for her miserable state of mind. "Like I said, though, I'm swamped."

"Good. The not making a bad impression part, not that you're swamped. Although I expect for you, that is a good thing."

Cindy smiled, nodded, took another step back. Waved again. Maybe it would be all right. Maybe she could manage to get away for dinner with him and Gina and the others this weekend. Maybe they—

He went and ruined it, rushing across the small distance between them and kissing her.

Hard.

On the lips.

Well, not exactly on the lips. He started there and mashed his way across to her cheek. Or perhaps she'd moved her head and that's how he ended up there. Either way, she hadn't given him any indication she'd welcome it. Truly. None at all.

In a black and white movie, she might have smacked him. Instead, she took several more steps backward, sucked her lower lip beneath her front teeth—hoping that wasn't his onion bagel she was tasting—then spun on her heel without a word and marched in agitation back to Cinderella Silks.

Chapter Eight

Yanking the door open, Cindy hurried into the store. Before venting, Cindy glanced around to make certain there were no customers. From the third floor, she heard the slight mechanical hum from the sewing machines, indicating the assistants were at work. Somehow, even though voices remained trapped up there, the light, pleasant drone always filtered down through the walls. Acoustics, she supposed.

"Cindy!" Jasmine cried from behind the counter. "How was your date?"

Cindy walked up to her and right on by toward the storage room to hang up her coat. "Don't want to talk about it," she said.

Jas dogged her footsteps. "Bad?"

As Cindy neared the inner door, Peg popped out carrying several boxes for delivery. Cinderella Silks offered local delivery for free. 'Off the rack' or custom made, the items were delivered in the signature pink box with the glass slipper logo.

Cindy and Peg nodded to each other. Normally, the girl was more talkative. She'd probably noticed something in Cindy's expression.

Shirking her coat from her shoulders, Cindy hung it on the coat rack and turned to face Jasmine. "As dates go, not the best. I don't really remember dating. It's been too long. But I don't think it's supposed to end after less than half an hour with the guy kissing you so hard he almost breaks your teeth."

Jasmine's eyes flew wide. "He didn't!"

"Yeah. He did." The bell above the front door tinkled. Cindy rushed out in time to see Peg exiting with the packages. "As I was making a hasty departure to return here," Cindy went on to Jasmine, much as if there'd been no break in her rant. "Followed me outside and wham."

Jas's hand flew to her mouth. Behind her fingers, Cindy spotted the telltale twitch of a stifled laugh.

"It's not f-funny," Cindy stammered before she, too, began laughing. It was always like this with them. If Jas laughed, Cindy did, and vice versa. Many a tense moment was diffused in their recognition of humor in a situation, no matter how odd or slight. When they finally stopped this time, Cindy wiped tears from her eyes. "Really," Cindy wheezed out, "I gave him no indication I wanted him to kiss me. At the very least, it was rude."

"Maybe it was meant to be a peck on the cheek and he missed? Stumbled, maybe?"

Picturing it, Cindy laughed again. "If so, poor guy, but I don't think so."

"And dinner this weekend?" Jas asked.

Cindy gave her a look. An eye-rolling, are you kidding look.

"So, back to square one," Jas said, her expression somewhere between not surprised and already starting to plan. Cindy ignored her and went upstairs to check on the assistants.

Around seven that evening, Cindy's mom brought Gran home from the hospital. Jas assured Cindy she could handle the evening with Peg staying a little later than usual, and sent her off. Cindy stopped at a drugstore and purchased a frame, then drove over to Gran's. She walked in with the framed photo to Mom insisting Gran could no longer live alone at her age, and Gran's declaration that at her age she could darned well do what she pleased. They both turned and glared at Cindy, as if her interruption had somehow taken the sharp prick from each other's point.

Cindy strode over to the mantel above Gran's little-used fireplace. Several frames already took up most of the surface, pictures of Pop, Pop and Gran, their kids, grandkids. One with Cindy stood at the end. Cindy had no qualms pushing that photograph to the back and settling the newly framed picture in a place near to Pop's smiling face. Knowing the history, there seemed no reason not to.

"Thank you," said Gran, the argument with her daughter temporarily forgotten.

"You're very welcome," Cindy answered, studying the framed family row. "What did the doctors say, exactly? Mom didn't mention."

"A medication change, and a new one added. Otherwise, I'm fit as a fiddle," Gran declared.

Cindy avoided her mother's look, concentrating on Gran instead. She didn't think Gran's assessment far off. Moving across the apartment she possessed spryness to her step, either due to the enforced rest or the change to her surprisingly small drug regimen, although the latter seemed a little too soon.

"Seriously, Gran, you do look great, considering you were flat on your back in a hospital bed last night."

Gran shrugged her narrow shoulders. "I do sometimes feel my age, Cinderella."

"To be honest," Cindy quipped, "I sometimes feel your age, too."

They both laughed. Mom stood by, frowning.

"Tea?" Gran offered.

"I'll make it," said Mom, and strode the short distance into the condo's small kitchen. Opening and closing cabinets with her back to them, she added in an offhand manner, "I spoke with Jeremy yesterday."

Cindy bit back a groan. They spoke quite often, her mother and Jeremy, so no surprise there. Knowing where she might be headed with the mention, Cindy decided to forestall her. "Did he tell you he's been dating Sheila Bradford? They're going to the Garland Ball. I think it's getting pretty serious."

Her mom whipped around with her fingers looped through three mug handles. Her brow lowered and her eyes sparked. "No. He didn't. How do you know?"

"I ran into him a few nights ago. We talked. We always talk, Mom."

"Of course, you do. Which is why I don't understand—"

Gran's chuckle interrupted what Cindy knew her mom was going to say. Leaning toward Cindy, Gran said in a stage whisper, "Get my tux ready, sweetie."

Cindy gave Gran a thumbs up and a smile.

"Mom," said Lacie, still struggling with her aggravation. Whether at Jeremy for not telling her about Sheila or the fact Cindy already knew and didn't seem devastated by the news, Cindy couldn't tell. "Cindy will have a date for the ball. Won't you?"

Cindy grinned. "Sure. Gran in a tux. We're all over it." Gran laughed again.

Lacie threw up her hands. "You two are hopeless."

Cindy exchanged a glance with her grandmother, who winked broadly and deliberately. They discussed the ball, then, but not on a personal level. More about the plans, the décor, how the ball affected Cindy's business. Once they'd finished tea, Cindy set her mug in the sink, readying to return to the store. She slipped back into her coat and jerked her chin toward George Martin's photo. "When's the last time you heard from George, Gran?"

Gran's eyebrows flicked upward and then down as her brow furrowed in thought. "Not since a year or so after his wedding? Yes, I think it must be. He and Frank had opened their gallery the year before they got married. I went to see it once. George is such a wonderful artist, and his husband's sculptures are amazing. We didn't see or talk to each other near as much as we would have liked once he moved, and after a while, well, you know what happens."

"Don't I," Cindy said. A few minutes later, she hugged them both and left, driving back to the narrow garage in the alley behind the shop. If she'd had anything bigger than her compact vehicle, it never would have fit. Before letting herself in the back door to the store, she stood a moment searching again on her phone for George. This time, she entered George Martins, artist. And found him.

The gallery website referred to him in the present tense, so that was promising. He also looked great in his photo, nearly the same as the one gracing Gran's mantel now. Older, sure, but great. Healthy and happy. Cindy scrolled through the artwork featured on the site. His work was, indeed, amazing, as were the various sculptures popping up in between. She located the contact information, found an email address, bit her lip, considered reaching out to him for Gran's sake.

But would Gran thank her? She seemed more

resigned than unhappy about the changed circumstances. Gran had many friends, some a great deal younger, and spent much time engaged with them. More than Cindy did with her own. For Gran, George might just be someone from her past, now. A fond memory. Moments well spent, but over.

Sort of like Cindy and Harry.

"Right," Cindy said out loud, dropping her phone into her purse. She hurried through the storage room toward the store, from which she heard multiple voices humming as she yanked off her coat and hung it up. She found two women had pulled a dress from a rack for viewing and discussion. A third had Jasmine cornered by the ball wall, where the outfits from the open house were displayed. The short woman held a gown up against herself, asking the towering Jasmine whether she'd wear something like it. Apparently, the woman admired Jasmine's personal style. Jasmine's eyes met Cindy's over the woman's head. Cindy hurried over to lend a hand.

The remaining evening proceeded in a like manner until closing time. Finally able to breathe, Cindy grabbed a package of almonds from the box beneath the counter and ripped it open. She plopped her phone on the counter, brought up the gallery website she'd been viewing earlier. Crunching nuts loudly, she scrolled through the images again. George Martin's paintings were quite lovely. Cindy knew nothing about art except what she liked, and she liked George's ethereal style. According to the site, he worked in oils and acrylics, painting lovely, mysterious faces, or the occasional building in Philadelphia, looking almost misty, haunting.

"What are you looking at?" Jas asked. She had her coat in hand, but seemed to be in no hurry to leave.

Cindy showed her. Jasmine scrolled through the website as Cindy had done. "This is Gran's friend?" she asked Cindy. Cindy nodded. "Talented."

"Very," Cindy agreed.

Jasmine lifted the phone, gave it a little side to side waggle before returning it. "Do you have a particular reason for looking?"

"Curiosity." Not the entire truth, but Cindy didn't want to say more. She slipped a few more almonds into her mouth. "Any plans for tonight?" she asked around them.

"No," said Jas. A rather short answer for her. She usually had something going on.

Cindy chewed and quickly swallowed. "Me either," she countered with a laugh.

"So, Selwyn's definitely out?"

"I think so. He hasn't texted since the semi-aborted kiss. Maybe he's just embarrassed or is waiting to see what I do. He was very touchy-feely as we talked. Well, he talked for the most part. I didn't care for that, either. The touchy not the talky. Not with someone I don't know. Otherwise, sure, he seemed nice enough."

Jasmine snorted.

Cindy returned her phone to her pocket. "And before you say beggars can't be choosers, remember: I'm not begging."

"I know," Jasmine said soberly.

Cindy's brow creased. "You okay?"

"I want to talk to you," Jas finally said. "I've wanted to talk to you."

"About Harry?" Cindy asked. She didn't want to talk about him but obviously, if Jasmine needed to, she would.

"Yes," Jas said. "You seem a bit put off by him. I thought you liked him."

"I did," Cindy said. "I do. You should have told me. I felt a little sidelined."

Jasmine reached out, grasped her hand. She squeezed Cindy's fingers. "I'm sorry. Are you okay with it, now, though?"

Cindy squeezed back. "Of course, I am."

Jasmine hugged Cindy hard. Stepping away, she smiled broadly. "Good. I'm glad. I'll see you tomorrow. I think the Garland Ball is going to give us a record-breaking season." At the door, she paused, swung back around. "He likes you, too, you know."

"Well, that's a good thing, considering," Cindy said, hoping she sounded as enthusiastic as Jas expected her to feel.

Jasmine smiled, blew her a kiss. "See you tomorrow. Wouldn't it be wonderful if it's as busy as today?" Pausing outside on the sidewalk, she pointed in exaggerated fashion at the Garland Ball poster with both hands. When she walked away, Cindy swore she heard her singing. She began to wonder how much Jasmine-in-love she could handle.

In her nightly ritual, she checked the day's receipts. She thought about Selwyn as she flipped through them, wondered how she would tell Gina things hadn't worked out. That was the problem with being fixed up by one's friends. How the heck did you let them know you had no interest in someone they felt would be the perfect date? Maybe even the perfect match? Or at least, someone to fill a space in one's life?

Perhaps Selwyn would be the one to let Gina know they weren't a good mix. Cindy decided she wouldn't think about how to handle imparting the news, and turned off the overhead lights. She left on the few at the door, a deterrent to break-ins, as was the spotlight over the back door and the alarm. Crime happened sometimes, even in this small town. Not a lot, but precautions were better than losses.

Turning away, she caught a shadow passing across the door. Heart leaping into her throat at the timing with her thoughts, Cindy whipped around. She spotted Dan's familiar profile right before he knocked. She hurried to open the door.

"Dan," she said, letting him in. "What's up?"

"Sorry. I meant to call. Then I figured if I ran, I'd get here before you closed."

He wasn't even breathing hard. Not surprising. Cindy knew he regularly ran most mornings and had even competed in local runs.

Occasionally, if she happened to be down in the store early enough, she'd see him pass by in his daybreak ritual.

"Is everything all right?" she asked.

"Dandy," he said. He swiped his hair off his forehead. Sometimes, like right now, he looked a great deal like the boy he'd once been, rather than a father of three. "I was wondering, do you make gowns for—" He held his hand out palm down, about four feet or so above the floor. "Littler ladies? Younger ones?"

Cindy's mouth curved up. "Rena?"

"Yes." He smiled crookedly. "She's my date for the Garland Ball."

"Oh, that's adorable!" Cindy cried with heartfelt warmth. "And yes, of course. If you want to stop by with her one day this week or next, she can pick out a style and I'll measure her and get started. Maybe I can show her around the works the same day. She did seem interested."

Dan appeared pleased Cindy remembered. "She'd love that," he said. "Thank you."

"Not a problem. It'll be fun. I'll only charge for the materials, though, okay?"

"No, I won't—"

"I insist," said Cindy. "This just might get me into the mood for the whole Garland Ball thing." At the expression on his face, she immediately regretted her admission. "It's nothing against the ball. I'm just feeling a little overwhelmed, that's all. Making a gown for Rena will cheer me up."

"Yeah?"

She nodded. "Absolutely."

"If you're sure…"

"I am."

He stood a moment just smiling, suddenly recalled himself and started backing toward the door. "What about you?" he asked, placing one foot behind the other.

"What about me?"

"Date?"

Cindy shrugged, shook her head in a quick movement. "It's my plan to buck the whole process and go solo." She placed a finger to her lips. "Mum's the word."

He mimed pulling a zipper across his mouth. "No one will hear it from me," he said and stepped out into the night. Chill air rushed in behind him. Cindy hurried forward to relock the door.

The phone rang while she was climbing the metal staircase to her apartment. She paused on the landing and looked down at the screen. Mom. Slightly panicked, Cindy answered straightaway.

"Is Gran all right?"

"Oh, she's fine," said Lacie. "Or insisting she's fine, which amounts to the same thing."

"Okay," Cindy said slowly. She turned, looking up and down the alley. Soon, it would be Thanksgiving, followed by the ball, her birthday, and then Christmas. The cooler months, the holiday season, usually energized her. Cindy shivered a moment in her shirt sleeves. She'd left her coat in the stockroom.

"What?" she said. "Sorry, Mom, I missed that." Hastily, Cindy shoved the key in the door lock and went inside, reveling in the apartment's warmth.

"I said, there's a lot of excitement about the ball. I'm so proud of you, honey."

Cindy pulled the cell away, stared at it, switched over to speaker and set the instrument on the counter while she gave Shakespeare his nighttime treat. "It's not all me. I've had help. A lot of it. As far as popularity, I think we can blame it on the nostalgia-starved masses."

Lacie giggled. *Giggled.* Cindy's brows gathered into a tight knot. "What's up, Mom? Speak."

"I can't lie. I was a little disappointed with the Jeremy news—"

"Really, Ma? After all this time? We split up more than five years ago. You dwell about my marriage's demise more than I ever have." Cindy bent and gave Shakespeare a treat, only remembering she'd already given him one after he'd gobbled the second treat down. "You can thank your grandma for that," she said as she kissed him on the head.

"What'd you say?" Lacie asked. "Did I just hear you tell your *cat* I'm his grandma?"

"Well, you are. I don't have any kids."

"You could've—"

"Nope," said Cindy. "Not going there."

Jeremy had wanted kids, and she hadn't. This wasn't the reason they broke up. Or at least, not the major reason. Jeremy had been counting on the fact there might still be time to convince her. Then other issues had crowded in. Small things that had added up to the big thing. A recognition their marriage wasn't…whatever it wasn't. They'd split up and become better friends. Sometimes that happened.

Cindy released a breath. "So, grandma," she said, "why did you call me?"

A full second passed before Lacie answered. "You know Judy, yes? My friend since, I don't know, nearly as long as you've been in this world?"

Cindy frowned again. "I'm not senile, Mom. I know Judy."

"Do you recall her son, Hugh? The one who roomed with your brother at college?"

"Vaguely. I haven't seen him in years. I remember him more from kicking his butt at dodge ball when we were kids. Wait. Is he okay?"

"He's fine," Mom said. "Relatively fine. He recently divorced—"

"No," said Cindy. "No, Mom. No. You're not matching me up. I don't need a date for the ball, no matter what was decided. Yes, despite my vote in favor. Momentary insanity. I will happily be the odd man out. Marching to a different drum, and all that. Do not, do not, do not give him or any other male person my cell phone number. Got it?"

Lacie was silent.

"Mom? Come on. I'm a grownup. I can figure it out myself. And like Gran says, I'm old enough to do what I please."

"I was just trying to help," Lacie retorted, somewhat icily. Or maybe it was a guilt-trip sulk.

Cindy couldn't decide.

"I love you, Mom. You know I do. But I don't need that kind of help. Gina tried and I can tell you, it kind of sucked."

"What do you mean?" her mom asked, perking up again. "Have you been out with someone recently?"

Cindy headed into the bedroom. She kicked off her shoes, dropped her hips down onto the mattress edge. "Yes. Today. Lunch. No fun. Or not much."

"Maybe he just needs a second chance—"

"Yes. With someone else. Look, Mom, I want to get out of my clothes, take a shower, relax for a while. It's been a busy day." Shakespeare jumped up on the bed. Cindy scrubbed him behind the ears, smiling at his purring response.

"But I want details!"

Arms wide, Cindy flopped back. "Sorry, gotta go," she shouted to the phone that had fallen from her hand to land a couple feet away on the bedspread. "Love you!" Rolling onto her side, Cindy depressed the button to disconnect the call. Shakespeare sat beside the cell, staring her in the face.

"Oh, not you, too," Cindy muttered. She started unbuttoning her blouse. The phone rang again. "Mom," she growled to herself as she snatched the cell up.

Not Mom. Harry's number. Crap. She only had him in her contacts because Jasmine had insisted she should. Perhaps so Cindy wouldn't ignore his calls. But Cindy hadn't looked at the paperwork since she'd skimmed through it in a less than efficient perusal. She didn't want to admit to that. It seemed rude, at the least. She pressed the button on the cell's side, sending him to voice mail. Even as she did, she knew she would have liked to talk to Harry. They used to have such wonderful discussions.

A long time ago.

Chapter Nine

Gina called in the morning and said she was sorry things hadn't worked out with Selwyn. She promised never, never, ever to try something like that again. Cindy had no idea what Selwyn had told Gina. Still, Cindy was glad he'd spoken up, because she really hadn't known what to say. She made a few positive comments about him to Gina, admitting that yes, despite how nice he was, they weren't really suited, and Gina hung up, somewhat mollified.

As the days progressed through the weekend and into the next week, Cindy began to feel like a washing machine set on heavy soil in a constant cycle of work, sleep, work, repeat. One morning during an unexpected lull, with Jasmine out on a run for coffee from Gina's bakery, Cindy pulled Harry's paperwork from the drawer. For a few seconds, she again admired the cover, a textured black with his company's logo embossed at the lower righthand corner. She knew she didn't have time for a heavy examination, but she took a moment to skim the contents again. And again, she found nothing objectionable, nothing that didn't make sense. Following the proposal would likely grow the business, sure, but she already had enough to handle. Jas had hinted multiple times—more than hinted—that Cindy ought to give up the reins, hire managers if Cinderella Silks expanded. Spend her time on designing, not supervising every detail. Meet with customers, yes, but not be the one to assist them with every step of their decision making.

Cindy sighed. The bell above the door tinkled. She shoved the proposal back into the drawer, shut it, and looked up, ready to greet Jas with eager hands reaching out for hot coffee. It wasn't Jas who entered.

"Hi," Cindy said to a man who looked slightly familiar. Where had she seen him? In a store, or the bank? Perhaps Gina's? "How may I help you?"

"Cindy Michaels?" the man asked, pausing halfway across the floor. Cindy always noticed clothes first. His were casual. Not a whyever-did-you-leave-the-house-wearing-that kind of casual, but comfortable. Well-worn jeans, a maroon sweater with the hint of a tee shirt at the neckline, an old, maybe vintage, leather jacket. Light brown hair trimmed to the collar. She guessed his age at mid to upper thirties. His faintly familiar face was friendly enough.

"I am," she answered hesitantly. Was this going to be a solicitation? She got them from time to time. The 'no solicitations' sign was subtle and sometimes missed.

The man strode closer. "I haven't changed that much. Have I? Herb. Herb Bancroft."

Cindy had been preparing herself for an introductory handshake. Her fingers slapped down to her thigh. "You're Judy's son."

"Yes."

"Dodgeball."

"What?"

"Nothing. We used to play."

He thought a moment, brow wrinkling. "I don't remember."

"Probably too traumatic losing every game," she said.

"No," he breathed out, and then laughed. "I definitely think I would have remembered that."

"Every game," she repeated. She didn't know why she was taunting him. They'd been kids. She changed course, smiled in welcome. "It's good to see you again after all this time. How have you been?"

Cindy knew how he'd been, or at least the most recent part thanks to Mom. Her mother had probably sent him to the store to skirt the admonition about not giving out Cindy's cell phone number. If not, his appearing in the store today was an extraordinary coincidence.

He gave her a small, head-rocking, shrug. "Been better. Anyway, nice store. I've heard good things about it. From your brother most recently."

"Thank you," Cindy said. He was a silent a moment. A small, embarrassed smile played out on his lips.

"I have a confession," he said.

Cindy had to admit his expression was rather endearing. Unfortunately, she figured she had an inkling as to his confession already. Even so, she encouraged him. May as well get it over with. "Go on."

"Your mother suggested I stop by. She thought we might…reconnect."

"For another game of dodge ball?" Cindy suggested, because it had been that long since they'd spent more than a few minutes in each other's company.

He laughed, shrugged again. "Moms, huh?"

"Moms, yeah," she agreed. Her glance went quickly to the door. This would be an opportune time for Jas to return from her coffee run. No sign of her yet.

Herb cleared his throat. "I think they're trying to match us up."

Straight to the point. "That would be like mothers," Cindy said. "No matter what age their children are, they can't stand to see them single, I guess."

Her stomach sank. Now he would know her mother had told her about him, about his divorce. Crud.

He didn't seem to mind, however. Perhaps he had expected the news to be passed on. "The divorce was final a few months ago. Yours was longer than that, though, right?"

"It was."

"Maybe we can get together one evening and, you know, just talk."

Talk. Commiserate, more likely. She wasn't sure how much commiseration he'd get with her, with her marriage having dissolved years ago in a friendly manner. She supposed she could listen, though. Give him an ear…

Cindy pulled herself up short, opened her mouth to make some excuse. He spoke first.

"How about a drink at that pub in town? On the funky corner. What's it called?"

"The Sitting Duck," Cindy said. Seemed quite the fitting name suddenly.

He laughed. "That's what it's called? I wonder where they came up with that?"

"There's a sign inside the front door explaining it. Cute story," she added with some reluctance.

"Really? I look forward to reading it when we're there." He jerked his thumb toward the door's vicinity. "I have to go, but I'll text you?"

"Sure," Cindy said, barely grinding her teeth. She thought her countenance might even resemble something pleasant. She doubted it. Either way, Herb didn't seem to notice.

"I'll need your number, though. Here's mine." He pulled a card from his jacket pocket. A business card for a sound studio for voiceovers. Interesting. This could make for some entertaining discussion after all. She could ask him about his business and ward off divorce talk. Cindy set the card on the counter and grabbed one of her own, penning her cell number on the back.

"There you go," she said, handing the card to him.

"Great. So, I…so, I'll text you?"

"Sure. My days are pretty long, but we'll see what we can work out."

He nodded, lifted his hand in a wave, and headed for the door. Jas entered as he made his exit. They did a little dance together in the doorway. Jas stepped aside to let him out and strode up to the counter with the coffees and a quizzical look on her face.

"Um, what was up with that guy? They don't usually come in alone," she said.

Cindy took her cup, held it to her face, breathed in the aroma, reveled in the warmth, took a second to settle herself. "He's the son—the newly divorced son—of my mother's friend."

"Oh," Jas said, and then, "ohhh."

"Yep," said Cindy.

"He was kind of cute." Jas took a sip from her cup and smiled, a wicked twinkle in her brown eyes.

"Stuff it. I don't have time and I don't like being set up."

Jasmine's head cocked to one side. "You told him that, I presume?"

Cindy growled, drank more coffee, swallowed. "Of course not."

"You're a coward," said Jas.

Cindy blew out a breath. "And you're a pain."

Jas headed to the storeroom with her coat. "I work hard at it," she called back. "It gives me joy."

Snorting a short laugh, Cindy returned to her work day, temporarily dismissing Herb Bancroft from her mind. She made a mental note to call and thank her mother, sarcasm intended, once the store had closed. That evening, when she climbed the stairs to her apartment tired and annoyed and hungry, she received a text from Herb. A text appealing to her stomach.

Hi. It's Herb. Since you said your days are long, how about something beforehand? Like breakfast?

Breakfast was a long way off, and she'd need dinner in between, but she could always use a hearty meal before morning crazy began again.

Are we talking tomorrow? she asked.

If that works. Is 6:00 a.m. too early? There's a diner outside of town. The Pepper? You probably know it.

I do, she answered. *And 6:00 is not too early. I will meet you there. Thanks.*

Cindy decided to wait before calling her mother to complain.

*   *   *

In the morning, the thermostat outside the window showed twenty-two degrees. Cindy could barely see it in the pre-sunrise gloom and had to shine an angled light on the numbers through the glass. Just spotting those digits made her shiver, despite the cozy temperature in her apartment. She determined to dress practically rather than work-ready. Breakfast shouldn't be a lengthy meal. She'd be back in plenty of time to change her clothes.

With the sun barely up in the sky, Cindy clanked down the stairs in her coziest, fleece-lined boots, jeans, a bulky sweater over a long-sleeved tee and a rather unfashionable, down-filled jacket. Besides being warm, the outfit didn't scream 'date.' This was breakfast, plain and simple.

Unlike Selwyn, she at least knew Herb. Or had once, in vague memories. Since he still spent time with her brother, she might have seen him at other times, yet she couldn't bring them to mind. As with Gina's sister's brother-in-law, however, any connection was bound to make it awkward when Cindy called it quits after a non-date breakfast. Because she would. She knew she would. Breakfast would be a meal, they'd talk—or he would talk about his ex-wife more likely—Cindy would get back to work, and that would be it. Possibly, they'd both talk and would have a good time, but it still would end there. It had to. She didn't possess the frame of mind for romance, or even dating. As far as needing an escort for the ball to meet the expectations of the evening, she was comfortable doing without.

Driving from town, Cindy noted certain shops already had hints of the upcoming holiday season in their windows, to explode full blown at Thanksgiving. In nearly every window or door the posters for the Garland Ball were prevalent, too, a reminder to her of how much she still had to do. Eyes front now, she avoided looking at them, yet continued ticking off in her head the remaining tasks. The bigger items had been settled, fortunately, such as the venue, the menu, the catering, the band, and the like. Final numbers were still needed. There was no cut-off date for ticket sales, which made a headcount a little tricky. Back in the day, Eleanor had used the amount sold as of two weeks before the ball, and then added fifteen percent for last-minute sales. It seemed risky, perhaps had even been the reason for the event's demise in terms of cost overrun, but really, there seemed no other way to do it and still have everything needed.

Blowing out a breath, Cindy turned right outside Connor Falls and headed to the diner about five miles away. The building resembled a larger version of an abandoned establishment pictured on one of her mother's favorite record albums. Unlike the luncheonette in the photo, the Pepper wasn't abandoned but functioning quite heartily. Even at this hour, cars dappled the lot, with two more pulling in as she did. Cindy checked the dashboard clock. Right on time. She didn't know what Herb drove, so had no idea if he'd arrived yet. The best thing would be to go in and check. If he wasn't there, she'd get them a booth and wait.

Satisfied with her plan, she parked and got out.

"Cindy!"

Whipping around on her heel toward the voice, she spotted a familiar face. Jeremy. With Sheila. Cindy waved. They came over, arm in arm.

"Cindy," said Jeremy, "you know Sheila."

"I do." Cindy smiled. "How are you?"

"Great," Sheila said. "We're here for our Wednesday morning breakfast!"

"Every Wednesday?" Cindy asked. "That's a treat."

"Yes," Jeremy answered. "It's our Wednesday thing. Plus, they have fabulous specials on a

Wednesday morning." He and Sheila grinned at each other with intimate amusement, more entrenched as a couple than Cindy had realized.

"Good to know," Cindy said, glancing around the lot to see if Herb might be exiting a car.

"Are you meeting someone?" Jeremy questioned, following her gaze.

"Supposed to be. He might be inside already."

"Don't see his car?"

Cindy turned back to him. "I don't know what he drives."

"Oh," said Sheila. Another looked passed between her and Jeremy. Cindy's breath caught.

"We knew each other when we were kids. I haven't seen him in a while," Cindy said, her statement a half-truth that seemed the easiest explanation. She compounded equivocation by adding, "He came to the store yesterday. We're just catching up."

Catching up. Sounded better than matchmaking by mommy. Especially at forty. Almost forty. She still had a few weeks before that clock turned.

Sheila tugged on Jeremy's arm, saying to Cindy as she pulled him away, "Well, if your guy's a no-show, come eat with us."

Ouch. Was that a dig? Probably not. Sheila wasn't the type to be malicious. Cindy nodded. "I will. Thanks. In fact, I'll follow you in. He might be inside already."

She climbed the stairs behind them, holding back as a woman came up to them, greeting Jeremy and Sheila by name.

"Three today?" the woman asked, peering

around them to Cindy.

"I'm meeting someone," said Cindy. "I just happened to walk in with them."

The woman grabbed two menus and led Jeremy and Sheila away. Cindy took the opportunity to peer around. She didn't see anyone resembling Herb Bancroft in either direction. When the woman returned, Cindy asked for a booth and told her a man named Herb would be coming to join her shortly.

Shortly became fifteen minutes, and he hadn't yet arrived. Cindy reopened her menu for the third time, tapped her finger twice on the omelet heading, considered again ordering without him, and picked up her phone instead.

Sorry, I won't be able to wait much longer. Are you almost here?

"I am here," said a voice near her shoulder. She looked up to find Herb, his cell on his palm. He slid into the seat across from her. "Sorry I'm late. You still have time to eat, yes?"

Cindy nodded, studying him in a quick onceover. His hair was wet, his coat collar damp, as if he'd jumped from the shower to the car. He hadn't shaved.

"Oversleep?" she asked, figuring it likely based on his appearance.

"I was up late," he said. "Went out with a couple of the guys, had a few laughs." At her widening eyes, he added, "I work from home, so there's no rush for me to get back and into other clothes. I guess that's not the case for you. You probably need to change before your day starts."

"I'm dressed for work," she said, pretending offense. He started to mumble an apology and she laughed. "Kidding. Sorry. I'm dressed for warmth is what I'm dressed for."

He smiled halfheartedly in response and reached out, sliding the second menu from under her arm. "What are you having?" he asked.

"Not sure." Cindy lifted her own menu, taking her time needlessly perusing it again. She glanced up at his face once or twice, found him squinting in concentration at the choices. He looked a little…off. Cindy straightened. "Are you okay?"

"Fine," he said. "Why?"

"I don't know. You just look like maybe you're not feeling well? We could have rescheduled."

He shrugged, his mouth lifting to one side. "I'm just a tad hungover. It'll pass after some coffee and pancakes."

Hungover, Cindy mused, on a Wednesday morning. Could be he was definitely taking his divorce a lot harder than she had hers. She looked around for the server, ready to order, eat, and get on with her day.

"I'm sorry," he said. "Making a wonderful impression on you, aren't I? It just…it's been hard."

Cindy's gaze shot back to him. Were those tears in his eyes? "It's okay," she said. "I understand." Despite her calm and willing compassion, inside her head she fervently wished she were still in bed cuddling her cat.

"I thought you might." He reached across the table toward her fingers. She pretended not to see and raised the hand to catch their server's eye. The woman came over, pad at the ready.

"I'm going to have the garden omelet, minus the onions, white toast, home fries," Cindy told her, then looked pointedly at Herb. "You?"

He seemed a little stunned by her straight to business attitude. In fact, he greatly resembled a chastised child as he pointed at his menu and gave his order. Ding-ding went an alarm bell in Cindy's brain. Stifling misgivings as the server walked away, Cindy tried to steer the conversation to less traumatic topics.

"Working from home sounds great. Do you have a studio setup in the house?"

Herb took a deep breath. Cindy almost expected to hear a child-like shudder as he did. He seemed to have recovered, however, and unrolled his napkin to remove and carefully place his knife, fork, and spoon before answering.

He entered into a description of what he did, during which the coffee arrived. He explained what clients he worked for, and how most of his work was recording audio books and advertisements. "You and I could work up some ads for your store, for the local radio if you wanted." His voice lifted at sentence end, like a hopeful question.

"I have to be honest," Cindy said. "We've got that covered already."

"We?" he echoed, latching onto the word.

"My partner Jasmine and I." Cindy took a sip from her coffee mug.

"Your partner?" Herb said with a slight frown. "Your mother didn't mention that. Why wouldn't she have said something? How long have you two been—"

Cindy nearly choked on the brew sliding down her throat. "Business partner," she corrected him. "And friends. We've known each other since second grade."

"Ah," he said, looking happy again. "How's your business going? Like I said, I've heard great things about it."

While waiting for their food, Cindy gave him the general gist regarding Cinderella Silks, which brought the subject around to the Garland Ball. She hadn't meant to mention it. His pancakes, her eggs, landed on the table as she spoke.

Overhearing, the server said with a smile, "My husband and I are going. I'm looking forward to it."

"That's wonderful," Cindy said, and meant it, avoiding Herb's eye. She could tell he wanted to say something. Not to the server, but to her. Despite the server's chattiness about the event, the woman eventually had to get back to work. Cindy turned to face Herb across the table again.

"So, the Garland Ball," he said. "Seems like an outdated concept."

Cindy hadn't expected those words, exactly. She agreed while concentrating on smearing jelly across her toast. After taking a bite and swallowing, she explained the reasons for resurrecting and reinventing the event.

"It's a good cause," said Cindy. "If it's successful, it'll take place each year, raising money for charity."

"And the theme," he asked. "Mistletoe and Memories?"

Apparently, he knew something about the ball. Maybe Mom had clued him in, or could be he'd just read the sign on Cinderella Silks' front door before he came in the store.

"It's a throwback Christmas theme to various time periods. However, I figured there needed to be some cohesiveness, so the room will be decorated with vintage style lighting and ornaments grouped together, like little vignettes, rather than thrown about without any direction. As for the clothing, I've made a few designs for order harking back to earlier times. A bunch of old photos from the ball prompted that. The designs are proving popular. No one needs to dress up in theme, though."

"That's good," he said. "I'm not sure everyone would want to. I don't think I would."

"No, of course not. And no one has to."

Herb chewed a mouthful of pancake, watching her. "All this must keep you really busy," he finally said.

"It does."

He picked up his knife to saw the remaining pancakes into bite-sized pieces. He didn't look up as he said, "I guess that's why you don't have time to date."

Cindy paused with her fork halfway to her mouth. "Who told you *that*?" As if she didn't know.

He confirmed her suspicion. "Your mom told my mom. It's like high school with them." He smiled, stuffing more syrup-covered hangover food between his parted teeth.

"Well, to correct the gossip chain, it's been a choice, not a time constraint." Cindy stuck her own fork in her mouth, chewing more forcefully than necessary.

"But you do need one, for this Garland Ball thing."

Cindy lifted another piece of toast, waving it for emphasis before biting into the jelly-covered bread and talking around a mouthful. "It's not law. I'm not going to get arrested if I show up alone."

"But you won't show up alone. Will you? I mean, as you said, this has something to do with increasing revenue for charity. A guarantee two tickets will be sold."

Cindy fished bread crust from a tooth with her tongue. "I'll buy two."

"Or you can go with me. I believe your mother was hinting at it."

A small yet noisy breath rushed out Cindy's nose. She hoped he didn't hear it. "Considering the fact that I will likely be running around all evening making sure the darned event goes well, I wouldn't wish accompanying me on anybody."

Reaching out, he toyed with the clean spoon lying beside his plate. He'd taken his coffee black and hadn't used it. "I wouldn't mind. It would be nice to have someone to cheer me up. I really need it."

He glanced up at her, his expression pitiful and coy at the same time. Cindy didn't like coy looks. They always appeared practiced and offensive. She wondered, too, if he was still talking about the ball. The way he'd said 'cheer me up' and 'really need it' seemed like an attempt at seduction over a diner breakfast.

"Your guy friends from last night would probably be better at cheering you up than I would," Cindy said, scooping the last egg and vegetable smidge onto her fork. "But if you occasionally need to talk, you can call me. If I'm not in the middle of a hundred things, I'll be a good listener. Might even have something helpful to impart."

Herb considered her as she chewed, swallowed. She wondered if he was figuring out how to respond. Suddenly, he leaned forward, stretched both hands out across the table toward her, stopping short of her plate. His upper body was nearly in his own.

"A listener is good," he said. "Especially one as beautiful as you are."

Oh boy. She didn't like false compliments, either. She wiped her mouth with her napkin, remaining silent. His boot toe tapped hers beneath the table. She really, really hoped the contact had been accidental.

"But I have to say," he went on, "I'm looking for more. More than someone who listens. Someone who can help me get my mind off how bad things are."

Okay, now he was switching into high gear. Cindy's eyebrows crept up. "I'm sorry, but I'm not looking for anything like that. I can't help you. You need to help yourself, you know?"

Reaching into her purse, she took out a twenty-dollar bill, tossed it on the table, and stood. "This will cover my meal and probably yours, too. If it doesn't, I'm sure you don't mind getting the rest plus the tip."

By the time she reached her car, she realized this was the second occasion where she'd paid for meals eaten by men who had asked her to dine then subsequently followed up with behavior to make her cringe. The practice needed to be broken, she decided, sliding in behind the wheel. Mom needed a talking to, and everyone else needed to stay out of her business for a while. Anything resembling a good mood had abandoned her. Anything resembling a hankering for male companionship had, too. Not surprising. She figured such vague notions as the latter had been hanging from a thin thread for quite a while.

Chapter Ten

"You just need the right man," Jasmine said to her later that morning. Cindy tried to discern if her friend spoke seriously or in jest. "Like Harry," Jas added.

Cindy shook her head, fighting an eyeroll.

"What?" said Jasmine. "I really thought you liked him. You used to."

"I still do. He's a great guy. I'm not sure how many of him there are, though." Cindy shrugged her shoulders and smiled, hoping Jasmine would drop the subject. It occurred to Cindy that Jasmine's relationship with Harry might be the "one" for her. Jasmine would likely ask Cindy to design her wedding dress. It would make sense, of course, and Cindy would do it without hesitation, fashioning the best darned gown ever, but she couldn't stop her stomach twisting at the thought. Things would change. They had to.

Mid-afternoon, Cindy took a breather in the quiet storeroom and pulled out her phone, checking her to-do list. Some notations were purely personal, like making dessert to take to Mom and Dad's for Thanksgiving next week. Another: Gown for the ball. She really did need to get started on that. She had something in mind. Something elegant and timeless enough to still be in keeping with the throwback theme. She'd already picked out the fabric, a cherry-red, silk satin. Another said, email George Martins. Cindy had prepared the email, revised it, revised it again, and it still sat in her computer, waiting to be sent. The last read, decorate for Christmas/send out cards. That was both personal and business and she was way behind. She usually had them done and ready to be posted on Black Friday.

"What are you doing?"

Cindy glanced at Jas, standing tall in the storage room door. "Making like Santa," Cindy said. "Checking my list. Not gift list, though. I haven't even begun that one."

"I haven't either. But you know what I want?" Jas questioned with a grin.

"Peace on earth?"

Jas dipped her head from side to side. "Well, yeah, but on a more realistic level, I want you to agree to a spa weekend after the holidays. Just you and me. We'll get someone to take care of the store."

"No Harry?"

Jasmine appeared puzzled for a moment. "Not unless you want—"

"I was joking," Cindy interrupted. "Girls' weekend, it is. Something to look forward to, for sure."

Jasmine clapped her long fingers together twice before spinning on her heel and exiting. Cindy called out to her. She paused and looked back.

"I have to run upstairs," Cindy said. "I'll be right back."

"Checking on the ladies?"

"Nope. Something I want to check off my list. I'll only be a few minutes."

Cindy didn't bother with her coat. She trotted up the steps outside to her apartment, let herself in and found Shakespeare curled in the windowsill. With a quick pat, she passed him by and headed to her computer. Logging into her email account, she pasted the brief but informative message she'd drafted to George, gave it one last look-through, and hit send. She didn't really expect anything to come of the communication, was quite possibly overstepping boundaries in making it, but she couldn't forget how happy Gran had looked in the photo with George. She wasn't not happy now, but sometimes friends drifted apart without intention.

Pulling her cell from her pocket, Cindy removed the to-do item from her list.

*   *   *

Thanksgiving came too soon. The night

before, Cindy made her signature cheesecake and deleted the reminder. At one a.m.

The way things were going, Cindy would end up sleeping through a spa weekend and never experience any of the amenities. Exhaustion dragged at her bones. Her face in the bathroom mirror, her nearly-forty-year-old face, showed the signs. Of course, a bathroom mirror tended to show a person at their worst. Or so she told herself as she turned away and got dressed.

Downstairs and up, silence reigned. The store was closed. The assistants had the day off. Cindy had started decorating her apartment the night before while the cheesecake baked, and finished it in her pajamas before her morning shower. Another item checked off, sort of—because of the reminder's compound structure, she had to decorate the store and prepare and post both the business and personal Christmas cards before she could really remove it from her phone. Business greeting cards were easy. She had them printed every year along with the mailing list on labels. All she needed to do was slap the labels on the envelopes, shove the cards inside, and get them to the post office. Easy-peasy.

"Easy-peasy, my butt," she said out loud. Shakespeare looked a question at her. "Ignore me," she said to him. "Let's feed you now, since I won't be here this afternoon. Time to start messing up your schedule for the holidays."

The cat looked at her as if to say, *I'll eat whenever you feed me. I don't have a schedule.*

Which was true. Her ridiculous complaint proved Cindy's bad mood. Again. Or perhaps still. She needed to shake it. Thanksgiving was the official start to the holidays for the Michaels family. For most families, Cindy supposed. Friends, relatives, loved ones gathered around the table to eat until their pants cut into their waists and a near stupor ensued. What could be a better way to begin the season of excess?

"What is wrong with me?" she asked herself, quite loudly. Shakespeare chirped in consternation. "Sorry," she apologized before getting his food ready.

After putting on her coat and a hat—a light snow was in the forecast—Cindy grabbed the cheesecake in its container and a bottle of wine off the counter, lingering for a longing, sleepy stare at her unmade bed. Unmade at nearly two in the afternoon. Somehow, she'd broken a habit of centuries. Or at least her adult life.

Fighting the urge to set the wine and cake and her purse on the counter to take the five minutes necessary to make the bed presentable and more comfortable without all those wrinkles, she decided habits were meant to be broken. Doing so showed strength and determination and character.

Yep. That's what it showed. However, knowing the mussed bed would haunt her through the afternoon and evening, maybe even remind her of a time when a wrecked bed signified something more pleasurable than a restless night, Cindy gave in, plopped the items beside the sink, and restored her bed to its usual daytime state.

"There we go," she said. Shakespeare, who had already made a dent in the straightened bedclothes by marching across them, butted his head against her thigh. She scratched his ears, swiped his whiskers, turned and retrieved her things from the counter, headed out the door and down the clanging metal stairs.

Fifteen minutes later, Cindy pulled into her parents' driveway. Their house, the house she'd grown up in, sat a distance off the road between two open fields. The driveway provided ample room for the cars filling it. Full house, then. Mom hadn't really said.

Her parents always invited any aunts, uncles, cousins, their kids, friends, who weren't otherwise engaged. Due to the loose arrangement, the congregation tended to vary in amount and attendees. Mom always made enough. Too much, to be honest. However, as with friends and relatives, Cindy had no qualms bringing dishes anyway, accepting leftovers, and helping as needed. Many hands made short work the saying went.

Striding up the winding walkway to the front door, Cindy felt her tension ease. She really did love the holidays. The closer she got to the cheery, Thanksgiving-themed welcome mat, the more she recognized how different she'd been feeling this year. She lingered a moment with her feet squarely planted, listening to the voices inside. Knowing she had no need to knock,

Cindy grasped the doorknob. It pulled away from her hand as the door opened inward.

"Hi," Cindy said to her cousin Len.

He gave her a quick hug. "I was just heading out to my car to grab something. Be right back."

Cindy slipped in past him. For several moments she stood in the foyer without announcing her presence. Numerous aromas filled the house, both savory and sweet. Conversation continued unabated. Cindy heard her name mentioned. Twice. She focused in on the dialogue, curious. Whoever had been speaking had moved on already. Mom appeared from the kitchen, carrying a tray filled with various glasses. Cindy hurried over to help her, exchanging the items in her hands for the tray in her mother's.

"You're here!" her mother cried. "No one told me you'd arrived."

"Just got here," Cindy said. "Where am I going with this?"

"Set it on the coffee table, honey. People can help themselves." Lacie headed back to the kitchen with Cindy's cheesecake and the wine.

Walking through the living room proved a risky affair with a liquids-laden tray. Cindy stopped every few feet for greetings and cautious hugs. When she finally set the tray on the table, she straightened to discover Herb at her side.

"Hello," she said.

"Hi. How are you?"

"Fine. You?"

"Good."

Cindy waited, shifting a little to one side to make room for those reaching for glasses. Finally, Herb raised a hand, pointing his thumb toward the kitchen. "Your brother invited me."

"Peter's here? I thought he wasn't coming!" Cindy paused before heading into the kitchen, contemplating Herb for a second. "Seems weird we didn't run into each other more often, considering your friendship with Peter."

Herb shrugged, his gaze shifting to a point behind Cindy's back. He lifted his hand. From the corner of her eye, Cindy saw the fingers on a smaller, slender hand slip into his. A young woman, perhaps in her late twenties, stepped closer to Herb, smiling at Cindy.

"Hi," said the woman. "I'm Savannah. Herb's girlfriend." She glanced at Herb and tittered.

Cindy's brows went up. That was quick. Their aborted breakfast date, hers and Herb's, had only taken place a couple weeks ago. Apparently, he'd found the 'more' he needed. Suppressing surprise, Cindy greeted Savannah with a smile and then excused herself to find her brother. She found him mashing potatoes in the kitchen, his wife beside him adding butter to the mixture.

Cindy threw herself into both of their arms, receiving a spattering from the potatoes on the masher in Peter's hand. Quickly she stepped back. "Where are the kids?"

"In the yard," said Tracy. "Playing with Len's brood."

"I'm so glad you made it," Cindy said.

"So are we," Tracy responded. "We were going to do quiet this year. Quiet doesn't quite cut it, though."

Cindy laughed in agreement. A female voice spoke from the table's opposite end. Cindy peered around her sister-in-law and spotted Gran seated in the corner. Cindy grinned at her.

"Don't you go grinning at me like that, Cinderella Louise Michaels," said Gran. "I have a bone to pick with you."

"What? Why?" Cindy asked, hurrying over to kiss her grandmother's cheek.

"George Martins is why," said Gran.

Cindy jerked upright.

"Seems you reached out to him without letting me know."

With a nod, Cindy eased herself into the nearest chair. "I meant to tell you, but since he never got back to me—"

"He contacted me directly," said Gran. "I still have the same email address I've had for years, so he took a shot." Gran's expression was either angry, or just pretending to be.

"I thought...I don't know what I thought. I guess I was feeling a bit of my own remorse over letting old friends slip away. I shouldn't have gone behind your back, Gran. I'm sorry."

"Well, you've lost your date for the ball now, Cindy."

Goodness. Gran really was angry. Cindy scooted closer, sliding her chair across the floor. She took her grandmother's hand. "Don't be mad."

Gran's lips quivered as though she might cry.

What Cindy had thought a good deed had backfired. But no. Tears were not in the offing. Instead, Gran laughed.

"George is coming up to visit. He's taking me to the ball, Cinderella." She grinned with sparkling eyes.

"George?" echoed Peter from behind them. "Your artist friend?"

"You remember him?" Gran asked.

"Sure," said Peter. "How could I not? Back when you and Pop used to do the Thanksgiving thing, he was there. And he was around other times, too."

"He was older then," Cindy said to Gran. "I didn't recognize him in the photo from the ball. I should have."

Gran patted her hand. "No worries, dear. Not even about being a busybody."

"Pardon me?" Cindy said.

"I'm glad he contacted me. We've had a wonderful time catching up. He said he still dances when he can. I better get into shape myself if I'm going to keep up."

Picturing Gran and George in the photo, Cindy stood with a satisfied smile. She'd done good after all. Turning, she checked to see what else needed doing in the kitchen.

"Petey and I plan to be there," said Tracy. "Already got our tickets. Who are you going with? I hear Jas has gotten herself someone tall, dark, and delicious." Tracy glanced at Cindy's mom when she said this.

"I think Mom has a bit of a crush on him

herself," Cindy said, "but yes, Mom's description describes him pretty well. They've been friends since college. Not this sort of friend, though."

"Who are you going with, anyway?" her mom asked from the stove. "Figured it out, yet?"

Mom spoke those words as if she hadn't sent Herb Cindy's way, and as if he wasn't standing in the living room this minute with his speedily acquired girlfriend. "You mean since Gran's now taken?" Cindy said. "Shakespeare. I'll be getting started on his tiny tux."

Everyone laughed.

"I know you," Tracy whispered. "You'll buck tradition and go alone."

"Tradition?" Cindy echoed. "You do realize the ball was defunct for a long time?"

"But it's not anymore. It's new tradition now. You'll keep it going."

"Let's see how this one goes first," Cindy said with a rueful smile.

Caught up in meal preparation with family and friends, Cindy didn't think about the Garland Ball again as the Thanksgiving festivities progressed. Around four o'clock, she headed down into the finished basement with her sister-in-law and several others, carrying the food to lay out along the bar and across an eight-foot-long folding table. Other folding tables had already been set up with tablecloths, utensils, glasses, plates. As per tradition, a Christmas tree stood in the corner. An artificial one for downstairs, and not yet decorated except for warm, white lights and strung popcorn. Mom had always done this, ever since Cindy could remember. Seeing it, Cindy's heart swelled a little.

Tracy paused beside her. "Seriously," she whispered, "who are you going with?"

"Oh, not you, too, Trace," Cindy groaned. "I'll figure it out. Or not. Easiest solution, I'll pay for two tickets and no more to be said. It'll serve the same purpose."

Tracy grunted, tossing her hair, and then laughed. "Okay. Understood. But if you want, I do have a single cousin—"

"I'm fine," Cindy interrupted her. "Truly."

Tracy nudged her with an elbow and walked away. Herb, who had trooped down the stairs empty-handed except for his girlfriend, twisted his mouth in commiseration from across the room. Pretending she hadn't seen, Cindy returned upstairs for more food.

With nearly all hands helping, setup was quickly completed. Family and guests moved to gather downstairs. Cindy hung back in the kitchen, letting the voices drift off. A footstep sounded in the hall. Her father appeared.

"Dad," she said. "I didn't even get to say hello to you yet."

"It's Thanksgiving. I didn't get to say hello to half of these people." Making his way to the refrigerator, he opened the door, reached in, grabbed a beer bottle. "Want one?"

"I'm good," Cindy said. Her father straightened, pushed the door closed. He stood taller than her brother, possibly the tallest of his own siblings. His shoulders hunched a little more each year, but he still towered over them all.

"What are you doing in here all by yourself?" he asked her.

"What are you?"

He lifted the beer bottle in teasing response, took a swig, swallowed, and smiled. "Like you, I need a little quiet before I head into the fray."

Cindy nodded. "Always. Just a second or two to reboot, right?"

Bob Michaels nodded his gray head sagely. "I'll head down. I'll tell them you're in the bathroom. See you in a few minutes." He started for the door, hesitated, looked back. "You're your own person, Cindy Lou. You do what you need to do. Don't let anybody push you in the direction you don't want to go."

Cindy smiled. A tremulous smile. She blinked moisture from her lashes. "Thanks, Dad."

Once he'd disappeared, Cindy leaned her back against the counter, crossed her arms. It didn't matter how old she was. Encouragement from her dad always teared her up a bit. Maybe because he didn't say much. He'd always been a quiet man. But when he spoke, he often came out with some gems.

Abruptly, the cell phone in her pocket gave its indication a text had been received. She pulled the phone out. The message came from Jasmine, wishing her a happy Thanksgiving. Cindy texted her back with a few, relevant emojis and slid the phone toward her dress pocket. The tone popped one more time before she got the cell inside. Cindy lifted it again, expecting something more from Jas. It was Harry this time, with his own Thanksgiving sentiment. Staring at the phone, Cindy sucked in a slow breath, let the air out.

I hope you both have a wonderful day, she typed, then erased the words. He and Jasmine weren't necessarily together at Jas's parents' house. Instead, she pecked out, *Same to you.*

The message seemed rather pathetic. *Family filled and happy, I hope!* she added. Afterward, she silenced her phone and stowed it away. No need to get into lengthy texting with Jas's boyfriend.

As much as she might have liked to. Goodness, she was pathetic.

Chapter Eleven

Thanksgiving blurred into a wonderful but whirlwind memory, even though only four days had passed since families had gathered to feast and be thankful. An employee from Luke's Tree Farm arrived in town the day after, hanging wreaths high up on every third lamppost along Main Street. All the shop windows soon possessed their holiday displays and the countdown to the Garland Ball began in earnest.

Cindy's phone alarm played its morning tune. Cindy hit snooze but with a sudden start, she threw off the blankets and hurried out the apartment door wearing the sweats and tee shirt she'd slept in. She rushed up the stairs to the third floor barefoot, keys jangling in her fingers. Letting herself in, she clicked on the lights, nearly panicked. But as the rational part of her brain expected, she found everything as it should be.

Breathing a sigh of relief, wondering what bad dream had caused her panic, Cindy went to each work station, checking for open orders. Two boxes held a slip each, the third empty. Dresses and gowns in numerous colors filled the rack along the back wall, tags with the owners' names carefully clipped to each. A great many had already been collected by their purchasers, or delivered.

Sliding her rump into the nearest seat, Cindy closed her eyes, going over the list in her head. Hall: the last installment for the deposit delivered yesterday. Decorations to be put into place the evening before the ball, including the enlarged photos: boxed up and ready to go. Caterer for the buffet and bartenders had already called with follow up confirmation. Cindy continued in this fashion through all the details and tasks she could recall. Most everything had been donated or discounted thanks to the friendly interaction and persuasive abilities of Jasmine and others.

Yet, with each passing day, Cindy dreaded the ball more. Even so, she made sure her attitude didn't affect her commitment to seeing it through, to making the ball a memorable event for everyone attending. They deserved it. All who came into the store or recognized her or Jas on the street seemed unable to hold back encouragement and compliments. Their kind words and enthusiasm lifted Cindy's spirits. Even so, something continued to dampen her holiday mood.

Christmas, the entire season, was her favorite time of year. Cindy was usually energized by festive enthusiasm. She could always be counted on to eagerly join in every holiday event. But she hadn't even signed up for caroling in the park yet, and only yesterday morning had switched the satellite radio to seasonal tunes in the store. Normally, her cards would have been mailed the day after Thanksgiving. They were out, but this year they likely wouldn't arrive to their destinations before Christmas. Her apartment contained only a few candles and lights and fake holly above the door. As for the store window, well, Cindy's half-hearted décor had become a source of quiet contention between her and Jasmine. Yet, Jasmine made no move to correct the problem. She knew the window was Cindy's thing. So, instead, Jas went into passive-aggressive mode, pausing at the open door each morning, her face turned toward the lackluster display in the window beside it with a comically aggrieved expression.

Well, not this morning. In a tossing, sleepless moment, Cindy had come up with a brand-new idea. She might have enough time to execute it before Jas came in.

Grabbing an empty box, Cindy hustled around the room collecting items she needed. Partially empty spools of colorful thread. Varied ribbons from the basket where odd-sized lengths were kept. Smaller scissors that caught the light even in the dim room. She picked up several other oddments, dropped them into the carton under her arm, then returned to her apartment to get dressed.

Cindy's phone dinged as she was putting on her shoes. She glanced at it, saw a text from her mom. Of course it would be Mom. She knew what time Cindy rose in the morning. Remembering the early hour, however, sudden alarm shot through Cindy's blood. Quickly, she read the message. She groaned loudly. At the noise, Shakespeare bolted under the chair, latent survival memories still stored in his brain from the days before Cindy had rescued him. "Sorry, bud," she whispered and studied the text once more, to make sure she hadn't misread it. She hadn't.

Herb broke up with his girlfriend. There's still time. I'm sure he'd be happy to hear from you.

His girlfriend of FOUR DAYS ago? Cindy texted back in disbelief. *The one he felt so enamored with that he brought her to your house for Thanksgiving? Thanks for the update, but I'm not interested. I love you, Mom, you know I do, but you really need to stop.*

Shaking her head, Cindy opened her closet door and rummaged through the crowded shelf for more things she visualized needing. "Okay, Shakes," she announced to the cat while adding the items to her box, "I'm heading down to finish that darned window."

As usual, Jasmine wasn't wrong. The front window displayed a sweet yet totally uninspired little scene. Nothing in it screamed Christmas. It also didn't stimulate curiosity, any Christmas sentiment whatsoever, nor did the contents invite the onlooker to come inside, to view what lay beyond.

In less than ten minutes, Cindy had the window stripped down to nothing. She set everything to go back into the window to one side and the rest in another box from the storeroom. She glanced at her wrist. Barely six-thirty.

A weak sun glazed the display area in soft hues, providing enough light to see by. Cindy clicked off the overhead, not wanting to call attention to what she was doing. Spotlighted by the fixture, she'd been feeling a bit like she was on display. Maneuvering the artificial tree back inside, Cindy stood it in the corner rather than front and center, and plugged in the light strands. The warm, clear glow sparkled on the frosted glass and made indistinct, soft-edged shadows on the walls. Cindy observed the effect with a smile.

Something tapped the window. Cindy jumped and whirled about.

"Sorry! Didn't mean to startle you!" Dan stood in strange motion on the sidewalk, his whole body bobbing up and down.

"Do you want to come in?" Cindy shouted back.

Shaking his head, he pointed to his still moving legs. "Out for my morning run. I thought your window was finished?"

"So did I. But it needed re-doing due to lack of...nearly everything."

He laughed, shuffled his running-in-place form a little closer to the window. "Can I bring Rena in this evening?"

Cindy had thought he'd forgotten or changed his mind. "What time?"

"You tell me." He ran in a tiny circle on the sidewalk until he bobbed before the window once again.

"Seven-thirty?" Both Jas and Peg would be in the store, so Cindy could sneak away to take measurements, pick a design, and then show Rena the third floor while they were up there. "Is that too late?"

"I'll make arrangements to have Rena dropped off to me and we'll be here. She can even spend the night with me. It's not their usual day. She'll love that."

He waved and jogged away, but a moment later he returned. "Thank you." He sped off.

"You're welcome!"

Cindy discovered the grin still on her face five minutes later. Nice man, Dan Hayes. Great dad. The Garland Ball planning and implementation had brought him into her sphere more frequently than usual. She welcomed it, with everything else going on.

Hastening back to work, Cindy tried to recreate the scene she'd visualized while sleep eluded her, a display combining the modern Cinderella tale with Christmas tradition. She had already removed all the silver balls from the tree and now arranged the spools wrapped in bright thread to hang from the branches, along with the bright, shining scissors and shimmering ribbons. Deciding the tree could use a little silver after all, she returned some of the balls, then stepped back, arms crossed, to study the presentation.

So far, so good. But she had to hurry if she wanted to complete the display before Jas's arrival.

Cindy placed an old wooden stool she'd purchased at a flea market to one side. On the worn surface, and on the floor in front of it, she set up several resin mice which had graced the window sill on the third floor. Colorful ribbons trailed from their little hands, as well as a spool from which bright green thread wound across the floor. A silvery pumpkin someone had given her a long time ago stood behind the mice, as though awaiting their transformation to horses and it into a carriage. Next, she lined the window with traditional faux greenery, neglected in the storeroom this year but now fastened top and bottom, left and right, with duct tape concealed by gently coerced fake pine needles. Real greenery would have been nice, but it wouldn't last in the window, so this would have to do.

The final touch remained in her apartment. Glancing at her wrist again for the time, Cindy raced back upstairs and down again, manhandling the antique dressmaker's dummy through the store and into the window, where she placed it front and center. Hastily, she moved the small spotlights on the ceiling to highlight the items, and then she hustled into the cold morning air to view her work from outside.

Her breath huffed from her lungs, frosting the air. Something was missing.

Standing with her arms crossed and her teeth in her lips, light and rapid footfalls caught her attention. She turned her head and spotted Dan heading her way. He paused beside her, somewhat sweaty despite the cold air.

"What's wrong?" he asked, still performing the jogging in place. She figured he must do that until cooldown and stopping.

"Something's missing," she said.

He circled around her, eyeing the window from

different angles, and came to an abrupt stop. She could see their reflections in the glass, side by side, the top of her head nearly at a level with his shoulder. In his casual, worn-out running gear, he looked slightly disheveled and definitely fit.

"I like this much, much better than what was in there," he said, "but I think you need something on that dummy. Something that ties in to the upcoming ball?"

Cindy followed his gaze. She nodded her head in a fashion that moved her whole upper body, as if her neck didn't bend. She turned and grinned at him. "You're a genius, Dan." She squeezed his upper arm. Yep, muscular under the tattered sweatshirt. She realized she'd been holding on a tad too long when an amused expression appeared on his face. She dropped her hand to her side.

"Sorry," she said.

His smile deepened. "No problem. Glad I could be of help." With a small salute, he was off and running in the printshop's direction. Her gaze trailed him until he reached his store. She felt like an idiot. Groping an old friend's arm. A fellow businessperson's arm. What the heck was the matter with her?

Blowing out a long breath, Cindy returned her attention to the dressmaker's dummy, giving it a narrow-eyed inspection. She knew exactly what would make the window shine.

*　　*　　*

148

"What is your gown doing in the window?" Jas demanded the second she walked in the door.

Cindy lifted her chin. She didn't plan to back down. "Advertising Cinderella Silks," she answered calmly. "And tying the Christmas-Cinderella-Garland Ball theme together."

"This is not what I meant when I said the window had no flair."

"Maybe not," said Cindy, "but it does now, doesn't it?"

"Grrr," Jas showed her teeth and wrinkled her nose. "Yes. Yes, it does." She stomped into the store and up to the counter, where she shrugged her coat from her shoulders. "If this is some way to avoid going to the ball—"

"By not having a gown? That makes no sense. Especially since I do have one. It'll come right off that dummy when I'm ready for it."

Pacified by Cindy's logic, Jas's expression smoothed out. She walked her coat into the backroom and returned holding a small bag. "For you," she said.

"Me? What is it?"

"Open the bag and look, or don't and keep guessing."

Cindy pulled the top open and peered inside. Confused, she pulled the object out. Contained in the smallest frame Cindy had ever seen was a photo. Cindy squinted at it, unable to decipher at first the parade of color or the shape. She held the photo up to the light.

Now she saw exactly what the photo showed, right down to the words emblazoned across the jacket back: Carter and the Cool Cats.

"How? Where?" she stammered.

"Harry gave it to me for you. Last night."

"Last night?" Cindy echoed.

"Yes. Where did you think I'd gone to last evening?"

"I don't know." Cindy said. "Your time is your own. I don't usually pry."

"That's true," Jas agreed. "You don't. Why not? Especially when it comes to Harry. I mean, you *know* him. You and he were almost inseparable way back when. I used to think you two had something going on. But you never really did. Did you?"

Cindy didn't want to be reminded. For all those many hours spent together, nothing had ever progressed. A couple years following graduation, she'd run into him somewhere. She couldn't even remember what the occasion had been or where it had taken place. He had called their friendship a missed opportunity for something more. She'd kissed him a few times in those college days, fumbled around in an easy, not quite urgent way, but beyond that, nada. It hadn't bothered her as much as she'd expected it would. It hadn't seemed to concern him either. He said there was time. And then there wasn't. Everyone moved on into their own adult lives.

She hadn't even been sure he meant those words. She'd suspected he had a thing for Jas the whole while.

Cindy looked up, away from the photo. "Did he say why he wanted me to have this?"

"So that you'd remember."

Remember? Cindy thought. Remember what?

"He said," Jas added, "you didn't recall the jacket, but when you did, you both couldn't stop laughing. At the tavern?"

Cindy understood Jas's reference. She nodded. They used to laugh a lot like that.

"I remembered," said Jas. "Who could forget how much time you devoted to making it. He loved that thing. Still does, apparently."

Smiling, she took the frame from Cindy's fingers for a close examination and then returned it. "Silly man," Jas said affectionately.

"Definitely," Cindy agreed and set the frame aside on the counter where she could see it if she wanted to, but in a place where it could also be easily ignored. "Oh," she said as Jas turned away. "Dan—from the printshop?"

"I know who you mean," said Jas.

"He's coming with his daughter at seven-thirty so she can pick out a gown design and get measured. She had some interest in seeing the machinery upstairs, so I'll be running up there, as well. I know Peg is here, but if at any time you need me, just grab me."

Jasmine swung back around. "Is Rena going to the ball?"

"She is," said Cindy.

"At twelve years old she probably has a date, at least."

Cindy ignored the jibe. "Yes, she does. Her dad."

"Oh my gosh," Jas gushed, pressing her hand to

her mouth, "how sweet is that?"

Cindy smiled, as warmed again by the thought as Jas appeared to be. "Very. Not to change the subject, but besides your complaint about my gown, what did you think of the window?"

"I love it," said Jas. "A big improvement. When on earth did you do it?"

"The butt crack of dawn," Cindy answered.

Jas shook her head and crossed the floor to take another look at the display from behind, peering through the opening. "Cinderella-Christmas. You totally captured it."

The door opened while she stood there, admitting a queue of women who made straight for the counter. Any chance for further conversation vanished.

A busy day sped by after that. Before Cindy realized, the alarm she'd set on her phone to remind her of Dan and Rena's appointment chimed. Five minutes later, they arrived right on time.

"Dan, hi," Cindy greeted him, meeting his gaze quickly while she tried not to think about the embarrassing arm-squeezing. "Rena, how are you?"

"Excited," the girl said, jumping a little on her toes. Rena was an animated little thing. 'Little' being relative, since she was quite as tall as Cindy. Still, Cindy found her refreshing. So many girls Rena's age possessed preoccupations Cindy didn't quite understand, including spending an inordinate amount of time on their phones ignoring everything around them except whoever or whatever had their attention on the screen. Cindy nipped her thoughts short with another: *I sound like my mother.* She inwardly groaned.

"Great. The assistants have all gone home, so we'll go straight upstairs," Cindy said. "I can show you designs and the work area at the same time. Is that okay with you both?" She glanced at Dan, figuring she should include him in the decision. They both nodded, Rena's enthusiastic and Dan's quietly amused. Still.

Jas waved them off with a similar look. As soon as Dan and his daughter's backs were turned, Jas pointed at Rena, then pressed both hands over her heart. Cindy smiled in agreement.

They clambered up the stairs, pausing on the second level so Rena could peer over the railing down to the alley below. Everything seemed to excite her. "What's behind that door?" she asked, pointing to Cindy's apartment.

"That's where I live," Cindy said.

Rena's blue eyes widened. "You do? That's so cool!"

"Apparently, she thinks you're the coolest," Dan whispered.

"Dad!"

Cindy laughed. "I am pretty cool," she said with a wink at Rena.

They climbed the next set of stairs to the third floor. The twelve-year-old was fascinated with everything Cindy showed her. Willingly, gladly, Cindy answered all her questions in detail, turned on the various machines to give the girl a demonstration. Dan stood quietly by the doorway, leaning against the wall with his arms crossed over his chest and a closed smile on his face.

"Can I come work for you?" Rena asked.

Cindy didn't glance back at Dan, as much as she wanted to. This seemed like an important question for Rena. One to be respected and owned.

"You don't mean right this minute, I'm assuming," Cindy said to her.

"When I'm older," said Rena.

Elbow on the table, Cindy dropped her chin onto her hand, meeting the girl's gaze. "I always appreciate when people take a genuine interest in what I do here, so sure, if it still appeals to you once you're older, yes. I'd be happy to have you work for me. As long as your parents are okay with that," she added, looking back at Dan for a second before returning her attention to Rena. "Who knows? You might even have your own design ideas by then we could work on. I didn't always want to do this, you know. My head was all into softball. And then one day…well, my interests changed. Yours could, too. But that would be okay. You could still visit me even if you're not working for me."

Rena looked over at her dad, eyes on him for longer than Cindy's had been. "I can, can't I, Dad?"

"In a few years," Dan said softly. "If you still want to."

Rena turned back to Cindy, grinning. She lifted her hand into the air. Cindy did, too, and Rena smacked her palm against Cindy's.

"Does that, like, seal the deal?" Cindy asked jokingly.

"Yep," Rena answered.

Cindy glanced at Dan once more. He appeared proud and a little sad, perhaps thinking about his daughter growing up and away from him. Cindy's breath caught in her chest. She gave him a small, encouraging smile.

"How long have you known my dad?" Rena asked abruptly.

"Since I was younger than you," Cindy answered after a brief hesitation. "Went our separate ways as adults, but we've maintained our friendship to one degree or another."

"I think my dad's happy about that, because he thinks you're cool, too."

Dan laughed, perhaps both shocked and genuinely amused. With an embarrassed grimace, Cindy steered Rena's attention away from the subject and to the computer monitor, where Cindy brought up designs she hoped would be perfect for a girl Rena's age.

Following a half-hour review and discussion, Rena picked a design and fabric. She looked to her dad for approval, which he gave. Cindy then quickly measured the girl in keeping with the chosen gown style. Only then did Cindy check the wall clock for the time.

"It's almost nine!"

"I guess you need to get down and close the store? Sorry to have kept you so long." Dan apologized.

"Jas and Peg can handle it. I'm just thinking of the hour and the fact it's a school night," Cindy said.

"I've been up later than this," Rena interjected.

"For special occasions," her dad said.

Rena stood up from the stool where she'd been

sitting and stretched. "This is a special occasion, Dad. Besides, my homework's all done, we've had dinner, I can shower in the morning, and we're ten minutes from the house." She went over to stand beside him. Dan ruffled her russet-brown hair.

"I can't argue with any of that," he said.

Cindy walked them back downstairs and through the store, pausing at the front entrance with the door open. Chill air rushed in. A few snowflakes, too.

"Goodness," she said, "it's beginning to look a lot like—"

"Christmas," Dan finished. They both laughed. Rena looked from one to the other, her brows knitting.

"Finishing someone's sentence can be annoying, Dad."

"Sorry," he said to Cindy with a broad wink. Rena rolled her eyes. She grabbed his hand and tugged it.

"You're letting out all the heat. Isn't that what you always say to me? Besides, it's snowing. I want to be in it."

"One second," Dan said. "I owe Cindy a deposit on your dress."

Cindy waved him away. "It's okay. No deposit necessary. Besides, I know where *you* live."

He laughed outright. With his free hand, he took Cindy's fingers and gave them a quick squeeze. "Thanks." Together, father and daughter strode away into the flurries.

On impulse, Cindy stepped out after them, allowing the door to close behind her. Tiny frozen flakes settled on her cheeks as she watched the pair walk down the block. As if sensing her eyes on them, Dan turned at one point, spotted her and gave her a small salute before continuing down the sidewalk hand in hand with Rena. Cindy's breath slowed, almost stilled.

"What on earth are you doing out there?"

Spinning on her heel, Cindy faced Jasmine in the again opened door. "Just seeing them on their way."

"That Rena is so darned adorable," Jas said as Cindy eased past and into the store. "So's her dad."

Cindy's step hitched a bit at Jasmine's words, knowing exactly where Jasmine was headed. "Always has been," she said and went on to begin tallying the day's receipts.

Jas shut and locked the door, and set about turning off all but the nighttime lighting. "Too bad he already has a date," she added in Cindy's ear upon passing.

"Ha, ha," Cindy muttered. Her hands paused in their work. "Rumor has it he's seeing somebody. Besides, I would never risk my friendship with him by asking him to do me a favor like that."

"A favor?" said Jas. "I'd think he'd be happy to help out." She disappeared into the backroom.

The suggestion Dan escorting her to the ball would be his way of 'helping out' stung a little. Frowning, Cindy continued with the paperwork. Maybe if she were more open, like Jasmine, this wouldn't be an issue. Maybe she needed to stop being so judgmental, cautious, content with being on her own…

Wow, she sounded like she *wanted* a date. She didn't. She was perfectly happy to go it alone, to the ball and in her life. And if she decided she needed a companion at the Garland Ball? Shakespeare would be in his best tux.

A couple hours later, exhausted, and ready for sleep, Cindy clicked off the bedside lamp, snuggled down beneath the covers, and stared at the ill-defined shadows made by the string of tiny, colorful lights outlining the window above her bed. In the morning, she would purchase her own ticket. Two of them. She couldn't understand why she'd delayed this long. Two tickets, and that would be that.

No Prince Charming needed for this Cinderella.

Chapter Twelve

For possibly the tenth time since the Garland ball became a reality, Cindy reiterated her intentions to Jas. She wouldn't lie to her best friend. Jas seemed unimpressed by her statement. Not angry, or annoyed, or disappointed, but more as though she felt sure this wasn't Cindy's last word on the matter and things would change before the ball's date. She even said as much.

"The ball is only two weekends away," Cindy reminded her.

"I know," Jasmine answered with an arch to her brow.

Cindy's own brows crunched downward. "You're not planning something dastardly, are you?"

"Goodness! Me? Why would you think that?"

"Maybe because I've known you forever?" Cindy countered.

"Has it been that long?" Jasmine sashayed her way in exaggerated fashion to the front door, where she flipped the sign Cindy had forgotten from closed to open. "How time flies."

"There are no Prince Charmings," Cindy said as she returned. "Or if there are, they're already taken. I'm going to be running around all night anyway. You probably will be, too, but at least Harry has patience. Or I assume he does?"

"He's a very patient man," Jas agreed.

"Because he waited for you?"

Jas paused, turned on her heel. "I suppose he has, hasn't he?" She walked on into the backroom, where Cindy heard her doing something with the coffee pot. No take-out from Gina's today, apparently. They both much preferred Gina's coffee to what they brewed here, but it seemed Jas had opted not to make her morning run. Jas returned a few minutes later with a mug for each of them.

Suddenly, the door opened. Dan came in, along with a waft of cold, fresh air. He wore a knit cap over his hair, forcing it into curls along his collar.

"Well, look who's here," Jasmine whispered.

"Stop that," Cindy responded before smiling at Dan. "Hi. What's up?" she said to him. Because he looked like a man with a goal.

He halted a few feet from the counter, held up two fingers. "Two things," he said.

"Only two?" Jas drawled before strolling away, cup in hand, and giving him a pointed look from behind his head.

"At the moment," he answered her over his shoulder. He turned back to Cindy.

"Would you like some coffee?" Cindy offered.

"Sure. Thanks."

Dan followed her into the storeroom, where the fresh pot's aroma filled the air. The scent mingled with the chill clinging to his coat and the apple-y aftershave he wore. Cindy found herself unusually aware of the fragrance as well as his proximity.

"Sugar?"

"Yes, please," he said, "but I can fix it myself."

"I don't mind," Cindy mumbled, hastily preparing then handing him his mug. He took a sip and smiled.

"Perfect," he said.

"Not as good as Gina's, though," Cindy countered inanely.

He smiled, took another sip. "Well, no coffee is a good as Gina's, I have to admit."

"It's like magic," Cindy said. "Like she puts a spell on it."

They both lapsed into silence. Cindy felt her cheeks grow warm. Darn Jasmine and her allusions. "So, what's up?" she asked again, squeezing past him and heading back out into the store. He followed, meeting her at the counter with his cell phone out.

"There's this," he said. "I hope it's not too late."

Cindy took the phone from him, frowned at it. "Is that fabric?"

"Yes. Do you recall Rena took pictures last night? She texted me this photo bright and early, and asked me to find out if she could switch the gown to the blue. This blue. She was torn between this and the one she picked out, if you remember. I told her it might be too late, and if it wasn't, she absolutely could not change her mind again." He looked at Cindy with an apology and hope.

Behind him, Jas raised her hand to her ear, pinkie and thumb extended, and gave it a little wave. Cindy understood the implication. Dan caught the gesture when he turned to follow Cindy's gaze.

"I'm sorry. I guess I could have called," he said to Cindy.

"No, you absolutely should not have," said Cindy. "Or at least, I don't mind you coming in to tell me. Better now than after the dress had been started, right?"

Slightly flustered, Cindy looked closer at the phone in her hand. After a moment, she returned the instrument to him. She glared at Jasmine, who strode across the store, pretending a focus on something there.

"I haven't started the gown yet, so really, there's no problem." As for Jas's inference, she didn't know what to say. Sure, he could have called, but there was also no reason he couldn't stop in. This was important to him. To him and to Rena.

"So, you don't mind?" Dan asked.

For a second, Cindy thought he was referring again to coming to the store rather than calling, until she realized he meant the change in fabric. "This is a special thing for Rena, right? The dress should absolutely be the color she prefers."

Dan inclined his head, reached out, lowered his hand onto hers on the counter. "Thank you."

Cindy avoided looking at his fingers. "No problem."

He released her hand. Another silence ensued. Dan gulped more coffee down, winced when he burned his mouth. "Ouch," he said quietly.

"You okay?"

He nodded.

Cindy smiled. "What was the other thing?"

"The what?"

"You said 'two things' when you came in the door."

"Ah, yes, I did." His mouth twisted.

"Go on," Cindy said, sipping from her own mug.

"The website states 'music' but doesn't say what kind. Rena wanted to know. Just in case her dad might make a fool of himself on the dancefloor."

Movement on the store's far side caught Cindy's eye. She tried not to look, but couldn't help it. Jasmine clutched her hands together beneath her chin, mimicking a swoon, but swiftly adopted a normal position when Dan's head turned.

"All types," Jasmine said, lifting her mug back off the table. "All eras. From whatever the kids are gyrating to today—if they are—to the waltz."

"That's a bit of an exaggeration," Cindy said. "The band is talented, but not that talented. Music from various eras, however, is correct."

Dan pivoted his attention back to Cindy. "So, there will be a waltz?"

"Yes."

"That's what I was afraid of. Do you waltz?" he asked her.

"Barely."

After taking another short sip from his coffee, Dan set the mug back on the counter. "I'll have to find somebody else to teach me, then."

Jas made a small noise, quickly stifled.

"My gran could help you there," said Cindy, only half-joking. "She still performs ballroom dancing twice a month."

Dan placed one foot behind the other, backing toward the front door. "I'll have to keep that in mind." He continued his backward step until his wrist struck the door handle. "Thanks for being so accommodating about Rena's dress." He ducked out quickly. Cindy didn't have time for a response. She shot a glance Jasmine's way.

"Why did you—"

"You're an idiot," Jasmine interrupted.

"Pardon me?"

"He wanted you to teach him how to waltz. Didn't you get that?"

Cindy made a face. "Me? Some teacher I'd be. I can barely do it myself."

"Bet he would have liked to learn with you, then," Jasmine said, crossing back to the counter.

"Stop it, Jas. I told you, I heard he's dating someone. Besides—"

"Then why isn't he taking her?"

"What?"

"Why isn't he taking the woman he's dating to the ball, instead of his daughter?" Jas clarified.

Cindy lifted her chin, feeling peculiarly defiant. "Probably because Rena wanted to go and he's a great dad."

"Admirable, yes. Love the way you defend

him, by the way." Jasmine snatched Dan's mug from the counter. "I'll just take this, shall I? I'll wash them both and put them away."

Staring after her, Cindy resisted the urge to stamp her foot like a petulant child. "And for all you know," she called out, "he could be taking his girlfriend, too. There's nothing saying you can't buy three tickets!"

Jasmine didn't answer. Cindy's mouth twisted. Catching a glimpse of the jacket photo from Harry, Cindy tipped the frame facedown onto the countertop. Jas with perfect Harry just wanted everyone to be settled. Sweet, but unrealistic.

When Jas returned a few minutes later, Cindy apologized to her. "I don't know what's wrong with me," she said, "but I'm sorry for being disagreeable. If you're good here, I'm going to take a quick walk."

Jasmine acknowledged her words and her intention with a small nod. "Don't forget your hat. It's ridiculously cold out there."

That was the problem with a two-second commute. Cindy spent only a moment outside and didn't really get a good gauge on the weather. "Thanks, Mom," she said, and scurried into the storeroom for her coat, and the hat she'd stuffed in the pocket. Pulling the garment out, she yanked it down over her head, not caring what it did to her hair.

"Need anything while I'm gone?" she asked Jasmine as she passed.

Jasmine looked up from something under her hand on the counter. Cindy saw it was the overturned frame. Jasmine stood it back up. "A new best friend?" she said.

Cindy stopped short. "Jas, I'm sorry."

"And I'm kidding," Jas responded. "But it would be nice to have my old one back at some point."

Cindy's shoulders dropped. "I have been acting a little weird, haven't I?"

Curling her fingers, Jasmine extended her thumb and forefinger straight out and about a half-inch apart. "A wee bit. Enjoy your walk. Clear your head."

"I will. Thank you. For everything."

Jasmine shooed her off, smiling.

Outside, Cindy turned right and headed toward Dan's shop. She wanted to clear the air between them. He had seemed rather flustered when he left Cinderella Silks. Jasmine might be right. Maybe he had wanted Cindy to teach him the waltz, or as much as she could remember from when Gran taught her years ago. Jas's implication was an interest in Cindy, but he had only been asking as a friend. And as a friend, Cindy should have been paying closer attention.

Outside the printshop door, Cindy paused. She didn't want to have this conversation with him if he was busy. She peered inside and quickly backed away. She saw he was not busy, but otherwise engaged.

Cindy ducked away before he spotted her. She headed for the park, increasing her pace, deciding on a nice long walk among the evergreens and the trees in their lovely, nearly winter starkness. The girlfriend rumors were apparently true. He'd been engaged in a somewhat intimate clinch with a blond woman inside the store. In fact, was in the act of planting a kiss against her cheek. Not a moment for interruption from a friend who'd come to apologize and offer to teach him the waltz after all.

Shoving her chilled fingers into her pockets, Cindy strode along the sidewalk with her head down, feeling suddenly and ridiculously vulnerable. She called herself an unfriendly name. In a whisper, she thought. But no, it was loud enough a passerby jerked his head in her direction. She yanked her hand free from her coat and gave him a brief wave.

"Bad day," she said.

"We all have those," the stranger answered. "Hope it gets better."

"Thanks."

Head down once more, Cindy entered through the always-open iron gates. The park was a popular place for young and old, strolling, jogging, eating on a bench. Cindy avoided looking around the first few minutes, watching the placement of each foot instead. After a time, the slight noise of speech and footsteps around her abated. Cindy stopped, lifted her gaze. When had it started snowing? Flakes caught in her lashes, melted, ran down her cheeks like tears. Or were they tears?

"Idiot," she called herself again.

She wiped the moisture away, tasted a drop from her fingertip. No salt. Not tears. Yet, the melancholy continued. If Cindy had been the swearing type, she might have let out a few choice words. Instead, she just huffed out a breath, clouding the air before her face. She walked on, following the loop closest to the gate, until she came back around. In the time she'd been gone, a crew had arrived to decorate the new gazebo. Right. For the caroling on Thursday evening. The first event. Usually, several sessions were scheduled up until the night before Christmas. Cindy hadn't signed up for any of them.

Other workers took spools wrapped with lights from a cart, preparing to put them on the trees before the various displays were set up along the pathways. Recognizing Jimmy and his sister, both employed by the township, Cindy said hello and moved on. No use standing around watching other people work. She had her own to attend to, most importantly Rena's dress. She planned to do it herself, rather than handing the task on to an assistant. For one thing, it wasn't necessary. The work had slowed down somewhat and Cindy had the time to do it herself. For another, she looked forward to making the twelve-year-old's gown. Except for the equipment's modernization, it would be like old times.

Passing the printshop, Cindy didn't look

inside. She had almost reached Gina's bakery when she heard someone running up behind her.

"Cindy!"

Recognizing Dan's voice, Cindy spun and continued a slow stride backward. "Hi, Dan."

"You walked right by me," he said, amused.

"Sorry. I have a lot on my mind," she answered.

"Are you alright?"

Cindy pushed her hat up off her brow and came to a stop. "Yes. I'm just…look, I'm sorry about earlier. I can teach you a serviceable version of the waltz. Gran taught me, and I think I retained something from it."

He took a couple steps closer and stopped, too, looking regretful. "No worries. But funny thing, I do have someone to teach me. Me and Rena, both. I didn't realize she knew how, but—"

"Oh, that's fine," Cindy stammered out. "That's good. I—okay. We'll talk later. I've got to get back to the store." She turned and started away, but hesitated, looking back. "I'll be cutting Rena's dress this afternoon. I think she'll love it."

He nodded. She hurried off. He bellowed a loud 'thank you' after her. At her own store front, Cindy paused outside, studying the display inside the window. "Not bad, Michaels," she said under her breath. The gown made it. Her gown. Shimmering and strapless, flowing like water and catching the light in dulled, ruby sparks.

"Yeah, not bad Michaels," she whispered, yanking open the door and going inside. "At least you do some things right."

She found Jasmine on her cell. Cindy spotted Harry's face on the screen. She could also see Jas's live and upfront, and highly animated. Belatedly noticing the bell tinkling from the opening door, Jasmine turned and waved Cindy over, angling the phone in her direction.

"Hi, Harry," Cindy said, yanking the hat from her head. Her static-filled hair crackled and followed the garment upward. She attempted to smooth it down. "How are you?"

"Great. You?"

"Same, sort of," she answered with a laugh.

He grinned that infectious grin of his. Jasmine cut in.

"Harry is coming this weekend for a visit. And guess what?"

That would make it two weekend visits in a row, considering the ball the following week. Must be love. Or a stunningly strong infatuation. Who could tell? Although, Cindy recognized the difference this time for Jas. For one thing, Jas seemed inclined to include Cindy more than with any other beau in recent years. Usually, Jasmine kept them separate, her love life, her friend life. She liked her privacy.

"I'll bite," Cindy said. "What?"

"Harry's bringing a friend. Someone you might remember."

Cindy caught her breath, twisting her knit hat in her hands. "Who might that be?"

Harry opened his mouth, but Jasmine spoke

first. "Brad! You remember him, right? Harry's dormmate in college? And fellow bandmember to this day?" she added with a proprietary smile.

Cindy lifted her chin, preparing to nod. Jas seemed beside herself with excitement. Cindy was afraid she knew why. "Yes," Cindy said, completing the nod reluctantly. "I remember him. A massive amount of curly blond hair? And a goatee, right?"

"Still has both," said Harry. "Well, not so much hair, but yeah."

"And you're bringing him for all the fun and excitement in little ol' Connor Falls?" Cindy said.

"No, silly," said Jas, again before Harry could answer. "He wants to get together with all of us, catch up. I'm making reservations for us four to have dinner on Saturday night."

Four. Which probably meant Brad was unattached. Cindy felt as though her smile had frozen. Maybe like a rictus in death.

"Is that alright with you?" Harry asked in a sober tone.

Backing away, shirking her coat from her shoulders, Cindy said, "It'll be fun. Great idea." In truth, it would be nice to see Brad again, she supposed. He'd been an awkward, quiet, polite guy. Getting him to talk hadn't always been easy. But they were all older now. People changed.

Still, it rang like a setup.

Sighing, Cindy hung up her coat. She yelled out to Jas she was going to start Rena's dress. Climbing the outside stairs, she noticed she'd forgotten to unplug the lights strung on the second and third floor railings, their multiple colors hardly visible beneath the clouded sky. Snow had gathered on the bulbs. Cindy pulled out her phone, framing the nearest for a photo. Staring at the captured image for a moment while tiny flakes swirled around her head, she started to smile. An honest smile. A heartfelt one. Christmas was coming. Her favorite time of the year.

She just had to hold onto that sentiment.

Chapter Thirteen

Saturday morning, Dan came to Cinderella Silks with his daughter for her final fitting. "I have to head back to the shop," he said. "I'll come and get Rena when you're finished."

"Really, Dad?" drawled Rena in response. "I can walk half a block by myself."

Dan exchanged a look with Cindy and lifted one shoulder in a small shrug. "All grown up, I guess."

"Dad," said Rena again.

"We can walk together anyway," Cindy told her. "As soon as we're done, I have to run to the bakery." She had no real plan to go to the bakery, although she wasn't opposed to stopping in and saying hi. However, Cindy could plainly see Dan's discomfort at his daughter walking alone from Cinderella Silks to the printshop. Rena probably did a lot worse on her own he didn't know about, but Cindy figured she could at least put his mind at ease on this one. Despite the low crime rate in Connor

Falls, he couldn't help being a dad.

"Oh, okay," Rena agreed. "I haven't had breakfast. Dad, if you give me some money, I'll pick us both up a cupcake and a coffee."

"Cupcakes? That's some breakfast," said Dan, but he pulled out his wallet and handed the girl a ten-dollar bill. "And when did you start drinking coffee?"

"Dad," Rena said once more, this time with obvious affection.

Rolling his eyes, a smiling Dan backed away from the counter, turned, and strode to the door. Cindy's gaze trailed him until he'd exited. "He just loves you, you know," she said to Rena.

"Yeah. I know," the girl answered. "I love him, too. But I'm not a little kid anymore."

Cindy started toward the storeroom. "I think he realizes that. He can't help but want to protect you forever, though. Humor him. At least for a little while longer."

Behind her, Rena snorted. Grinning, Cindy led the way out to the stairs. On the second floor, Rena paused. "Dad says you have a cat."

"I do," Cindy said.

"He said he remembers you showing the cat to him on the sidewalk when you got it from the shelter."

Cindy thought a second. "I did. I forgot."

"I'm pretty sure he's seen your cat since then, too. Hasn't he been to your place?"

Cindy considered. He had, but not frequently or recently. "Yeah. Once or twice. I invited him to a small party I had here last year, too. A very small party. There's not much room inside."

Rena laughed.

"Do you want to meet Shakespeare?"

"May I?" Rena asked, politely and with proper, endearing grammar.

Cindy reached for the knob, stuck her key in. "Sure. Shakespeare likes company. Doesn't get a lot of it."

Rena followed her inside. "How come?"

"I keep to myself mostly." Cindy pushed the door shut behind the girl and called Shakespeare over. He studied Rena in a quick onceover before jumping from the sill and trotting to her side. Rena squatted down slowly, reached out and scratched the cat's head.

"He's sweet."

"Yep," agreed Cindy.

"So, why do you keep to yourself a lot?"

Cindy released a short breath. "I don't know."

Rena gave her a look, a very grownup look, and didn't pursue her question. "May I peek around?"

"For a minute or so," Cindy said. "We really should get on with your fitting."

Rena made her way through the apartment, peering at books, plants, knickknacks, the furniture. She looked in the bedroom, too, then came back out, Shakespeare at her heels.

"I love it," she said. "I want to live someplace like this when I grow up."

"Me, too," said Cindy.

It took Rena a split second to get the joke, and then she grinned. She bent and picked up a framed photo. "Is this you?"

"I think I mentioned to you I was into softball. My mother came across that photo last year and framed it for me."

The girl looked at Cindy in her uniform a few seconds longer before carefully placing the photo back where she'd found it. "Do you have any kids?" she asked, her eyes on the wall and other pictures hanging there.

"Yep. Keep them in the closet," Cindy said. Rena whipped around. "Sorry. Just joking. I do not have kids."

"I figured that," said Rena. "Or else they didn't live with you. This is your place. Only yours."

Cindy's brows lifted. "Yep. Mine and Shakespeare's."

"Got a boyfriend?"

Cindy's brows crawled up a millimeter more. "Nope. How about you? Any boyfriends?"

Rena scrunched up her nose and suppressed a shudder. Cindy barely held back a chuckle.

"There's plenty of time for that," she said to the girl. "But not for getting your gown finalized. I think we ought to get to it."

As they exited onto the metal stairs, Cindy eyeballed her apartment with cynical consideration. Was her life so obvious even a twelve-year-old could figure it out in a few minutes' time? Or was Dan's daughter just that astute? Either way, it didn't matter. Cindy liked her life.

For the most part.

They climbed to the third floor. Cindy unlocked the door and let Rena in first. The girl squealed.

"Is that it?" she cried, running across the room to where the dress hung. Standing before the garment, she jumped a little on her toes, her fingers clutched together under her chin. "May I touch it? My hands are clean."

"Sure, but be careful. There are still a few pins in it."

Rena lifted the skirt, pressed the fabric between her palms. "It's so soft."

"I don't use straight satin for that reason. I like fabric to move and not look like it's been pulled out of an old trunk by night's end. You can go into the bathroom and try the dress on. Don't get stuck by a pin. If everything fits to your liking, I'll finish sewing later and you and your dad can pick the dress up tomorrow."

Rena left the door cracked an inch and continued talking from inside, rattling on about a school project, a friend she didn't name, Cindy's cat, and a few other rapid-fire topics Cindy didn't quite catch. Suddenly, the girl went silent.

"Are you okay in there?" Cindy called.

The door opened in slow motion. Rena came out, walking on her toes, her fingers to her mouth. Her eyes shone with moisture. She dropped her hands. "Look at me," she whispered.

Cindy's lips twisted. Rena was so thrilled, Cindy almost cried a little, too. "You look quite grown up," she said, truthfully. She didn't know if Dan would be charmed by the results or inclined to a few tears himself. Possibly both.

"And it fits. It fits perfectly." Rena spun once. "I love it, Cindy. Thank you."

"You're very welcome," Cindy said, having to clear her throat first. She tipped her head, studying the garment with a critical eye. The girl was right. The dress was a perfect fit. "Change back into your clothes and I'll hang that up. Then we'll head out."

Again, Rena nearly closed the door, still speaking through it. "You don't have to walk me to Dad's, Cindy. He's being silly."

"He's being a dad. Better than not caring at all, yeah?"

Rena made no response. Cindy remembered that age. Wanting to be grown up, thinking you were, and yet not quite there. Dads could be viewed as a pain-in-the-butt. Moms, too. Both holding you back from some scary but thrilling freedom calling out to you.

After using her cell to take a photo of the gown returned to its hanger, Rena zipped her coat closed and followed Cindy down into the alley. Cindy texted Jas and told her she was walking Rena back to Dan, with a stop at the bakery, asking if she wanted anything. Without waiting for a response, Cindy led Rena to a narrow walkway between two other stores which took them out onto the sidewalk.

"How'd you get started? Sewing," Rena said. "Making clothes."

Cindy considered a minute. "I think it was the time I saw this neat shirt in a catalogue. I showed it to Mom and asked her if she could buy it for me. She asked if I'd looked at the price. I hadn't. I was floored. I decided I'd give making it myself a try."

"Did it work out?"

"Heck, no," Cindy said. "The results were laughable. But I tried again until I learned to get it right. And in all the trying, I found I really enjoyed the process and kept going."

"I wish that would happen to me," Rena said quietly. "I'd like to have a thing I could do that was special."

Cindy didn't answer right away. It seemed Rena should be talking with her parents about this, but Cindy remembered her old piano teacher and how many times Cindy had solved her own problems after discussing them with the woman. Sometimes you needed a different head, a different voice, a different perspective.

"What do you enjoy doing?" she asked Rena.

"Dreaming," Rena answered flatly. "That's what Mom calls it. I'm always dreaming about wanting to do, to be, something else."

"Well, I told you about the softball, right?"

"I saw the picture," said Rena.

"Yes, well, softball was my life way back

when. But even then, I thought about other things. After I got into designing and making clothes in earnest, I still wondered what it would be like to be…let's see, there were so many. An architect was one. A nurse. A teacher. An author. An archeologist. A botanist. Yes, a botanist," Cindy repeated with a laugh. "And all that daydreaming, wondering, learning, helped me to be who I am, to shape my interests, but I ultimately knew I wanted to do what I'm doing now."

"Do you ever, you know, regret not doing those other things? Like, being a botanist?"

"Teaching myself in small ways what botanists do is how I learned about flowers and things. And I love flowers. But I realized I wouldn't want to study them in a scientific way. I'd rather plant them and enjoy."

Rena gave her a skeptical look. "You don't have a lot of room for flowers, though."

Cindy shrugged. "True, not anymore. But I still help my mom with hers. It's a joint effort, keeping her sprawling garden going. Oh! Here's the bakery. Are you really having a cupcake for breakfast?"

"Definitely," said Rena and marched up to the door, holding it wide for Cindy to precede her.

Ten minutes later, after an exchange with Gina and an introduction to Gina's niece, Cindy arrived at the printshop with Rena. She'd only meant to watch her get safely inside, but they'd still been talking and she'd fallen in beside the girl without thought. Dan met them at the door.

"How'd it go?" he asked, stepping aside for Rena to enter.

Rena stayed on the sidewalk a moment, leaving her dad in limbo. "Perfect," she said. "I love the dress. And did you know Cindy once wanted to be a botanist?"

Dan's face twitched in amusement. "I did. I happened to be there when she decided it. Or at least, when she shared it with me and everyone else standing within ten feet."

"Oh, crud," said Cindy, "I'd forgotten about that."

Dan grinned, accepting the coffee cup from his daughter. Rena slipped past him, taking the cupcakes and the other coffee to the counter. Dan hung onto the open door, watching her for a second or two before he turned to face Cindy again. "We used to talk a lot when we were kids, you and me. Sometimes you told me things I didn't really want to hear."

"Did I?" Cindy countered. "I'm sorry. I really shouldn't burden anyone with half the crap that goes on in my head."

He made a dismissive noise. "I didn't mind. I did the same with you. A *quid pro quo* sort of arrangement, I suppose."

They smiled at each other, long enough for Cindy to feel a fluttering in her gut like moths on steroids. Mentally, she backed away in a hop, chastising herself for her reaction. Dan was her *friend,* for crying out loud. A taken friend. Much like Harry was.

"I need to get my pitiful behind back to the store," Cindy said. "Rena's gown will be ready for pickup tomorrow. Prepare for a shock. Not the price," she added, as Dan's eyes widened. "How very grown up your daughter looks in it."

"Thanks for the heads up," he said with another smile. Rena yelled thank you from inside the store, already elbow deep in her cupcake. "I'll see you tomorrow," Dan added. "Bright and early."

Cindy nodded, a quick movement, and hurried to Cinderella Silks. Jas was waiting for her, fluttering paper order slips in the air. "Two late orders for dresses. Should I call the girls back in?"

"Sure," said Cindy. "Will the customers need fittings beforehand?"

"They were both pretty adamant about what size they wore. I had them try on something similar in their sizes to be sure."

"Great. Yes, maybe get Sandi in. She was looking for more hours. In the meantime, I just want to run up and put the finishing touches on Rena's dress. Text me if you need me."

Jasmine waved her off, unperturbed. Very little bothered Jasmine. Good thing. The way Cindy had been reacting to everything lately, she might otherwise have been without her best friend.

Cindy heard footsteps on the stairs as she was hanging Rena's completed gown on an old-fashioned, pink padded hanger. Special orders always came with them. It was worth the expense as a keepsake for the customer. Cindy turned to find Sandi opening the door.

"Hi. Thanks for coming in on such short notice," Cindy said.

"Thanks for the hours. It's going to be an expensive Christmas this year. The water heater broke."

"Oh, no!"

"It's fine," said Sandi, swiping her short curly hair off her forehead. "My brother's a plumber, so he's only charging me for the unit."

"That's good," Cindy said. She waited until Sandi had removed her coat before going over the two orders with her. Prior to leaving, she asked the woman if she'd finished her own gown yet. All assistants paid cost for the materials and used the shop machinery to make their dresses.

"All done," said Sandi. She nodded toward the wall where Rena's dress hung. "That's a small one. Teenager?"

"A twelve-year-old. Dan Hayes' daughter."

Sandi's eyes lit up. "Ooo, that's exciting for her. I didn't realize kids that young would even be interested. You can't tell me she has a boyfriend who's willing to go, too?"

"She's attending with her dad."

Sandi appeared perplexed. "But I would have thought…"

"I know," Cindy said. "She wants to go, though. So, yeah, they're going together. Who knows? He might be bringing someone else, as well. There's no rule against it."

"That would be nice. And you—"

"There's no rule against going alone, either," Cindy added, cutting her off. She patted the woman on the arm. "Thanks again. They're some cookies in the tin over there if you want some. And it you want a coffee, give me a shout. I'll bring one up."

She exited as quickly as she could, avoiding the

inevitable question about who she might take to the ball. On the landing in front of her apartment door, Cindy's cell chimed in her pocket. She pulled the phone out, spotted a text from Harry which she almost ignored. When a photo popped up a second later, she looked at both. The text read: *You know Jas better than anyone. Help me pick. And don't tell her!*

The photo? Two diamond rings side by side on what was obviously a jewelry store counter.

Chapter Fourteen

Cindy's lungs emptied. Abruptly, she sat on the garden chair, the only one she kept out through all four seasons. The chill from ice-cold metal cut through her leggings. Her breath frosted the air. She lowered her head, bringing the phone closer and away from the sun. Two rings. Two gorgeous rings. One purpose. Not merely a Christmas gift. A promise. For now, per Harry, also a secret.

Cindy studied the rings. Decision weighed heavily. She didn't want to be the one to choose. It wasn't her place. Besides, what if she picked the ring based on what she believed to be Jasmine's preference, and Jas didn't like it? Did a person exchange an engagement ring for something more appealing? Not likely. Wasn't this why both parties had a say? To avoid something like this? But Harry had opted for surprise and to stick Cindy with the responsibility.

Pushing away any grumpy rumination, Cindy scrutinized each ring again. She knew which one she would prefer, but she and Jas rarely had the same style likes. Closing her eyes, Cindy attempted to visualize the jewelry she'd seen Jas wearing, and which pieces, which stone cuts, stuck out as Jas's favorites.

After five minutes, Cindy texted Harry back. *Sorry, I need to think about this some more. Is that okay? Hasn't she given you any indication?*

He texted a response right away. *That's fine. And you know Jas. Beating around the bush doesn't work with her. I might have to ask her straight up after all. It'll ruin the surprise, but probably the best move.*

Give me a few hours. I'll figure out some way to get you an answer.

Thank you, he said. *You're the best.*

Right. The best. She didn't particularly feel like the best. Especially not the past few months. Telling him congratulations might be in order, she mused, but she'd hold off on that until Jasmine gave him an answer. Cindy figured it would be yes, but with Jas, one never knew.

Continuing down the stairs, she realized he probably needed an answer in short order. Very likely, he planned to pop the question this weekend, maybe even when they were all together. Yes, Cindy along with her best friend and the guy Cindy still remembered crushing on, as well as Mister I-Never-Say-More-Than-Two-Words-In-A-Row, who might be coming along so Cindy wouldn't be dateless to the ball. Or, because once the question was popped, Cindy and

Brad might be asked to fill two important positions in the wedding party.

Grumbling under her breath, Cindy passed through the storeroom, pulling herself together before she came face to face with Jas. She found the store empty. Unattended, because it was too early for Peg to be in.

"Jas?"

Nothing.

"Jasmine?" Foolish, to continue calling out. Cindy could see into every corner around the store with one, sweeping glance. Nevertheless, she said, "Hello?" before heading for the front door. She pushed on it. Not locked. If Jasmine had to run out somewhere, not only would she have made sure Cindy knew first, but she would have locked the door, put up the sign.

Cindy stepped out onto the sidewalk, a little worried. She looked first one way, then the other, locating Jasmine talking rapid-fire to someone Cindy didn't recognize. The man handed Jasmine a business card, shook hands, and walked away. Jasmine noticed Cindy as she turned. She hurried in Cindy's direction. "Sorry. I could see the store, if anyone went in. I—"

"It's fine," Cindy said, grabbing the door and holding it wide. "You're alright? Who was that?"

Jas glanced at the card in her hand. "Ward Smith. He's a journalist, writing for that glossy magazine in the city."

Cindy knew which magazine she meant. How often Cindy had dreamed of her store being the subject of an article in it. Or even of being able to afford an ad at the back. "What was he doing here in Connor Falls?"

Jasmine grinned. "An article. On our little town. And on the Garland Ball. He left before I got his name, so I chased after him. He's going to be calling to set up a time to interview you."

Speechless, she followed Jas back inside. "Us," she finally said.

"Us?"

"If he's going to ask anything about Cinderella Silks or how the Garland Ball was reinstated, he needs your input, too." Cindy reflected for a second. "He's left it kind of late, though, hasn't he? The article will never make it into the magazine before the ball."

"He said that, this—" Jas peered down at the card again. "Wade. He said it would be coming out in February. A combination Valentine's and after-Christmas summary of events in the area or something like that."

"Huh," said Cindy. "Well, this could be good."

"Good? Excellent!"

"Okay, excellent." Cindy grinned back at her. She grabbed Jasmine's hands. Together, they jumped up and down a few times, laughing and sobering only after a few subdued war cries into the air above their heads.

Jasmine headed toward the counter with the card. "We could discuss the new plans," she said.

Cindy halted behind her. "Wait. You didn't

mention anything to this Wade guy, did you?"

"Of course not. But it would be perfect timing, wouldn't it?"

"No," said Cindy. "Because nothing's been decided."

Jasmine harumphed. "Well, fine. The least we can do is give Harry's company a boost by mention, then." She stowed the business card away in the box they kept for that purpose.

"Okay," Cindy agreed. "We can say we'd had a marketing plan drawn up for the new year, but with no mention of any changes here. Not yet." With Harry's recent text in mind, Cindy went closer to the counter, eyeing the jewelry Jasmine wore.

"What are you staring at?" Jas asked, somewhat testily for her. Cindy knew Jasmine didn't like the fact she kept stalling conversation about the marketing and new direction. Both required some serious thinking on Cindy's part, and she just wasn't ready to do that. She didn't want to say 'no' outright, because some positives existed in it. A happy medium was required. Until after the holidays, Cindy had enough on her mind. Figuring out what came next would have to wait.

"That ring on your finger," Cindy said. "Is it new?"

Jas lifted both hands, due to the several rings she was wearing. "Which one?"

Cindy pointed at a sapphire she'd seen before, noticing now it had a similar setting to the lefthand ring in the photo Harry sent. Not as spectacular, but close enough to perhaps get an idea from Jasmine's response. "I don't remember this one," Cindy said. "I like the way the stone is cut."

"Me, too. I've had it for years. Are you telling me this is the first you noticed?"

"Well, no. Now that I see it better, I recognize it. Must have been the light hitting the sapphire," she fibbed. "You wear that ring a lot, don't you?"

Jasmine frowned. "Yes, I guess. Why?"

"Just changing the subject, dear." Cindy smiled at her. Jasmine returned the gesture with a withering glare.

As soon as she could, Cindy ducked into the bathroom to answer Harry's question. She made sure to mention she only suggested the choice based on the ring Jasmine often wore. She didn't want the final responsibility to be hers. He said he understood.

See you this weekend, Cinderella, he said, ending the exchange.

Her reading of the words echoed with an odd intimacy in her head. Like they were long-standing friends rather than former friends. Like there had once been something more. She knew, though, they hadn't shared anything other than an exciting friendship and an exciting crush. Nearly twenty years ago. She'd mostly forgotten Harry Carter until seeing him again. The affection she'd felt from him when they were younger had obviously just been his way, a way he still had, displayed in his mannerisms, his speech. As for the kissing and all that back then? Friends, the saying went, with benefits. Rather small ones, in retrospect.

See you this weekend, Cinderella. Yep. No matter how it resounded in thought, it was no more than a friendly comment passed by Jasmine's guy.

Time to get a grip on reality, on life, Cindy chastised herself. Time to figure out what the heck was going on with her and what the heck she wanted.

* * *

Cindy repeatedly checked her phone throughout the day when Jas wasn't looking, studying the ring photos, and hoping Harry did more than rely on Cindy's suggestion before making the purchase. Several times, she considered texting him to repeat what she'd said earlier, or to tell him to call Jasmine. Something.

Around seven-thirty, she and Jas ordered some take-out delivered to the store. Not their usual practice, but they were both hungry. The temperature had dropped and the sidewalks were peopled only by those folks in a hurry to get out of the cold. Jasmine took a seat by the door, her meal in her lap. Cindy remained standing at the counter, her frequent position for eating in the shop or in her kitchen. Seasonal music played at low volume through the overhead speakers.

"Did you finish your Christmas shopping?" Jasmine asked. "You said you were behind."

"Not yet. There are a couple gifts I'm having trouble finding."

Nodding, Jas took another bite from her veggie wrap and said around it, "I haven't gotten anything for Harry yet, either."

"What does he want?" Cindy asked.

"Nothing, he says. No help. But he does like surprises, so…"

Cindy glanced down at her cell phone and back up at Jas. "Any idea what he's getting you?"

"Nope. He likes giving surprises as well as getting them, apparently."

Cindy's gut gave a little roll. "That's still nice. You'll love whatever he gets you, right?"

"Depends," said Jas. "I am particular about certain things, as you know."

"Like your undergarments," Cindy teased with a laugh.

"Oh, he's not giving me underwear of any sort," Jasmine retorted. "He knows better." She smiled, took another bite.

"You really have no idea, then?"

Jasmine shook her head from side to side, honey-colored curls dancing on her shoulders. She looked happy, sitting there eating, complacent in her relationship with Harry.

"But you would be thrilled by anything not underwear?" Cindy pressed.

Jas's head tilted to one side. "Why are you so concerned? Do you know something I don't?"

Cindy swallowed, and lied. She didn't like doing it, but she also felt she needed to honor Harry's request. "No. Your relationship with Harry seems very special. I guess I was curious about the expectations. Especially at Christmas. You know, you're hoping for one thing and your boyfriend brings you a pair of socks with dogs on them, or something."

Jasmine laughed so hard she nearly knocked the plate from her lap. "No underwear, no socks! Those are the rules!"

"A box of chocolates?"

"Not unless it has one of those sheets telling you what filling is inside each and every one," Jasmine shot back at her, still laughing.

"Cookware?"

"Stop!"

"A garden hose could come in handy."

"Stop it!" Jas doubled over, holding her meal out with one hand so she wouldn't land her sweater in it. Cindy wiped tears from her eyes, struggling to end her own laughter.

The door opened. Dan stood there, his breath steaming in the cold air swirling around him. Jasmine straightened up, swiped at her own eyes. "Hi, Dan," she said.

He lifted his hand in greeting, eyeing them both uncertainly. "Did I interrupt something?"

"Cindy just thinks she's funny," Jasmine told him.

"It seems she is, the way you two were carrying on when I walked in." He moved toward the counter, stopped halfway there. "Should I come back?"

"Of course not!" Cindy cried. "We were just discussing what gift Jas might anticipate from her boyfriend."

Dan's lips curved. "You weren't laughing at the possibility of an engagement ring, were you? Because that wouldn't be very nice." Still smiling, he looked at them both, expecting a laugh. "Oops," he whispered.

Jasmine stared at Cindy's stricken face. "Cindy?"

Cindy shook her head. "Nothing like that, Dan. We were talking socks and garden hoses."

His brows went up. "Do I want to know?"

Jasmine stood up with her plate. "Cindy?"

Cindy stepped around the counter. "Have you come for Rena's gown?" she said to Dan, avoiding Jas's gaze.

"Cindy?" said Jasmine again. "What do you know?"

Dan started moving backward toward the door. "I'll come by later."

"No, stay," said Cindy.

"Yes, later. That would be good," said Jasmine.

He slipped out the door, the bell tinkling.

For a long moment, Jasmine stared at Cindy and Jas stared right back. Finally, Cindy released a breath. "Are you in love with him, Jas?" Cindy asked. "Or do you love him?"

There was a difference. She and Jasmine had discussed this so many times, Cindy knew she would understand the question.

For nearly half a minute, Jas said nothing. Thinking. Obviously thinking. Cindy's heart sank a little for Harry. Jas's mouth twisted. Close enough to her now, she reached out for Cindy's hand with her empty one. "I love him," she said.

Non-laughing tears pricked at Cindy's lids. She squeezed Jas's fingers.

"I love him," Jas repeated. "Now tell me what you know."

"No," Cindy said. "But I think you should go call that boyfriend of yours. I'll see you tomorrow."

Wordlessly, Jasmine retrieved her coat and bag and left. From the open door, Cindy watched Jasmine for a few seconds. Jas's cell phone was already freed from her purse and at her ear.

Chilling quickly, Cindy hurried back inside, started cleaning up the refuse from their evening meal. Passing the counter, she found a text from Dan on her phone.

I'll come by in the morning. It seems I might have interrupted something.

No problem, she texted back. *The morning works, though. Thank you.*

She set the phone on the counter again, snatching it up when it chimed.

Enjoy your night.

Cindy smiled. *You, too.* She wondered what he did with his nights. Spent them with the kids, Cindy supposed. Or with the blonde she'd seen him with in his store.

After depositing the trash in the storage room can, she tied it, closed it, ran it outside to the dumpster. Still coatless. When she returned, she sat in the chair Jas had vacated, her hands folded between her knees. Even with the Christmas music playing, the store seemed unusually quiet. Conversation came through from the sidewalk in snatches. In between, Cindy went back to her thoughts. After a time, a long time it seemed, Jasmine came back inside.

"I've gotta run," she said, looking a bit dazed.

"Are you okay?"

"I'm heading down to Harry's."

Cindy smiled at her. "You do that."

Gathering her things, Jasmine left without saying anything more about her conversation with Harry. Cindy returned to the counter and her end-of-evening work there. Finally, after counting down the minutes until nine o'clock, Cindy closed the store and slowly made her way up the metal stairs to her apartment.

Chapter Fifteen

In the morning, Dan texted her he was on his way. Cindy figured he must be on his morning run, but he also knew Cindy was often in the store early. Slipping into her boots, Cindy hurried down and through the store to let him in when he appeared in his casual running clothes outside.

"Everything settled from yesterday?" he asked. "Not that it's any of my business."

"Not sure," Cindy said. "Jasmine left me a message she was taking half the day off. She drove down to Harry's last night. I haven't heard anything since. I think he's going to propose, and that's not something you do over the phone."

"You think, or you know?"

"Think," she said. "He asked my opinion on a ring, but it could just have been a nice gift."

He made a small face. "I won't mention anything."

"Please don't." Cindy said, relocking the door and leading him back through the storeroom. "I'll let you know what happens," she added, not sure why she had.

They climbed the stairs. Cindy paused outside her apartment door. "I ran down in such a hurry, I didn't feed Shakespeare yet. Do you mind? We'll only be a minute."

Dan followed her in, stood near the small table in the kitchen while she put food in Shakespeare's bowl and freshened his water. Cindy was very much aware of his proximity observing the morning ritual. But also, how at ease he seemed, his hips against the table edge, his arms folded across the worn sweatshirt covering his chest.

"Rena's coming into her own," he said. "I didn't think being twelve would make that much difference, but it has."

Crouched on the floor, Cindy glanced up at him with sympathy. "I was late coming to that stage. I started to feel the difference in the eighth grade, if I remember correctly. Rena's a sweet girl. Smart. A good head on her shoulders. I don't think you need to worry."

Dan scuffed his boot across the rug beneath the table legs. His mouth twitched up at one corner. "Thanks."

"No problem." Cindy straightened. Despite his recent run, she could still smell the light apple scent she'd come to associate with him. "I offer free encouragement whether you need some or not."

He chuckled, head turning, his eyes taking in the space, the living room beyond. "Cozy. I think I'd forgotten that."

"Is that another way of saying 'small'?" Cindy

taunted with a smile, following his gaze.

"No. Well, yes. It is small, but I meant cozy. It seems perfect for you."

"Thanks." Cindy grabbed her keys from the counter where she'd tossed them. She looked around again, dispassionately she hoped, wondering what he might be thinking and concluding about Cindy now he'd been inside her apartment again. Not that it mattered. He knew her, and her home reflected who she was.

"She likes your apartment, Rena does," he said, as if following her thoughts. "She spent an hour talking about it after she was here. Right now, she's aspiring to be you, I think."

Cindy jangled the keys in her fist and laughed. "Good lord, I hope she changes her mind."

Shifting his stance, Dan shuffled sideways and grabbed the doorknob. "I know you're joking, but your place is welcoming and charming and interesting for a reason. Rena doesn't like just anybody." He opened the door and stepped out, climbing to the third floor ahead of her. Cindy followed a short distance behind, observing his easy stride up the stairs from her vantage point beneath, thinking about what he'd said. Welcoming. Charming. Interesting. Some might not think those words as praise to warm the heart, yet they warmed hers. Her cheeks, too. Dan Hayes, who had never done anything to make her blush. Well, at least not as an adult.

Blushing like mad now, she remembered he'd tried kissing her. An odd time for that memory to come rushing back. Right around her thirteenth birthday, it had been. A clumsy, uneven attempt by the both of them behind the huge shed in her parents' backyard. To make matters worse, she abruptly wondered what it might be like to kiss him in the present, now he'd had years of practice.

"Crap," she muttered.

Dan looked back. "You alright?"

"Yep."

"You look a little flushed."

"It's all the rushing around," she said.

He moved aside when Cindy reached him so she could insert the key. She held her breath to avoid the apple scent drifting into her nostrils and making her think of other things. Things she shouldn't about another woman's man.

Really, Cindy? she grumbled internally. *Are you making a habit of this?*

Squeezing past, she preceded him to the wall where the gown hung. She threw back the protective cover. A different warmth ran through her at the low 'wow' that escaped him.

"Rena showed me the photo, but it doesn't do the dress justice," he said. "You are one talented lady. It's beautiful. I'm sure Rena does look all grown up in this. Of course, it doesn't matter what I think so long as Rena loves it. Which she does."

Thrilled, but avoiding his gaze, Cindy pulled the garment cover back over the gown and carried it downstairs to the store. At the counter, Dan paid the bill with more expressions of gratitude.

"Stop thanking me. I enjoyed making it. The process reminded me of the reason I started all this."

"That's always good," he said. "I need an occasional reminder myself, even though I took over from my dad. Not what I wanted, really, but what I'd always daydreamed about doing would never have paid the bills. Well, it might have, but the chances were slim." He laughed.

Cindy struggled for a split second to recall his dream occupation and suddenly did. "You haven't given up writing altogether, have you?" He'd shared some tales with her. She thought them marvelous. Then again, she'd been a teenager. What did she know.

"Honestly?" he answered. "No. How can I? It's who I am."

"Then don't give up," Cindy said. "Don't ever give up." Her inflection, the encouragement in her voice, seemed a little extreme. She felt embarrassed by it. He looked pleased.

Dan lifted the dress from the counter, folded the garment bag over his arm. "Thanks. You always did believe in me."

Had she? Then how had their friendship drifted into passing comments, a visit here and there, brief moments until recently? One thing she did know. She was happy to have Dan in her sphere again. She would make a better effort to keep him there. Him, his kids...and whoever the blonde he'd been embracing in the printshop might be. Package deal.

He backed toward the door. Always backing away rather than turning away. That meant something.

"So," he said, pausing, "like the shoemaker in the tale, I'm thinking you might not have your gown made yet?"

"You'd be wrong," Cindy said. "I do. It's been ready. It's the one on the dressmaker's dummy in the window."

Dan gave a little start, pushed open the door, and spent a few seconds studying the dress through the glass. He looked back, nodded, raised a thumb at her. He moved his mouth to say something but appeared to decide against it. His expression changed, and he merely waved before disappearing toward the printshop.

*   *   *

"What are you smiling at?" Jas asked when she entered the store around mid-afternoon.

Cindy's head jerked up, away from what she held. Briefly, she studied Jasmine's face, looking for an indication as to what had transpired with Harry and not able to discern an answer. "A card from George Martins," Cindy explained. "Thanking me for giving him the idea to get back in touch with Gran. You're smiling, too." Cindy stated the obvious. Did the smile appear brighter than usual? "What's up?"

Gazelle-like, Jas hurried across the floor, her left hand held out before her, fingers curved, palm down. Cindy took her hand, grinning at the ring with its pear-shaped diamond.

"You knew," Jas said. "I know you did."

"I knew nothing," stated Cindy. "Harry asked me for my opinion about a ring but I had no idea what it was for."

"He asked me if you spilled the beans. I told him you hadn't revealed anything, that I had a feeling after you reacted to Dan's joke. I told him you insisted I call him, though. He's not mad. I think he was happy not to have to keep it a secret anymore."

"It's your left hand," Cindy said, "so I'm assuming not just an early Christmas gift—"

"Yes," said Jas. "He asked me to marry him."

Cindy experienced a strange swirl though her stomach and out into her limbs. She recognized the sensation. Joy. Splendid, wonderful joy.

"And?" Cindy prompted.

With her hand still in Cindy's, Jas began to jump up and down in small hops, squealing. "I said yes!"

Cindy darted around the counter, threw her arms around Jas's waist, and joined her in the hopping and squealing, an exercise exuberant enough the force moved them in circles across the floor until Cindy's foot struck a chair leg. She stumbled backward. Jas caught her, laughing.

Grinning still, Cindy said, "Well, congratulations to you both. Did you set a date, or…?"

"We were talking sometime around next Christmas," Jas answered. "But, you know, we'll have to figure that out."

Cindy could already visualize a Christmas wedding: the gowns, the setting, the music. She stopped herself. Not her wedding. "I'll make your gown, if you want," she said.

Jas looked down into Cindy's gaze, dark eyes

smiling. "Of course, I want."

"Did he…go down on one knee?"

Jasmine made a face. "Aren't you the romantic? No. We were sitting side by side on his sofa."

"Well, that's a bit of a letdown," Cindy said, and laughed again. "Jasmine Williams, almost married lady. Wait until I tell Mom and Dad. Can I tell Mom and Dad?"

"You can tell whoever you want," said Jasmine. "Even Dan. Now he'll understand the funny little exchange you and I had yesterday that chased him out the door." Something in Cindy's face gave it away. Jas's brows lowered and she turned her head slightly to the side. "Did you—?"

"I might have mentioned my suspicions to him when he stopped by early for Rena's gown. I told him I knew nothing for sure and he promised to keep mum."

"Anyone else?" Jasmine drawled.

"No one." Cindy crossed her fingers swiftly over her heart. "I promise."

"Well, you can blab as much as you want now. You're off the hook."

Following a quick hug, Jasmine went into the backroom, presumably to hang up her coat. Cindy remained where she was, feeling undeniably happy. Any ambivalence had fled. Jasmine and Harry. Harry and Jasmine. She needed to call Mom and tell her. Her mother would be thrilled. She'd probably follow that up with some statement about Cindy's single status, but Cindy would ignore her and gladly.

When she returned, Jasmine was already speaking as though continuing a conversation begun in her head. "There's one thing we have to decide between now and then, though."

A hundred things entered Cindy's brain simultaneously. All of them exciting. All of them fun. None took into account what Jasmine said next.

"Where we're going to live."

Oh. Jas meant a decision she and Harry had to make, not she and Cindy. "Right," said Cindy.

This would take some getting used to. So would the idea Jasmine might sell her small house and move away. Might? Would. She'd have to. The place was way too tiny for her and Harry to co-exist. Plus, he had his business. Would Jasmine leave the store, as well? Had she possessed some inkling where her relationship with Harry was headed when she pushed for changes to Cinderella Silks? After all these years and years as friends, would she and Jas rarely see each other? What—

"Cindy!"

Cindy jerked her rampaging thoughts up short. "Sorry. You were saying?"

"Actually, nothing," said Jasmine. "Your blank stare stopped me. Are you okay?"

"This is a lot to take in. You moving away, and—"

"Did I say I was going anywhere? Nothing's been decided."

"I know," Cindy hastened to say. "And it's not my concern." Cindy took a step closer. "It's your life. A wonderful new life with Harry. And I'm so happy for you. You know me. Sometimes I can't help—"

"Worrying?" Jasmine interjected. "Wanting to sort things out in your brain before they have time to be real? Yeah, I know."

Cindy sighed, laughed, shook her head. "We'll always be friends," she said.

Jasmine nodded agreement. "And we will always make time for each other."

Always. It sounded like a vow meant to be broken.

Later that evening, once the store was closed and Shakespeare attended to, Cindy drove to her parents' house to share the news with them in person. She interrupted them watching some television show, likely a favorite at her dad's reluctance to leave it to come greet his daughter.

"I didn't know you were coming over," Mom said. "Tea? I've got an open bag of cookies we can finish off."

"Hi, honey," said Dad. "Good to see you. But do you mind if I—" He jerked his head toward the living room and the television.

"Go," Cindy responded. He wouldn't be as gaga over the engagement news as her mom anyway, and could hear it later. "Enjoy." She followed her mother into the kitchen.

While her mother got out the cookies, Cindy filled the teapot with water and set it on the stove. She grabbed two mugs, two teabags, and the sugar bowl, carrying all to the table.

"So," said Lacie, her back to Cindy while she made short work of dumping the cookies onto a plate and arranging them. "What's wrong? You don't usually make impromptu visits at this hour."

"What hour?" Cindy glanced at the clock. Ten-fifteen. "Oh. Sorry."

"So, nothing's wrong?" Lacie sat, scooting the plate across the Christmas tablecloth and closer to Cindy.

"No, Mom. I just wanted to share some news."

"You have a date for the—"

"No." Cindy picked up a cookie, took a bite and chewed it aggressively into tiny, masticated pieces.

"I'm waiting."

"It's Jas," Cindy said. "She's engaged."

For a moment, Lacie said nothing. Cindy wasn't even sure the woman was breathing. But she suddenly blurted out, "To that hunk?"

Cindy sighed. "Hunk? Isn't that word a bit outdated?"

"That is who you mean, though. What's his name again?"

Cindy took another bite. This time, she didn't bother to swallow before speaking. "You know his name, Mom. Harry. Harry Carter. From Jas's college days?"

"That's right. Weren't you and he—" and she made an indecipherable gesture with her fingers dancing against each other, "—back then?"

"No," said Cindy. "We were friends. More than friends. But we weren't doing this." She imitated her mother's odd hand motions.

Lacie started to chortle. She jumped up to answer the teapot's whistle, hurried back with it, centering the pot on a pad protecting the tablecloth.

"You're funny, my sweet Cinderella," she said, plopping into her seat once more.

Cindy rolled her eyes.

"Well, when did this happen? I'll have to call Jas and congratulate her."

"Sometime between last night and this morning, I expect. You should see the ring. It's beautiful. I helped pick it out."

"You did?" Lacie seemed less than convinced.

"Sort of," Cindy admitted. "Harry asked my opinion." She shrugged.

Lacie poured water into both mugs, passed Cindy's to her along with a teabag. "Well, tell me all. How did he propose? When's the wedding? What's it going to be like?"

"Mom," Cindy interrupted her. "Did you not hear me say the proposal happened sometime between last night and this morning? *This* morning?

"Of course, I did. Jas is your best friend. She has to have told you every little detail in the hours between then and now. I mean, she's getting married!"

Cindy heard a footstep behind her. She turned to find her father entering the kitchen. He looked from Cindy to his wife and back again.

"Who's getting married?" He stared at Cindy. "Not you?"

Cindy dropped her forehead onto the cheerful, patterned tablecloth and left it there.

Chapter Sixteen

Cindy half expected the weekend dinner to be cancelled. Even before Harry's text with the rings, she'd thought the reason for the get-together might be a special occasion. However, despite the premature proposal, dinner was still taking place. Cindy now figured the plan possessed more basic intentions. Food, catching up, and possibly pushing her and Brad together. She tried not to think about it. Which only made her think about it more.

Saturday came with Peg and Sandi taking the evening hours for the store. Reservations were for seven. Before Jasmine headed out at five-thirty, she advised Cindy to wear something nice.

"I was planning sweats and a tee shirt," Cindy retorted. "Comfort above style, that's me."

Jasmine frowned as if Cindy were serious. "We're going to Smith & Sons. I thought I told you that."

"You did," said Cindy. "Five times, in case you lost count. I do know how to dress at my age."

"Of course, you do," said Jas. "I'm sorry. I just want this evening to be—perfect."

For what reason, Cindy couldn't imagine. Perfect was for dates, special occasions, showing off a beau to your parents, not catching up with old friends. But if Jas sought a perfect evening, then Cindy would do her best. She did, however, opt to drive herself. Just to be on the safe side with any Brad intentions by Jasmine and Harry.

Arriving at the restaurant a few minutes before seven, Cindy parked her car and walked toward the front door along a sidewalk lined by warm clear lights wrapped around lamp posts and on the trees. This was their daily display, but they'd added fresh wreaths for the holiday vibe. Cindy paused to admire one. She stood on her toes to breathe in the lovely balsam and pine scent. Instrumental music drifted through the air from hidden speakers in the eaves. Christmas was a little under two weeks away. In her head, she knew this. But her heart, where she truly felt the season, appeared to be swathed in bubble wrap. A buffer against sentiment, against the winter mindset she enjoyed so much. She didn't like feeling this way, but she didn't know how to shake it.

"Pop that bubble wrap, Cindy," she whispered to herself.

"Do what?"

Cindy spun toward the voice. She squinted at the stranger standing nearby. "Sorry," she said. "Talking to myself." She started again toward the door. The man reached out, lightly grabbed her coat sleeve.

"It's me, Cindy. Brad. Har and Jas sent me out to fetch you. We could see you through the window. Jas insisted you'd spend all night out here smelling the wreaths if someone didn't make you come inside."

Cindy stared at him a moment longer, trying to fit the face to the young man she remembered and finally finding it. A face rounded a bit by time, less hair on top, and gray spattering the goatee he still sported in a rather attractive way.

"I guess I've changed a lot since the last time we met," he said.

"I'm sure I have, too," Cindy answered, recovering. "Good thing they pointed me out to you."

"Nah," said Brad. "You've barely changed at all."

Cindy smiled her gratitude. "Thanks, Brad, that's kind. It's good to see you again. And if you paid attention at all when we were younger, you'll remember I talked to myself a lot."

He laughed, held out his arm and bent it, as if he expected her to tuck her hand into his elbow. After a short hesitation—one she hoped he didn't notice—she fit her fingers into the folds in his sleeve. The arm beneath felt taut, muscles ropy and raised. She wondered if that came from beating drums on a regular basis. She assumed playing drums was still his place in the band, still his instrument of choice.

At the door, she released Brad's arm so he could open it for her, which seemed his intent. Cindy didn't recall these gentlemanly tendencies in the past, but to be honest, she hadn't spent a lot of time with him.

"This way," he said, touching her behind the elbow now, steering her through the tables. Cindy looked past the diners for Jas's syrupy curls. Suddenly, she realized she didn't see them anywhere near the front window. A second later, Brad explained, "Jas reserved a private room. This is it," and stepped right up behind her. She bumped into him when she tried to back up.

"Sorry," he said quietly. "They told me to do this. Jas didn't want you to run away."

Oh crap, oh crap, oh crap, Cindy thought, just as her eyes adjusted to the dimness past the rollback dividing wall. The room was packed. The lights came on. Jasmine jumped up front and center, shouting, "Surprise!"

Cindy burst into tears.

*　　*　　*

"Thank goodness for waterproof mascara," Cindy mumbled to Jasmine as her friend led her through the gathering toward the table reserved for the four of them. Brad hadn't exactly lied. The table did have a view of the sidewalk outside. Amidst calls of happy early birthday, Cindy skirted the table and took a seat facing the room. Given a chance, she would have played dumb, chosen a different chair, one where she didn't feel so much on display, but Jasmine had taken precautions against such an event. The chair designated hers was draped with a cloth bearing Cindy's name, and centered on the plate before it was a ridiculous tiara. Once Cindy sat, Jas plopped the crown on Cindy's head. The people at the other five tables, Cindy's family and friends, clapped. A few hooted. Cindy glimpsed the server rushing to close the door separating the room from the main dining area.

At the next table over, Cindy's brother lifted his fork and tapped his water glass. "Speech!"

"Petey," Cindy said to him, "you know better."

He laughed, as did others. People who knew her, people she cared about, people she loved. She stood up, despite her words to her brother.

"I, uh, don't do speeches," she reiterated, looking around, registering faces. "But I do want to say thank you. To all of you. For being here, for being in my life. I don't quite know how I had planned to spend my fortieth birthday, except to say not like this. In fact, I pretty much expected to spend it watching movies all night with my cat in my apartment. Which does have its appeal, so I might still. On my actual birthday. But this is so much better. Again, thank you."

She resumed her seat to a round of applause. Across the table, Harry winked at her. Jasmine kissed her on the cheek. Brad stared at his plate. Cindy realized he was likely uncomfortable in this setting. His behavior outside had been different. Maybe she'd never understood how shy he was. More shy than aloof.

As the evening progressed, he became more talkative. When Cindy wasn't conversing with a party guest, she spent quite some time talking to him. For one thing, he sat directly to her left. For another, she found Brad's stories entertaining. He seemed intent on making her laugh. Several times, Cindy caught the glances passing between Jasmine and Harry. They apparently decided inviting him had been a good move. Perhaps it had been. Still, Cindy didn't like being fixed up. Ever.

Jas had specified no gifts, knowing how uncomfortable it would make Cindy feel. Cindy was happy to learn she'd done so. There were cards, though. Some, like the one from Cindy's parents, included a little something inside. Short of alienating them completely, she couldn't argue. Jasmine and Harry gave her a gift card for a massage.

"Because?" Cindy asked them pointedly.

"Because you're stretched like a wire," Jas said, holding nothing back.

"Well, I appreciate your concern, and thank you." Cindy waved the gift card before stuffing it back in the envelope with the birthday card.

Gina had placed a bakery gift card in hers promising free coffee for a month. "I'll be taking you up on that," Cindy said to her.

"I planned on it," Gina answered with a grin.

She hugged Cindy before leaving to return to work. Gina always had tasks to take care of in preparation for the morning, Cindy knew. The large cake sitting on a side table had come from Gina's bakery. No doubt it would be delicious. However, the hour was getting late and some people had gone for coats and returned wearing them.

"Wait," said Cindy, standing up. "Who wants cake? I can't take all that home with me. I don't think it'll even fit in my refrigerator. Please, take a few minutes and have a slice."

Hastily, Jasmine began shoving candles into the top. Harry and Brad joined in. Cindy erupted into laughter. They seemed hellbent on sticking forty-one candles in the creamy icing. When lit, the flames resembled a bonfire. Cindy struggled to blow them all out after an off-tune rendition of happy birthday by the remaining guests.

"Thanks," said Cindy, "for making me feel older than the hills. It was so nice having you share in this. It was the best birthday ever."

After consuming their cake, family, friends, came up to her to say goodnight. Soon, the room was empty save for the servers cleaning up and Cindy, Jas, Harry, and Brad. Cindy hugged Jasmine, hard. "Thank you so, so, so, so much," she whispered.

"It wasn't just me. Harry helped."

Cindy squeezed Harry's hand.

"Me, too," said Brad. "I got you in the door." He grinned.

"Well, thank you all. This night was so special and such a surprise. I truly didn't expect it. All your effort, all the people coming, meant the world to me."

"You sound like the night's over," said Harry.

Cindy, retrieving her purse, paused and looked back at him. "Isn't it?"

"We're going to the Sitting Duck," Jasmine announced. "All of us. I'm going to get you roaring drunk."

Cindy would have liked to turn her down, but she was in too good a mood to disappoint her best friend. "Right. Let's go. But nix the getting me drunk part, 'kay?"

"Promise," said Jas, probably with her fingers crossed behind her back.

*   *   *

It didn't take much to get Cindy even a little tipsy. So, she refrained after having three drinks and switched to soda. Of course, sugar was sugar in the system, so she wondered if the switch really did any good. When Cindy drawled a third teary congratulations to the newly engaged couple, she figured it didn't.

"I really have to go," she said, pushing up from her chair.

"You know where it is," Jas sang out.

Cindy hadn't meant the little girl's room, but she headed toward the door with its cute sign anyway. Inside, she splashed her face with cold water, patted it dry, frowned at the state of her hair, straightened her dress. When she opened the door, she found Brad waiting in the hallway.

"Hi," she said. "Wrong door. Yours is that way."

"I'm good," he answered. "Just waiting for you. Wanted to make sure you were okay."

Aw, she thought, that's sweet. But was it? Did people do that? Follow you to the restroom for a well-being check? Could be she was more inebriated than she felt. A condition visible to all except herself.

"I'm good, too," she said. "Heading home, though. It's been a long day."

"Don't leave yet." He stepped to the side, blocking her path. Not in an aggressive way. More like…something. Possibly he needed the wall to hold him up. Cindy scratched an itch on her face with a fingertip.

"What's up?" she asked.

"I…" He drew a deep breath, let it out. "I used to like you, did you know? Back then, when you and Harry were—"

"Friends," said Cindy. "We were never much more than friends."

"Okay. Then maybe you and I could go out sometime?"

Cindy eased around him through the small space he'd left on his right side. He turned, following her movement, fell in beside her, almost literally. He seemed a bit unsteady on his feet.

"You might want to sit down," Cindy said to him. "Let's go back to the table."

"Okay." He reached out, took her hand. She let him, only because she thought he might fall if she didn't. Both Harry and Jas pivoted simultaneously to view them as they walked up. Jas smiled smugly. Harry looked a little less pleased. Cindy figured he might realize how drunk his friend was, even if Jas didn't recognize the same thing.

Cindy removed her fingers from Brad's, stepped behind him. Reaching up, she placed her hands on his shoulders and coerced him into his seat. She looked at Harry over Brad's head. Harry gave her a small, perceptive nod. Cindy maneuvered around Brad's chair to her own to grab her coat and bag. Brad's hand snaked out of nowhere to latch onto hers again.

"Wait a second," he said. "I was supposed to bring this up. The Garland Ball thing. These two have been talking about the event. A lot. They said you need a date. We're doing it, right? Together?"

Cindy closed her eyes, pulled her hand away gently. "Brad, call me at some point and we'll talk about it, okay?" Yes, and Cindy would explain to him, when he was coherent enough to understand, exactly why she planned on going alone.

With a polite and exhausted goodnight, Cindy exited the tavern. She waited to don her coat until she stood on the steps, where she spent a moment welcoming a bracing chill on her face. She kept her gaze on the street leading to her shop and home, on the holiday décor still glimmering in the night. She watched the few people on the sidewalks, jumped a little when the church began to chime its subdued but clear midnight song. During the Christmas season, it was literally a few bars of an appropriate carol followed by the toll of the hour. She wondered briefly why no one ever objected to the noise in the middle of the night. Except it wasn't noise. Not like a clamoring bell. Cindy figured what it said to everyone who celebrated was "this is Christmas." No one else seemed to mind, either. As far as she knew, no complaints were ever made.

Cindy listened until the last notes faded into the night. The season of joy has come, the soft chimes said. With a sigh and a small smile, she finished fastening her coat. Behind her, the door opened. Cindy half expected to find Brad had followed her out.

"Dan," she said, with a small shock. "I didn't see you inside."

Dan came down the two steps until he stood beside her. "Hi. I didn't see you either. Sorry about missing your party. My normal evening guy was out sick and no one else was available to cover. Did you have fun?"

"I did," Cindy said, and meant it.

The door opened again. This time it was Brad.

"Cindy! I wanted to say—" Brad paused upon seeing Dan at her side. "Oh. Hey, man." He squinted at Dan as if trying to remember meeting him at the party. Unable to figure it out, he turned his eyes to Cindy once more. "I just wanted to say it was nice catching up and um…" His gaze went to Dan again and back to Cindy. "This ball thing. Pretty weird, eh? But yeah, I'll be happy to be your date."

"Brad, we'll talk about it, okay? Go back inside and get yourself a big glass of water. And it was nice catching up with you, too." Cindy waved the gloves she'd pulled from her pocket. She waited, wanting to make sure he returned into the building without any issues. He did appear to have had one too many. Brad stepped back inside, letting the door close. He continued watching her through the glass panes.

"Well," said Dan, his expression slightly amused.

Cindy yanked on her gloves. "We used to know each other, sort of, back when Jasmine was in college."

"Got it. Is your car in the lot?"

"I put it in the garage before heading over," Cindy said.

"Mine's behind the store. I'll walk you home."

They made their way side by side in companionable silence toward the alley that ran behind the businesses. At the stairs to Cindy's apartment, they paused. Facing him, Cindy backed up the steps until she stood at his eye level. She noticed the way the light breeze lifted his hair. The way the colored lights on the railings reflected in his irises. The way his mouth was slowly curving. She stared at the latter for too long and jerked her gaze away.

"You know me," she stammered. "I don't usually drink. But I did tonight, and I appreciate you seeing me safely to my door. Or almost my door," she added with a laugh, pointing her thumb toward the second floor. "Thank you." She started to turn away.

"Not a problem," he answered. "What's a Prince Charming for?"

She whipped around. Quite abruptly, she clasped his face in her hands and kissed him. If he kissed her back, she couldn't tell. Shock took over first. Releasing him, she stumbled backward up the next two steps, jabbering an apology. She clambered up the remaining stairs without waiting to hear his response.

Hands shaking, Cindy jabbed her key several times into the lock before she got the door open. She pushed inside, shut the door, locked it, threw her purse onto the counter. Her elbows followed her bag onto the hard surface. She pressed her forehead onto her open palms, heart hammering in her chest.

"What is *wrong* with me?"

Shakespeare chirped a staccato reply from the window sill. Cindy scooped him up and quickly turned off the kitchen light. She carried him into the bedroom and threw herself fully-clothed onto the quilted cover. After a moment, she relented and kicked off her boots. She awoke in the morning wrinkled, stiff, angry at herself, and with a distinctly foul taste in her mouth.

Chapter Seventeen

"You did what?"

Cindy flinched at Jas's tone. At the laughter following the question, she squeezed her eyelids shut. Wrinkling her forehead hurt, so she lifted her lids again.

"I'll have to apologize to him," she said.

"Why? He might have enjoyed it."

Cindy carefully rubbed her temples. "He has someone in his life."

"Are you sure?"

Cutting short a painful nod, Cindy raised her eyes to Jasmine's. "I saw them together. In his store."

"Huh," said Jas. "I'm not sure you told me that. Anyway, he probably knows it meant nothing. Better to just let it go. It didn't mean anything, right?"

"Right," Cindy echoed. However, she couldn't help recalling the impulse, the driving force behind the quick contact, lip to lip. In that exact instant, it had meant something. She just wasn't sure what. Desperation, maybe.

"Because Brad—"

"Jasmine," said Cindy.

Jas closed her mouth. Cindy rarely called her by her full name.

"I need some coffee," Cindy mumbled, turning toward the storeroom.

"Use your gift card from Gina," Jasmine said, stopping her progress short. "I'll go. Get us both one. You don't mind me using your card for mine, too, do you?"

"Of course not." Cindy came back to the counter, leaned her weight against it, fumbled underneath for her bag. "As for Brad..."

"Yes?"

"I'm not dating him. I'm sure it would be extra cozy, the four of us together, and he was nice enough to talk to. Really, he was. But I don't... I'm not going to lead him on. I'm really not interested."

Jasmine reached for the card Cindy pulled from her wallet. "You should at least give him another chance. You two were really getting along. You were laughing and flirting all night."

Cindy's brow wrinkled again. She decided to put up with the pain rather than go to the trouble to change her expression. "Laughing I remember. Flirting? No. I wasn't."

"You were holding his hand," Jas reminded her.

"He would have fallen down if I hadn't," Cindy shot back. "There was no other reason."

"Hmm," Jas grunted, snatching the card from Cindy's fingertips. "I'll be back in a minute, my hungover friend." Jasmine hesitated at the door, looking back. "You did promise to talk to him about going to the ball, though. I did hear that."

"And I will talk to him."

"Good." Jas opened the door and stepped out onto the sidewalk. "Because they'll be stopping by the store before they head back to the city."

"Fabulous," Cindy said aloud, reaching for her phone. She'd received a text while debating things with Jasmine. She saw now it came from Dan.

No worries about last night, it read, followed by a smiling emoji. She sent a smile back. Let off the hook. Done. Resolved.

Except it didn't quite feel that way.

Two coffees, an aspirin, some toast, and a few hours later, Cindy felt somewhat revived when Harry and Brad appeared at Cinderella Silks. Brad looked the worse for wear. He hadn't shaved, he didn't remove his sunglasses when he came in, and he had a tinge to his skin as though he felt queasy.

"Sorry," he said to Cindy, as soon as they walked in. "I don't usually drink like that anymore. I'm afraid I might have been a little inappropriate. Well, maybe not inappropriate. More like overly enthusiastic."

Cindy smiled at his spot-on apology. "No wor—" She stopped herself, remembering Dan's text. "I think we both had too much. And apology accepted. Not even necessary, really."

"Thanks," he said with a sheepish smile. "So, this is your business?"

Cindy showed him around, up and down, excluding her apartment. She didn't want any mixed signals. Harry, who hadn't seen the third floor yet, accompanied them upstairs. Both men seemed impressed.

"This is fantastic," Harry said. Brad kept walking in circles, pointing at various machines and asking what they did, clearly interested. When they returned downstairs, Harry said they'd come to take her and Jasmine out to lunch before they both went to their respective homes.

"There's no one else on today, but take Jasmine," Cindy said. "I'll be fine by myself. It's a slow day so far."

Jasmine and Harry left, with Brad trailing behind. He pivoted and came back in, striding quickly to the counter. "I hope we're good?" he said.

"We are," Cindy assured him.

"And what about this ball thing? Are we...?"

Cindy leaned forward. "Don't tell Jasmine this, but I always planned on attending by myself. It's going to be a crazy night keeping things running smoothly. The point of taking someone was to raise more money for the charity. You could still buy a ticket and tag along with Harry and Jas to enjoy the evening. Excellent food. Fun music. I'll save you a dance, as the saying goes."

She straightened. Perhaps due to the excesses from the night before, Brad needed to ponder exactly what she'd said. "Oh," he responded after a moment. "Okay. Deal. I understand. About what I said to you last night—"

"What happens in The Sitting Duck, stays in The Sitting Duck," Cindy quipped.

He laughed and left, his walk a bit livelier than when he'd entered.

"Have Jasmine bring me back a sandwich!" she called after him. He gave her a thumbs up. The door closed behind him.

Cindy released a long breath over her lips. Time to get on with her day.

*　　*　　*

Several quietly thrilling events took place as the date for the Garland Ball approached. The first was a call from Wade, the journalist, asking for answers to a few questions before he and his wife—also his photographer—showed up for the actual ball. They'd both decided it would be fun to go in person for a more in-depth piece and had purchased tickets a week ago. The full interview would come after. The next was the appearance of the writer from Connor Falls' local newspaper. Jas had taken out an ad for the Garland Ball back in October, and now the paper wanted to follow up with a small article. Cindy managed to answer his questions between several customers and, per his request, promised to email him some photos. The third came in as an email query through the store's website on Wednesday. One of the two young women Cindy had spoken to on the sidewalk was also a blogger, and she asked to do an interview pertaining to Cinderella Silks and the Garland Ball after the holidays.

After Cindy explained the woman's request, Jas lifted her hand in an effortless high-five. Cindy had to jump to reach it.

"Three more days until the ball, Cinderella," said Jas. "Are you seriously going to tell me you're not bringing anyone?"

"Seriously. I'm not bringing anyone," Cindy stated.

Jas lowered her softly enhanced lashes and glared at Cindy from beneath them. Shutting the notebook where she'd been making a few notes, Cindy stowed it beneath the counter.

"You can't really be surprised," she said.

Jasmine's right brow lifted. "Can't I?"

"You know me well enough. I rarely say things I don't mean."

"What about when you—"

Cindy raised a finger.

Jas stopped talking and laughed instead. "Fine. I give up. What's the plan, then? What time are we heading over? Are we getting dressed there, or going home again?"

Cindy had arranged for Peg and two assistants to cover the store the day of the ball until it closed at five o'clock. The sign letting customers know about the early closing had been hanging on the front door for the past three weeks. Beyond that, nothing had been mentally finalized for Cindy. She possessed an idea how the day should progress, but apparently hadn't verbalized it to Jas.

"What do you think about this?" Cindy asked her. "I'd like to get there around nine or ten, to finish up whatever decorating we don't get done the night before. We could head out to get dressed after the band arrives and the caterers start setting up. Five-ish, maybe? Is that enough time?"

"We have to be back in time for early birds," said Jas. "The doors to the reception room will be locked until quarter after seven, right? We should return no later than that. So, I'd like to be home to get ready by four, if that's okay."

"Of course, it is. I'll stick around until five, just in case."

Jasmine brushed her palms across each other. "That's settled then. Did I tell you Brad bought a ticket?"

"You did," said Cindy.

"He's driving up with Harry and spending the night. Maybe in the morning you two—"

"No, no. No, no, no, no. No."

"Well, I'm glad to see you're not ruling it out or anything. Honestly, though, you might have a good time on Saturday evening, after all."

Cindy didn't respond. Most of the night would be spent making sure nothing went awry, but in between she planned just that. A good time. A plain old good time, not one relying on a male companion she wasn't looking for. It would be different if…well, if. She tried not to think about her mouth on Dan's. Veered away from the humiliation following, as well as the blonde in his embrace inside the printshop. He wasn't the if. No one was the if. Cindy was perfectly capable of having a blast all on her own, surrounded by various friends and the other, numerous attendees.

Later that night, standing before the wall calendar with a blue marker in her hand, Cindy contemplated her earlier thoughts. Dismissing them, she made an "x" on the date. One more day closer to the ball, to her actual birthday, to Christmas. She'd been crossing off days leading up to events since she was a kid. Her brother insisted she should use her phone, like she was disabling herself some way by not following his example. She liked the physical presence of the calendar, the act of making her 'x' and not having to keep track on a teeny-tiny screen.

"Do you think I'm a misfit, Shakes?"

Shakespeare trotted over, rubbing his face and neck along her calf, purring.

"Me neither," she said. "I'm like the dentist elf in that old Claymation Christmas special. I'm in-dee-pen-dent."

Scooping the cat off the floor, Cindy carried him into the bedroom and tossed him gently onto the bed, after which she hastily shirked off her clothes and put on her comfy pjs. "It's only a few days until Christmas. I haven't watched a single movie yet. Shall we?"

Shakespeare chirped again.

"If not for you, bud, I'd have to be a little more upfront about talking to myself." Cindy smiled. "But that's okay, too."

*   *   *

In the morning, things started going awry rather quickly. It started with a call from Gran. She'd insisted over and over she wanted to wear the dress she'd worn to the last Garland Ball. The fabric had kept like new in a garment bag in the closet and the dress did fit, thanks to Gran maintaining her weight and basic shape over the years. The only problem was she'd just discovered the garment needed a repair.

"I'll come over this afternoon and fix it," Cindy told her, tallying up the things needing to be done today and when. "What? You have aquatic aerobics this afternoon?" Cindy looked down at her midsection, gave her stomach a pat. Semi-flat. Still, she might want to join the seniors in the water someday soon. "Of course, you do. How about tonight? No. Lunchtime? Okay, I'll run over then. See you later, Gran."

Jas, who had walked in on the last few sentences only, cocked her head to one side. "Is Gran okay?"

"Fine. Feisty as ever. She insists she's wearing what she wore to the final Garland Ball from before. Did I tell you that? It still fits her, but something has to be repaired."

"I'm surprised the whole thing doesn't need repairing. Or remaking. Or cutting up to make one of those memory quilts."

Cindy laughed and shrugged. "I saw the dress. It's amazing how certain fabrics last through the years if they're cared for."

"Sort of like human beings," said Jasmine, unfurling her scarf from around her neck.

"I like that," Cindy said. "Did you make that up off the top of your head?"

Without answering, Jasmine gave her a cocky grin and strode toward the storeroom with her outer garments. A few seconds later, Cindy heard her groan.

"You okay?" Cindy called out.

Jasmine returned holding her cell phone up, screen facing Cindy.

Cindy frowned. "I can't read that from here."

Jas's hand dropped to her side. "It's Gwen. From the caterers. There's a shortage of beef, or something."

"What?"

"Well, maybe not a shortage of beef, but something is up with an element essential to the buffet. I'll give her a call." Coatless, Jas walked out the front door, probably wanting to spare Cindy any distressing details until she'd resolved the matter. Cindy wandered after her, curious for details anyway. While standing there not able to distinguish actual words due to the muffling effects from door glass and cars driving by on Main Street, Cindy studied the gown on the dressmaker's dummy. Her gown. Her cherry red, strapless gown. Suddenly, she remembered she hadn't yet purchased the proper undergarments for it. Or shoes.

Yanking her cell from her trouser pocket, she sent herself a text in reminder. Added another to make sure she had a wrap to wear. If she couldn't locate one, she needed to make or buy it.

Jasmine marched back in while Cindy was typing in yet another reminder.

"It's all good," Jas said, passing her by.

"Is it?"

"Sure. If not, Plan B. It'll be fine."

Cindy closed her eyes, nodded. It will be fine, she repeated silently. It will be fine.

By lunchtime, a lunch hour in which Cindy did not have to leave to attend to Gran's dress due to a change in her grandmother's schedule, Cindy and Jas sat side by side in two chairs they'd dragged up next to each other. Lunch was in their laps. Neither ate. They both stared across the store at nothing.

"What a strange day," Jas murmured.

"Feels like we've been putting out fires all morning," Cindy agreed.

"Nothing we can't handle, though."

"Right." Cindy lifted her sandwich, lowered it again. "Right?"

"Right."

"I hadn't really anticipated not being able to

decorate the room until ten at night on Friday, though," Cindy said, taking a real bite from her sandwich, rather than the phantom ones she'd been working on for the past fifteen minutes. "Funny, the prior engagement suddenly requiring an extra two hours for their event."

"Well, we agreed to it."

"Had to," said Cindy. "Bad karma if we didn't."

Jasmine snorted.

Cindy swigged some water, swallowed. "I'm going to miss you when you move away, Jas. Heck, I'm going to miss you when you're married."

Jas dropped her hand onto Cindy's, gave her fingers a squeeze. "Never said I was moving away. Nothing's been decided there. And just because I become Sadie, Sadie, Married Lady doesn't mean anything changes between you and me. I'll still be the thorn in your side."

"Sounds painful." Cindy grinned. "And wonderful."

"I try," said Jasmine.

They finished their meal and were returning the chairs to their places when Peg walked in the door carrying Gran's garment bag. Cindy took it from her.

"Thanks, Peg. Saves me a trip. I'll run it back over later."

Cindy went upstairs to make the repair. Two, actually. Both minor. She'd finished in short order, but spent longer studying the garment's manufacturing, the different materials used. This fancy dress was not the one from the picture, but a style in fashion several years later. The black and white design was still beautiful.

Holding the garment against her chest, Cindy rose and walked slowly to the full-length mirror on the wall. She swung slowly from side to side, watching the skirt swirl. The dress was likely knee-length on Gran, but fell a couple inches below Cindy's. Cindy lowered her lids and continued swaying, thinking of old black and white movies and the couples' elegance as they moved around the dancefloor. She imagined, too, a room filled with people, some she knew and others she didn't, all enjoying themselves in an event that was a perfect lead-in to the holiday season. As much of a pain in the neck setting it up had been, Cindy realized the Garland Ball might end up a wonderful occasion for everyone attending.

She envisioned stepping into someone's arms for one of those elegant dances—a waltz—and glided gracefully around the sewing room, astonished she remembered the steps. But the waltz made her think of Dan. To think of him in ways she preferred to avoid, including kissing him on the staircase right outside. Even so, in the fading fancy she felt his arm at her waist, his fingers on hers, saw his smile that had changed very little since they were children.

Cindy's arms dropped to her midsection. The dress folded over them. She rushed across the floor and placed it back inside the garment bag.

Dan Hayes, attached family man. Cindy Michaels, unable to hold her liquor. A mistake in a vulnerable moment.

"Idiot," Cindy said out loud and hurried back to the store, to work, to real life.

Chapter Eighteen

"It normally takes me three days to decorate my Christmas tree. And we're doing five in the next couple hours," Jas griped jokingly. "Thank goodness we have help."

Several shopkeepers and townsfolk with a hand in the ball's planning had also volunteered with the decorating. Fortunately, Hannah's department store had kept their old window and store décor in storage, so much of the vintage style ornaments were on loan from them.

"Here's hoping we're done by midnight," Gina said, having overheard the comment. "I need my beauty sleep."

Cindy smiled at Gina and her natural good looks. "Is that your secret? Sleep?"

"It's what I'm claiming," Gina responded with a laugh.

Sophie from Sophie's Chandlery had shown up with a cd player and some holiday music. Jas scurried over and turned up the volume. The tunes were from a time before many in the room were born, but everyone apparently approved with loud applause.

"This should get us moving," Jasmine said, returning to the box she'd been emptying.

They sorted the trees—necessarily artificial, since they'd have to be removed on Sunday—the lights, and the ornaments, and divided into work groups, two people to each tree. Cindy worked with Jasmine. As Jas's hands flitted about fluffing up tree branches, her ring glittered in the overhead light.

"Your ring really is beautiful," Cindy commented.

Raising her hand and stretching her fingers out, Jasmine grinned. "Harry does have a good eye."

"I'm sure he has other good parts, too," said a voice at Cindy's back. Cindy spun on her heel.

"Mom! What are you doing here?"

"Lending a hand," said Lacie. "Just point me in the direction I'm needed."

"Well, okay," Cindy said, pleased to have her there. "You've always had the patience to untangle lights. Why don't you see who needs help with that?"

"Your mom's the best," Jas said, once Lacie had crossed the floor to perform some detangling.

"If you say so," Cindy muttered in a teasing tone.

"You know she is."

"Yeah," said Cindy. "I do."

Almost all the trees were standing and wrapped in lights when the door opened again. This time, Cindy heard it and turned her head.

Dan. And Rena.

Rena ran to Cindy's side. "Hi. We're here to help. What's next?"

"Hanging these ornaments." Cindy pointed to the box at her feet, watching Dan's approach from the corner of her eye. The temperature in her cheeks rose with each step he took.

"Good thing Dad's here," Rena said. "He's got long arms. We won't need a ladder. Could we sort them out on the floor so we can see them all at once? That's how we do it at home. Well, with Dad. Mom has a different way. It works, too."

"Sure," Cindy agreed. She dropped to her knees to avoid Dan's eye and began pulling the baubles out, placing them neatly onto the wooden floor. Dan stood nearby in silence. Cindy glanced up, spotted his gaze on her. She looked away again. "Thank you both for coming," she said, keeping her eyes focused on the task at hand.

"Happy to," said Dan. "And you can look at me, you know."

She did, and found him smiling. His easy, casual smile. A smile that said 'no awkwardness here.' Cindy's shoulders relaxed.

"I'll get the lights on, shall I?" Dan suggested. Without waiting for an answer, he picked up the strands and started on the task. By the time he finished, Cindy and Rena had nearly emptied the box.

Dan nodded toward the floor. "That's an old steeple. I haven't seen one like that since I was a kid. Want me to put it on top now?"

Rena followed his gaze. She started to giggle. "That's awful. Really awful. But in a fabulous way," she added. She looked at Cindy. "Dad says the trees are all supposed to represent different times. I guess this one is from bright and garish Christmas?"

Cindy burst out laughing. So did Dan. Cindy found she couldn't stop. Dan stood above her, a hand over his eyes, head shaking. Rena watched them both.

"What?" she said.

"Out of the mouth of babes, I think the saying is," Dan whispered, fighting back more laughter.

"Are you calling me a babe? Not only is the term outdated, it's sexist, Dad."

"Babe in this instance means child," Cindy explained. "I think the saying is an ancient version of kids say the darndest things. My mom used to use that one when I was growing up. It was the name of an old television show."

"Was it, like, a talk show with kids?" Rena asked.

"I'm not sure. You might find some episodes online somewhere." Cindy looked from Rena to Dan and back again. "That would be fun to watch together."

Rena's brow wrinkled. "The three of us?"

In a flash, Cindy's cheeks heated again. "I meant you and your dad and your brothers." She hurried back to unpacking the remaining ornaments. Dan picked up the steeple, tipped the tree on its stand, and fitted the clip-on steeple at its apex. Cindy glanced up at the brightly-colored, ultramodern ornament.

"It is rather gaudy," she admitted to Rena. "But it's jolly."

"Jolly. Yeah, that's…a word."

They smiled at each other and returned to sorting the ornaments on the floor before transposing their positions onto the tree. Cindy had to admit, decorating the tree in this manner did save time from the usual rearranging. When they'd finished, Cindy stepped back to admire the results, realizing for the first time that Jas hadn't been with them. Cindy spotted her helping Sophie and Sophie's friend finish another tree.

"Despite being *garish*," Dan said, turning his head to speak near Cindy's ear, "it's bringing back memories."

Cindy dug her nails into her palm to prevent the shiver forming over her skin from his drifting breath.

"Memories from when you were a kid?" Rena asked her father.

He nodded, appearing somewhat wistful, Cindy thought. She wondered what he might be recalling. She had her own special memories from childhood Christmases. Some included Dan and his family. They'd spent time together at parties and such over the holidays. Her favorites, though, were the quieter moments.

"I think my best memories now," Dan said to his daughter, "are from when you all were little."

Rena stood, looked up at her dad. "Do you remember when we got Roxie?"

The conversation had taken a personal turn. Cindy dropped to her knees and began folding the packing papers and returning them to the empty carton. Their voices, Dan's, and Rena's, continued over her head, discussing the dog, the Christmas they added her to their lives. Despite her attempt not to eavesdrop, Cindy couldn't help hearing their words, the animation in them, the affectionate recall. She smiled as she worked, warmed by the happy memories of people she cared about.

After a few minutes, Jasmine's voice cut in. "It's midnight, folks, and guess what? We have finished!"

Everyone stepped back to view the completed undertaking and applauded. From the photos on the wall, to the centerpieces on the tables, the lights everywhere, the decorated trees, everything looked suitably festive and wonderfully in keeping with the event's theme.

"Well done, everyone," Cindy said, turning in a circle to encompass them all, arms raised. "And thank you!"

The only thing left to do right then was store the boxes away until they would be needed again on Sunday morning. Afterward, they all walked out together into the night, parting ways in the parking lot to get into their cars and head home.

Jas, coat still open and revealing her seldom seen attire of worn, faded jeans and an oversized sweatshirt, waved as she hurried toward her car.

"Harry and Brad will be here first thing. I need to change all the sheets and clean the bathroom!" She laughed delightedly, unlocking the car and clambering inside.

"She seems happy," Dan commented. He and Rena had paused beside Cindy. Otherwise, the lot was empty and the last cars but theirs headed toward the exit.

"She is," Cindy answered. "I never thought she'd find someone she wanted to be with this way."

Dan was quiet. Rena's head tipped up to view her dad. "We should get going. Mom has some crazy plans for tomorrow. Um, today, I guess. She wants me to get *my hair done*." The girl shuddered in a theatric gesture.

"Right," said Dan, recalling himself from wherever his mind had gone. Cindy figured her remark might have prompted a quick contemplation about the woman she'd seen him with.

"I'll see you both tomorrow—er, tonight," Cindy said. "Thanks again for coming by to help."

"It was fun," said Rena.

"It was," Cindy agreed and unlocked her car with the key fob. Still, Dan stood there. Cindy saw thoughts moving in his eyes. Rena tugged on his hand.

"Dad."

"Right," he said again. "Goodnight, Cindy. See you in a few hours." Flashing a grin, he allowed his daughter to lead him over to their car. Cindy got into hers, started it, turned the lights on. Dan did the same, but he didn't pull out right away. Waiting to make sure she headed out first and safely, she supposed. A considerate guy.

At the exit, they turned in opposite directions. Dan, to drop his daughter off at his ex-wife's home and she, back to her apartment in town for another night spent cuddled around her cat.

Chapter Nineteen

Cindy had barely gotten dressed for the day when she heard someone knocking on her door. Given the hour, she hesitated before answering it, peering through the white curtain on the window. She yanked open the door.

"Brad! What's wrong?"

"Is that where your mind goes? To what's wrong?" he asked, stepping inside. "It's okay if I come in for a second, isn't it?"

"Of course. And yes, that's where my mind goes," Cindy said, pushing the door closed. "It's not even seven o'clock yet. What's up?"

Before answering, Brad moved his head in quick assessment. "Nice place. Cozy. Suits you, I'm thinking." First Dan, now Brad. Something was obvious. Brad turned his attention back to her. "As for why I'm here, I was told a text wouldn't work. You could ignore it too easily. The three of us—me, Har, and Jas—are going out to breakfast, and you're coming with." He jerked a thumb over his shoulder. "They're parked at the end of the alley waiting."

"I have to open the store," Cindy dithered.

"Yeah, at nine. That's why we're here so early." He grinned.

Plenty of time, Cindy estimated as she gave in.

"Let me get my coat."

When they stepped out onto the landing, Brad waved toward the alley's end, where Jasmine had exited a car Cindy could only presume belonged to Harry. Jas gave him a thumbs up. Halfway down the stairs, Cindy spotted someone running from the opposite direction. Less than ten feet away, Dan looked up with a start and completely stopped. Cindy smiled.

"Aren't you supposed to do the running in a circle thing, rather than stopping?" she said, trotting down the remaining steps to meet him.

"It's what I do. It's not official." He spoke the words to her, but his eyes were on Brad. Brad's gaze settled on him in return.

"Sorry, rude of me," Cindy said. "Dan, this is Brad. Brad, Dan."

Brad came down to the alley's rough surface, shook Dan's extended hand. "Nice to meet you," they said in unison. They both laughed with a sound not resembling the usual from either man. Lifting his right hand in a quick wave, Dan started away.

Cindy called after him, "I'll see you tonight!" He glanced back at her with a split-second smile and kept going.

"He looks familiar," said Brad.

"You probably saw him last weekend," Cindy reminded him. "Outside the Sitting Duck? He walked me home."

"I thought that was the guy." Brad watched him turn the corner. "What's his name again?"

Cindy strode toward the waiting car. "Dan. And we should get going. I don't want to be late opening the store."

Brad hastened to catch up. "I want to apologize again for last Saturday. I made some assumptions and said some things."

Cindy glanced at him and away. "I told you, really, no apologies necessary."

By his expression, Cindy couldn't tell if this was the answer he wanted, too easily dismissing an awkward few moments, but they'd reached the car. Cindy felt rather relieved. With Jas providing directions, Harry drove from town to The Pepper. The talk on the way was all about the Garland Ball, mostly fielding questions from Harry and Brad. What was it all about? When did it start? Why was it resurrected? What was the band like? By the time they reached the diner, they were all laughing hard. Harry and Brad had decided they might have to take over if the music wasn't up to par.

In the booth, Cindy glanced at her phone for the time.

"What's up?" Jasmine asked.

"Us," Cindy said. "We're up and out and eating breakfast. This is going to be a really long day."

"But a fun long day," Jas countered.

"Absolutely," Cindy agreed, pleased to find her smile wasn't forced in response. She loved Connor Falls and had so many friends there, many of whom would be in attendance. In all honesty, if she dismissed the stress, the extra work, bringing back the Garland Ball hadn't been a bad idea, at all. Next year, though, planning would begin early and the work would be spread out over the months leading up to it.

"Good," said Jas. "No more sour puss?"

"Sour puss? Cindy echoed.

"You haven't been your usual self. You know you haven't."

Cindy sighed, nodded, asked for coffee when the server appeared. No one had yet viewed their menus. Leaning back to read hers, Cindy bumped into Brad's arm across the seat back. His hand curled around her shoulder, then let go. He lowered his arm to the table, opening his own menu.

"Sorry," he said.

She grunted, gave him a small smile. She didn't think he noticed the sound or the gesture. He seemed absorbed now in choosing his meal. Having decided already what she would have, Cindy closed her menu and gazed around the diner. She spotted Jeremy and Sheila seated close by and gave them a wave.

"Not Wednesday," she said, not loudly, but loud enough for them to hear. They both laughed and shrugged.

"Who's that?" Brad asked. So, he was paying attention after all.

"My ex-husband and his girlfriend," Cindy told him.

"You're friendly?"

"Oh yeah." Cindy pulled the coffee just dropped off a little closer. "Could you pass me the sugar, please?"

Brad did, brushing her hand when he placed the packet-filled bowl nearby. Cindy pretended she hadn't felt the touch. Her text tone sounded. Cindy turned the cell screen side up, glanced at the words before tipping the phone away from Brad's probing eyes.

I see you two are getting along.

Cindy shot a swift look across the table at Jas before quickly typing back: *Do you WANT to wear my eggs when they arrive?*

Jas's phone was on silent, but Cindy knew the minute Jas read the return text. She started to laugh.

"Are you and Cindy texting each other?" Harry asked.

"Girl talk," Jas said.

"But we're done," Cindy added.

Harry and Brad exchanged a glance. Brad's arm came up again across the seat back. Cindy adjusted her seated posture to avoid leaning anywhere near his limb. When the food came, he had no choice but to return his arm to the front to use his knife and fork.

"The food here's good," he said after a moment.

"It is," Cindy said. She wouldn't be rude. She just wouldn't give him any indication they might be more than friends. She thought she'd made that clear, but she was getting the impression maybe she hadn't been as obvious as she hoped.

Talk around the table continued in a friendly, enjoyable manner, touching on as many subjects as they could fit into the time they had for breakfast. It was Jas who reminded them all they needed to wrap it up and get going, because the store was due to open. Cindy asked Harry to drop her off out front, climbing out with a thank you for breakfast when he pulled his car up to the curb.

"I'll be back shortly," Jas called out to her.

Cindy came back to the car, leaned in the window. "No rush. In fact, why don't you just take the day? Peg and Sandi will be coming in early. I'll be fine at the venue, too, and if not, I'll give you a call. Enjoy your day with Harry and Brad."

In the back seat, Brad leaned forward. "I could stick around—"

Cindy straightened. "See you all tonight!" Without looking back, she marched up to the door and let herself in.

With only two minutes left until nine o'clock, she left the door unlocked. First thing, she removed her gown from the dressmaker's dummy, examining the garment for dust or defect. Satisfied the sun hadn't faded it, no mysterious threads had come loose, and that the dress remained clean, she hung it on a hanger in the storeroom to bring upstairs later. After all her griping, all the stress, all the work still to come, Cindy was looking forward to the Garland Ball. Realizing as much had been a revelation during breakfast, but anticipation still danced in her consciousness. More for the townspeople, perhaps, but that was half the fun, seeing others enjoy themselves.

In the early afternoon, Cindy hurried over to the venue to see to any last-minute prep and issues. Gratified to find everything running well, she decided to give herself extra time to get ready and headed back to her apartment with plenty to spare. She went through the store first, checking with Peg and Sandi, then headed upstairs, gown in hand.

To find the apartment door standing open.

Chapter Twenty

Cindy's heart thudded to a stop. Her breath went into her lungs and didn't come back out. Hands shaking, she pulled her phone from her pocket, preparing to call the police. She hesitated. Everything inside looked untouched. She tried to remember if she'd forgotten to lock the door when she left, then recalled Brad had exited behind her. Even if she had turned the lock on the knob, he might not have pulled it closed all the way. It did stick sometimes, and the day had been breezy…

Her held breath abruptly rushed out. "Shakespeare!"

Calling his name again, Cindy hurried into the apartment, tossing her dress over the kitchen chair. She rushed through the few rooms, peering into the bedroom and bath before entering, then scurried back to shut the front door.

Shakespeare hadn't been in his usual place on the sill, but the door blowing open had surely frightened him into hiding. Now she knew her home hadn't been invaded, Cindy made her way again around the apartment calling softly for her cat, receiving no response. She peeked under the sofa, the bed, behind curtains, in every corner imaginable, one of his treats in hand. The second time through, moisture blurred her vision.

He'd gotten out. Her once feral rescue kitty had run out the open door. She couldn't imagine how afraid he must be. She couldn't imagine where he'd go. She couldn't imagine him coming back.

Pushing up from the floor where she'd been peering beneath the furniture yet again, Cindy took her dress and hung it on the back of the closet door. She put on her gloves, her hat, grabbed Shakespeare's carrier and the bag of treats, and headed out to find him. She left his bowl outside the door filled with food, hoping the scent would call to him.

Cindy started along the alley, calling his name, looking in open trash bins and the occasional dumpster. It hadn't felt unusually cold in the apartment, so she figured the door hadn't been open all day. With any luck, Shakespeare hadn't gone far. As she searched, she thought about how much her heart ached when she saw posters people put up, asking if anyone had seen their missing pet. It surprised her, really, that Shakespeare had left the apartment. Although he'd once been semi-wild before she took him in, he'd always been on the timid side with anything he didn't feel comfortable about.

She traversed the alley twice before pulling out her phone to check the time. Once she found Shakes and calmed him down, she'd have to take a record-breaking shower before dressing for the event.

Not finding him wasn't an option.

Spirits sinking despite her determination to be positive, Cindy went around to the storefronts and asked anyone she passed if they had seen a cat on the sidewalk. She showed them a photo from her cell. No luck.

Could he have run as far as the park? What were the actual chances of locating a runaway pet? Especially a cat?

She had to check, continuing to ask everyone she met while trotting through the park. Finally, deciding he might be the odd cat who actually decided to make its way home, she rushed back to the alley, visualizing Shakespeare eating from the bowl on the landing, greeting her upon arrival. But the metal staircase, the landing, were empty. She stood staring at his bowl, chewing on her lip and blinking back tears, the carrier's weight dragging at her right arm.

"Cindy!"

Cindy turned and leaned over the banister. Dan stood in the alleyway clutching a box for copy paper to his chest. He made a face.

"Where's your phone?"

"What?" Cindy responded. "In my pocket. Sorry, I've been out looking for my cat." She lifted the carrier, settled it at her side again.

"Did you find him?"

She shook her head, feeling more like crying than she wanted to reveal.

"Good," Dan said.

Cindy's shoulders jerked. "What?"

"If you'd found him, it would mean I had somebody's else cat tucked up in here." He lifted the cardboard container, which gave a little wriggle in his grasp.

Squealing, Cindy dropped the carrier, pounded down the stairs. She took the box from Dan, slightly lifted the lid, peered inside. Jammed into a corner, Shakespeare yowled rather loudly. "Where was he?"

"In the alley," he said, pointing toward the printshop. "I didn't find him. Rena did. She and her mom stopped by for a few minutes between, I don't know, whatever the heck they're doing before tonight's gala event. I'm not sure exactly what happened, but Rena decided to go out the back door and he was there. He ran right up to her. She scruffed him and we put him in the nearest box. Fortunately, it was empty."

Cindy grinned up at Dan, the tears she'd been fighting dribbling out. He lifted his arms, put them around her, pulled her close, or as close as he could with the box between them. Cindy relaxed in his embrace, wishing… Just wishing. After a moment he stepped back. Not awkwardly. There was that, at least. Cindy straightened, rearranged the copy box against her abdomen.

"I did text you. Called you, too," he said, sounding apologetic for not having reached her.

"I didn't know. How long ago?" Cindy asked, stunned she hadn't heard her phone.

"About ten minutes. No big deal. I figured I'd head down this way and wait."

"Wait? In the cold?" She envisioned him huddled on the freezing metal step or perched on the one chair she left out in all seasons. Huddled and clutching the box with her cat inside. A man with a big, kind heart.

"Well, not necessarily outside. I might have headed around into your store where it's warm."

"Oh. Yeah, absolutely," Cindy said.

"What? Were you picturing me like a waif shivering in the snow?"

She laughed. "Kind of."

He snorted. "Maybe we should get your little guy inside. I'll come up with you, get the crate out of your way."

They walked back toward her place, side by side. His was a comfortable presence, made even more so in recent months. She felt warmed by his friendship, and not just because he'd brought her cat home.

He took to the stairs ahead of her, mounting them two at a time. At the second floor, he picked up the empty carrier. "Keys?" he asked when she reached him.

Holding tightly to the box and its squirming occupant, Cindy cocked a hip in his direction. "In my coat pocket." It seemed an almost flirty movement. She didn't intend it that way but now she imagined it as such, heat flooded her cheeks. Again. That had to stop.

He didn't appear to notice. His hand dug in, past the odd wrappers, receipts, fortunately clean tissues, to the keys lying at the bottom. He pulled the ring out, held one key up.

"This it?"

Cindy nodded.

He unlocked the door, pushed it open for her and followed her inside. Cindy leaned her back against the door to make sure it had shut tightly before she crouched down on the floor and lifted Shakespeare out from his confinement. She held his tense body, petting him and whispering soothing words.

Dan watched for a few moments in silence. "Is he okay?" he finally asked.

Cindy lifted her head, catching an expression she couldn't quite read. Perhaps he thought her careless, or maybe foolishly attached. Finally, she recognized the tenderness in the look. He likely understood her emotion. He and his daughter had spoken fondly about Roxie, the dog now living with his ex-wife and her new husband. She wondered at a tangent if Dan had since found another dog to be his own. If so, he hadn't mentioned. They didn't often talk about personal topics. She realized she'd like to. Now they were close again, they should. Friends talked about all sorts of things, and he'd been hers in one way or another for a long time.

"He's fine," she answered, pushing the thoughts away. "Scared, but otherwise no harm done. Thank you, thank you, thank you, Dan. And Rena, too. So, so much." She stood, still clutching the cat in her arms. She expected Dan would want to get on his way, but he hovered near the door. A second later, he took a step back toward her.

"Are you going to be all right?"

"I...yes," she said. "Why wouldn't I be?"

He shrugged. "It had to be a shock, finding one of your best friends had flown the coop."

Cindy sighed. "It was. Thanks again. I know I keep saying that, but I can't help it."

Dan waved away her gratitude with a kind smile. "How did he manage to get out?"

Cindy's mouth twisted. "I'm thinking the door must not have been latched properly and then the wind blew it open? It was open when I came home. And before you say anything, I visually checked first to make sure no one had broken in before I came inside," she added, seeing his face contort.

"Mind if I have a look around?" he asked. "I'm sure you were thorough. It would just make me feel better."

Given the apartment's size, it took him less than a minute. "Nothing appears to be disturbed," he concurred. He then checked the doorknob, giving it a shake and a twist. "In working order."

Nodding, Cindy lowered the cat to the floor. Shakespeare immediately scooted into the bedroom and up onto the bed, where he watched her with an accusing stare. As if she'd somehow let him down.

"I think maybe Brad hadn't pulled the door shut all the way," Cindy said to Dan. "It sometimes sticks a little, but I've never had a problem with it. Probably because I know about the issue and always make sure the door's closed."

Dan released the knob, didn't quite turn around. "I guess you'll have to give Brad a heads up for next time."

Cindy wondered at his tone. Maybe he was annoyed on her behalf about what had happened, but it hadn't truly been Brad's fault. As for a next time, there wouldn't be one. Not that she could foresee. But it didn't seem worth wearying Dan with the details.

At her silence, he pivoted to face her. "I'll see the two of you later, then."

Cindy smiled. "Me and Shakespeare? Jas nixed that idea in the bud. Plus, I figured some people might be allergic to kitty dander."

He laughed, a little uncertainly, and left, shaking the doorknob from the other side for good measure.

"Thanks!" Cindy called after him. She waited until the clanging on the stairs died away before peering around the curtain. She made out his lanky form striding down the shadowed alley toward his store. Belatedly, she realized he hadn't been making a joke about Shakespeare. He'd meant he'd see her and Brad later.

Well, he would. Just not together. Clearly, he'd misunderstood the situation. And at this point, both she and Dan needed to hurry if they were going to get to the ball at all.

Chapter Twenty-One

Tipping her head from side to side, Cindy studied her reflection in the full-length mirror hanging inside the closet door. Hair? It would do. She'd taken the time to dry it in a fashion that flattered her face more than usual. Makeup? Just enough. Gown? Perfect. Any bodily flaws beneath were hidden quite nicely. She glanced at Shakespeare curled up on the comforter. He'd forgiven her and seemed none the worse for wear. Sleeping more soundly than usual, but he'd probably worn himself out with the trauma and his trek along the alley.

Cindy had already placed the few items she expected to need during the night into a small, handmade, beaded purse she'd bought at Sophie's Chandlery. Her shoes lay in the bottom of a canvas tote bag, the black, silk wrap on top. Right now, her feet were bare. She planned to wear boots to drive over and change before exiting the car. Looking down, she wiggled her painted toes, nails gleaming in a hue the same color as her gown. Her fingernails matched. Jas would be tickled pink when she saw.

Readying herself for the busy night ahead, Cindy drew a few deep breaths, letting each out slowly. She closed her eyes and repeated the exercise. Her phone chirped. Lids lifting, she bent sideways and grabbed it, reading a text from Jas.

Got here early. Where are you?

On my way, she texted back, and snatched up her boots.

Gathering her things, Cindy patted Shakespeare's head on the fly. She headed toward the door where she paused to yank on the boots, slip her arms into her coat. Outside, she double-checked the door was secure, then checked it again. After, she drove the car around to the front of the store and pulled up to the curb, getting out to assure herself Peg and Sandi had properly locked up before she hustled back across the sidewalk and into the car. Barring any unforeseen holdups, she'd be at the venue in less than twenty minutes. Plenty of time.

Somehow, she made it in fifteen. Switching footgear and leaving her coat on the passenger seat, Cindy hurried across the lot. She found Jas inside with the caterers, the servers, the venue manager, the band. Harry and Brad were nowhere to be seen.

"I left them at the house," Jas explained. "They'll be here soon. I can tell you, Brad's looking forward to this evening."

Cindy said nothing in response. She got the hint. No need to counter it. Looking around in one last check, she made certain all was in order.

Jas gave her arm a reassuring squeeze. "Relax.

We've done all we can. The rest is up to the Mistletoe fairies. By the way, love the nails."

They hugged each other in a quick squeeze. Jas had done something with her hair Cindy had never seen before. As always, it and she were absolutely gorgeous.

Soon after, guests began arriving. Cindy and Jas attempted to welcome them as they entered, but before long the influx was too much for personal greeting. From across the floor, Cindy saw Dan and Rena come in, accompanied by several other people, including the blond woman Cindy had spotted with him in his store—a woman whose name Cindy should politely ask Dan sometime. Beside him, Rena looked adorably grown up, less like a child playing dress up than a young girl approaching a new phase.

"Look at her," Jas whispered, having come up beside Cindy. "Great job with the dress. I think she might be the prettiest little lass here."

Cindy grinned in agreement.

Jas's parents arrived at the same time Cindy's did. With them were Gran and George. Something about the energetic entrance of those two octogenarians sealed Cindy's enthusiasm for the night. She greeted and hugged them all before hurrying over to the band's microphone to make the welcoming speech.

The defunct Garland Ball was back in a glorious way.

* * *

Dinner, buffet style, came before dancing, although the band played quiet music during the meal. Cindy listened to the comments about the food, the décor, the evening, as she strode across the floor with her plate to the table. Jas had saved her a seat between Harry and Brad, of course. The other four seats were taken up by Cindy's brother and sister-in-law and another couple, so there was nothing to be done about the arrangement. Cindy determined to enjoy the time with her friends and family.

"You and Jas did a great job with this whole thing," Brad enthused at her ear. "I didn't expect to like it so much. The idea seemed so…I don't know. Archaic."

"Thanks, Brad," Cindy said, tipping her head away from his warm breath. "There were a lot of people involved, and I think all their enthusiasm helped."

"Sure, but you and Jas did most of it from what Harry tells me."

"We did a lot, yes," Cindy acknowledged. "But it wasn't ever a solitary undertaking." Odd, saying those words, when on and off over the past couple months she'd felt exactly that way. Yet, underneath she'd always recognized the truth. Connor Falls was a community. They always came together for events and causes, for people in need, for each other.

Between Peter and Tracy's heads, Cindy could see Dan's table. She vaguely recognized certain people sitting there. Dan's family members, she thought, whom she'd seen even less than Dan over the years. The blond woman sat to his right, Rena to his left. Except when he turned to address someone else, Cindy mostly viewed Dan's wavy, longish hair curling over his collar, his suit jacket on the chair behind him. At one point he leaned back and stretched, lowering his arms over the chair backs to either side. The blonde tipped her head a little closer, said something to him. They both laughed. Cindy looked away, returned her attention to her plate.

"The food is delicious," Brad said. "I think I'm going back for seconds on the pasta. Want anything?" He addressed the table in general, but his gaze lingered on Cindy.

"I'm not yet finished, but thank you," Cindy answered.

Peter accompanied him. When they returned, Peter leaned closed to Cindy's ear. "Glad to see you're dating again. Nice guy."

"I'm not—" Cindy began, and let it go. No use getting into that discussion now.

Once everyone had eaten, Cindy announced the tables would be shifted closer to the walls to open up the dancefloor. When applying for the gig, the band had sent a video demonstrating a repertoire from modern tunes to classical, integrating a cellist and violinist in their midst. They would start off slow, allowing for participants' digestion. Making her rounds and avoiding the dancefloor, Cindy's thoughts went to Dan, wondering if he'd mastered the waltz after all. Jasmine had requested the band play the waltz last to end the evening on an elegant, somewhat romantic note. Brilliant idea, to be honest. Leave it to Jas to come up with it.

All around the large room, the decorated trees sparkled and shimmered and prompted conversation as certain guests found themselves nostalgic or merely charmed. Others gathered before the enlarged photographs, searching out family and old friends. The son of a committee member wove through the gathering, taking pictures for later posting on the website Jas had created. For those who wanted one or two or all, they could order them for printing at an exceptionally reasonable price, thanks to Dan.

Cindy's gaze strayed to where he danced with Rena in ridiculously loose-limbed movements in time to the music's faster beat. The nameless blonde watched from the sidelines. Cindy wondered where the boys were. Probably with their grandmother, since Cindy had seen Dan's ex-wife come in with her husband. Cindy pulled her attention away. Somebody grabbed her elbow.

"Harry," she said, looking up at him.

"Care to dance?"

"To this?" Cindy said with a laugh. "You know better."

"We'll wing it." He dragged her out onto the dancefloor, where he interlaced his fingers with hers, palm to palm, moving her like a chortling puppet in time to the music. Her stomach soon hurt from laughing so hard.

"What's so funny?" he asked. "You don't think we're the coolest ones on the floor? Look at them. They're all just jealous of these moves."

He gave her a quick spin and reeled her back in. She fell against him and straightened, wiping tears from her eyes with her free hand. "Stop. I'm going to pee my pants."

Harry came to a halt. Perfect timing, it seemed, because the music changed to something slower. Without missing a beat, he adapted his posture to continue their dance with the new song. "We used to laugh a lot," he said.

"I know," Cindy answered, remembering how much. "I can't believe how long ago that was. It's so weird."

"Yes. A lot of changes between then and now. And a lot that hasn't."

Swaying from side to side as they pivoted in a slow circle, Cindy raised her head, studying his smile. "Most significantly, you and Jas," she said to him. "I am so happy for you both."

"Thanks, Cindy. I'm happy for me, too. I always—"

"Had a thing for her. Even back then. Is that what you were going to say?"

He nodded, his eyes taking on a faraway gaze as their bodies continued to circle.

Cindy shook him a little. "You'll take good care of Jas. Not that she tolerates or needs taking care of, but you know what I mean."

The music stopped. Harry dipped his head. "I know exactly what you mean and I will. I promise." He bent and kissed her cheek. Jasmine appeared at his side, gave Cindy a wink. Together Jas and Harry moved off into the next dance. Another slow one.

"My turn."

Cindy arched a brow at Brad and agreed. He proved to be a pleasant dancer, not as good as

Harry, which made her feel a little more adequate. Cindy made sure to keep their conversation casual, warding off any flirting. He was funny, was Brad. She laughed with him, too. Yet, it wasn't quite the same as with Harry. Perhaps better. No old history rumbling in the background.

The next song had a much faster rhythm. Cindy started to excuse herself, but Brad took her hand, leading her into a few encouraging movements.

"This is where actually having alcohol at the bar would help me," Cindy joked. "I might not move like my joints are welded."

"You're doing fine," he said, and whisked her around, nearly making her dizzy. At the song's conclusion, Cindy thanked him and backed away.

"Little girl's room," she fibbed. What she needed was fresh air, but she didn't want company. Craving a few minutes alone, she snuck outside, finding several others apparently sharing the same need. Heads turned, nodded, mumbled greetings. Cindy gave them all a brief smile as she stepped further out onto the sidewalk. She recognized one.

"Having a good time?" Cindy asked her.

The blond-haired woman turned at Cindy's question. "Great time," she said, smiling.

Cindy took a step nearer, held out her hand. "I'm—"

"Cindy. From the dress shop. Your dress shop, I should say. Rena talks about you a lot." She lightly shook Cindy's hand and let go. "I'm Grace."

"Hi, Grace. It's nice to meet you." Cindy tried not to study every aspect of the woman's face. Yet, if she looked elsewhere, she saw in her mind the embrace in the printshop instead.

"What a fabulous idea, reinstating this event," Grace gushed.

"I agree," Cindy said. "The committee of business owners voted on it. Voted me in to spearhead the thing," she added with a crooked smile.

Grace laughed. "You've done a great job. Will the ball happen again next year?"

"I'm hoping so," Cindy answered, and meant it.

Behind them, the door swung open. Dan leaned out from it, his arm extended. "There you are," he said to Grace, wriggling his fingers to encourage her to come inside. "The band's taken a break, but they've promised a Charleston next. I don't think anyone even knows what that is. You do, though, and I'm not getting out on that floor alone."

Tittering, Grace hurried toward him and past into the hallway beyond. Dan looked at Cindy.

"She took a class. This is kind of her thing." He grinned. "And your grandmother's already cueing up for a demonstration with her friend. George, I think his name is? That's something I want to see. Are you okay?"

"Yeah, yeah, I'm fine," Cindy said. "Just needed some air."

"Don't be long." He smiled at her. "I believe Brad is looking for you."

Cindy stopped herself from rolling her eyes. "Thanks."

He backed away. The door started to close behind him. He pushed it back open, put one foot out. "By the way," he said, "you look beautiful."

Cindy's lips parted. Before she could say anything, he disappeared again. A second later the door opened one more time.

"Not that you don't always," he added, and was gone.

Chapter Twenty-Two

Now how was a person supposed to take a remark like that? Cindy mused, staring at the closed door. From a man whose girlfriend had just walked past him, no less. From a friend, she reminded herself, which perhaps made a difference. Excused what might otherwise be considered inappropriate or, at the very least, darned uncomfortable—despite the pleasure she felt at his words. Cindy wasn't normally flustered by compliments, nor did she court them or let them turn her head. Her recent considerations about Dan were clearly causing her to overthink this one. Dan was far too nice to display any intentions toward Cindy with the compliment when he already had a special someone in his life.

Yet, the smile remained plastered on her face as she made her way back indoors. She entered the reception room to Jasmine calling everyone out onto the dancefloor. "Gran and George here are going to give us pointers before the band starts playing," she was saying when Cindy drew near. Looking up, Jas saw her. "You, too," she said.

"I don't know the Charleston," Cindy reasoned, stopping short.

"Neither do I, but someone's got to look foolish enough to encourage the rest not to care. Hence, the lesson from your Gran and George."

Good point, Cindy agreed silently, and went to stand beside her friend. For the next five minutes, they mimicked Gran and George's moves, sans music. It was a bit surreal with no musical accompaniment, humiliating if not for the fact she and Jas kept bumping into each other, giggling with every step.

"Come on," Gran said. "It's not that complicated. Pay attention."

Grace, Grace who already knew the Charleston, arrived on the dancefloor with Rena. Neither wore shoes. Cindy glanced at her own and kicked them off. "You, too, Jas," she said. "If you stomp on my foot with those heels I'm going to need a ride to the hospital."

Even Grace couldn't compete with the ease in which Gran and her old friend moved, but she followed along good naturedly, helping Rena when needed. Which was often. Rena laughed through the entire process. From the perimeter of the growing circle, Dan watched them both with a broad smile. By the time the band returned from their break, nearly everyone was taking part in the impromptu lesson.

"Oh my gosh," Cindy said to Jas, "I can't believe how much fun I'm having."

Jasmine threw an arm around her shoulder, yanked her close, kissed the top of her head. "Me either. I think this is what we both needed."

"What we've all needed," concurred someone nearby. A second later, Brad pressed his way forward with an excuse me, and positioned himself next to Cindy.

"I'm ready," he said. "I was practicing by the table."

Cindy decided to just go with it. Whatever happened, happened. Whatever didn't, didn't. Dancing with someone, with anyone, was fun. If Brad had intentions beyond that, she'd kindly let him know hers when the time came.

From that point on, the evening progressed in wonderful, amazing fashion. For Cindy, at any rate, as she deliberately, consciously, enjoyed every minute. Family, friends, strangers, she decided she loved them all. She laughed hard and danced every dance she could manage, still barefoot. She danced another slow one with Harry, then with Brad—*hands where they belong Brad, I'm not kidding*—and then with Gran. She and Gran clung to each other like bear cubs, spiraling around the floor. Cindy didn't realize they were the only ones out there until applause broke from the crowd in a circle watching.

"Oh, my," said Gran. "Thank you."

George came to collect Gran for the next dance. Feeling oddly tearful, Cindy slipped away, losing herself behind the crowd. She eased toward the bar and the restrooms beyond, thinking she might hide out for a few minutes. Instead, she bumped into Dan. Literally. The cranberry juice in his hand slopped over his fingers and onto the floor.

"Step carefully—" he began, then pulled himself up short. "Oh, hi. Sorry. Did I get any on your dress?"

"Don't apologize," Cindy said. "I ran into you." She grabbed napkins from the bar and dabbed up the juice from the floor. Taking the glass from him, she gave him another napkin for his hand. "I never took you for a cranberry juice man. I like it myself, but for most people it's too tart."

"The juice is for Rena. I think it's making her feel grown up." He smiled. "Actually, she is grown up. Or growing up. I'm a little scared," he tacked on with a rueful chuckle.

Cindy walked around him to toss the soiled paper into the nearest can. "Where are the boys tonight?"

"With Jillian's mom. It'll be a night of Christmas movies and excess, I'm sure."

"That's always fun." Cindy came to stand beside him. For a few seconds, they observed the hall, its décor, the people, in silence.

"You've done the past honor," Dan said. "You, and Jas."

"And all of you," she reminded him quietly.

"Yeah, well, there's a difference between discounted print jobs and all of this." He tilted his chin toward the gathering. Turning his head to look at Cindy again, he gazed at her for a rather long moment, a crooked smile on his face. Cindy gazed back, her breath caught in her lungs. She cleared her throat.

"Dan, I—"

"I better get back," he interrupted. "Rena will decide I've run away."

Cindy nodded in agreement, watched him weave his way through the crowd and back to the table he shared with his family and his more-than friend. Glancing back toward her own table, she spotted Brad on his feet, clearly searching for someone. She figured she knew who the someone might be and continued to the women's bathroom.

When she came out, the band was telling the crowd they'd be playing two holiday favorites, followed by the last dance of the night, *My Favorite Things*, a song in three-quarter time to ease the event to its close. Cindy looked forward to watching Dan and his daughter dance the waltz together. In the meantime, she kept her distance from the dancefloor, performing a last-minute check with the venue's manager to make sure everything was in good order for the evening's conclusion.

Harry and Jas moved together onto the dance floor, along with many other couples. Cindy ducked away from Brad's searching eyes. Gina, who had come by herself, walked boldly up to him and asked him to join her on the floor. He hesitated only a moment before consenting. Seeing everyone enjoying themselves touched Cindy's heart in ways she hadn't anticipated. She watched them through the song's entirety. When the band slipped straight into *So This is Christmas*, the parties stopped dancing and the room broke into impromptu song. Cindy wouldn't have thought so many knew the words. She sang, too, tears in her eyes, not caring if she looked like an idiot crying on this special night.

"And now," said the band leader, "for the last song of the evening, folks. Those of you who have been waiting for a waltz, your time has come. Let's go. Fill the dance floor. There's plenty of room."

Cindy looked for Dan and Rena. She located them by their table. Rather than heading to join the others, they seemed to be having a rather intense discussion. Finally, Rena took Dan's hand and tugged him away from the table. Not to where everyone awaited the first strains, but around them all. Straight toward Cindy.

Oh goodness, Cindy thought, had something happened to Rena's dress? She glanced down at the girl's hem, thinking it might have come loose and Rena was afraid she'd trip over it. Seeing nothing amiss, Cindy raised her gaze. Closer now, Rena smiled at her, lifting something she held in her hand.

"Here you go." Rena handed Cindy the shoes Cindy had kicked off earlier. "Dad really wants to dance this one with you. He just won't admit it."

With that, Rena raced on her own bare toes back across the room. Cindy stared at Dan.

"She's not wrong," Dan said. "I do." Reaching up, he tucked Cindy's hair behind her ear. A very intimate gesture for a man with a significant other. Cindy took a small, sliding step backward.

"But what about Grace?"

Dan's brow wrinkled in confusion. "Grace?"

"If not Rena, wouldn't you rather be dancing with her?"

"Just because she taught me how to waltz?"

"No. Because she's your girlfriend or whatever."

Dan's face went blank, and then he laughed, sounding more relieved than amused. "Cindy," he said, "Grace is Jillian's sister. The guy with the somewhat shiny head standing right by her over there is Grace's husband. So, my ex-sister-in-law." He tipped his head to one side. "Okay?"

Wordlessly, Cindy nodded.

"While we're at it, I learned through Harry that Brad is not your boyfriend."

Cindy shook her head, her lips compressing. Dan took her shoes from her hand. He dropped down on one knee. Lifting first one foot, then the other, he slipped the shoes onto her feet and rose.

"Perfect fit, Cinderella," he said softly.

He held up his arms. Cindy stepped into them.

One curved warm around her waist, the other lifted her hand, fingers lightly holding hers.

"One, two, three, one, two, three," he whispered, and together they swept out onto the dancefloor as the waltz began.

Chapter Twenty-Three

Cindy rolled over in bed. She stretched, angled her head to look up through the slats on the window blinds. Snow flurries drifted in the air outside, light and sparkling in the risen sun.

"Merry Christmas, Shakespeare," she said. The cat barely lifted his eyelids in response. Cindy settled back down into her pillow, pulled the comforter up around her shoulders. She wriggled her toes beneath the sheet, smiling sleepily at…well, nothing and everything.

In the living room, the tree lights twinkled. She always kept them on overnight Christmas Eve. It was tradition. A tradition which, really, she'd inherited from her mother. Mom had always insisted the lights stay on, despite Dad's complaints about wasting electric.

Beyond the tree, the ribbons strung above the doorway held Christmas cards and a few birthday cards. She'd spent her fortieth as planned: popcorn, movies, Shakespeare, and a blanket. And on her phone for quite a bit. Let no one say she couldn't be flexible with the unexpected.

Outside, the church bells started their brief, Christmas refrain, followed by seven bells for the hour. Cindy had spent part of the prior evening with Jas and Harry. Later today, she'd be with her family. Everyone had their plans, their visits, their rituals.

Cindy's phone sounded its double-bell text tone.

Are you awake?

I am, Cindy texted back.

It's snowing.

Cindy smiled. *I see that.*

Walk?

Pushing back the covers, Cindy threw her legs out into the slightly chilly air and answered: *What? No running?*

Not today.

A walk sounds perfect, Cindy answered, already searching for warm and comfortable clothes to wear. Shakespeare observed through narrowed eyes, looking oddly pleased with himself.

I'll bring breakfast in a bag, Dan said. *See you shortly.*

Breakfast in a bag. Could be interesting. A walk with Dan? A lot more interesting.

Already dressed in her coat, hat, and mittens, Cindy fed Shakespeare with one eye to the window and the alley below. Spotting Dan, she shoved her phone and keys into her pocket and hurried outside.

"Merry Christmas!" she called as she trotted carefully down the stairs to his side.

"Merry Christmas," he said, his mouth widening into a grin. He handed her a bag. "You like bagels, right? I toasted them myself."

She peered inside. "Love bagels. Oh! And coffee! Where'd you get it?"

"That, I made," he said. "I wash out my to-go cups sometimes, so I can use them again. They last through a few refills. Kinda silly, huh."

Cindy took a deep swig from the cup. "Not at all. Where are we walking?"

"The park?"

"The park it is," Cindy answered, feeling exceptionally cheery.

Performing an about-face, they headed through the lightly falling snow back in the direction Dan had come. "You know what Rena told me on the phone last night?" Dan asked.

Cindy glanced at him with a smile. "A twelve-year-old? Could be anything."

"She said she'd never forget the Garland Ball."

I'm not sure I will either, Cindy thought. "Aww," she said instead. "Rena is such a sweetheart. But dressing up, dancing until midnight, what's not to remember? I bet it felt sort of magical to her."

Dan drank from his cup before saying quietly, "It felt sort of magical to me, too."

Cindy inhaled, her stomach churning in a not unpleasant way. She wasn't sure if he was thinking of her, or the time with his daughter. Either one felt right and good.

She opted for the latter when she answered. "I'm sure. A special night with your daughter before she gets too old to want you around. Sorry," Cindy added with a laugh. "Just speaking from experience. It'll change back the other way, though, after a certain stage."

He grunted, lips twisting, possibly to keep from laughing himself.

The alley ended at the park fence. They both climbed over, balancing half-empty coffee cups, their bags in their teeth to leave them a free hand.

"I really enjoyed the waltz," Dan said as they made their way through lower undergrowth to the path.

Cindy's cheeks heated in the cold air. She ducked her head. "So did I."

"Rena picks up on more than I think she does, sometimes."

Cindy's blush deepened. "Well, she's female, and she's twelve."

Dan grunted again. He turned right on the pathway. Cindy fell in beside him. Snow dusted the gravel beneath their feet in glimmering white and silver. Dan jerked his chin to the curve ahead. "Let's go to the gazebo. We can sit there and eat."

The gazebo had been built the prior year and had housed the carolers this holiday season. When they reached it, the open building was empty. Crisp snow coated the wooden seats inside. Cindy brushed a space off with her mittens and they took up positions more than a foot apart, setting the food down between them. Due to the angle in which they sat, their knees almost touched. Cindy glanced from her booted foot to Dan's. She told herself she ought to move a little away. She didn't. Instead, she moved her foot closer until it lightly contacted his.

"I'm glad the Garland Ball brought us closer together again," Dan said as he ripped into his bagel.

Cindy nodded silently. Beside her, he chewed and swallowed and lifted his head to gaze at the gazebo's rafters.

"It means a lot to me, having you in my life," he said.

Cindy bit her lip, nodded. "Me, too. Having you in mine," she added.

"Do you remember years ago when we decided we should 'make out'?" he asked. "It was an oddly conscious decision, as I recall, and didn't go too well."

Cindy nearly choked on the small section she'd torn off from her bagel and shoved into her mouth. "Behind the shed in my backyard? Yes," she mumbled after swallowing, "I had no idea what I was doing."

"Neither did I." He chuckled. "No idea."

"That was such a long time ago," she said.

"It was cold out. Might have been a holiday gathering. Our parents were inside, none the wiser about the fools we were making of ourselves outside."

Cindy laughed. "It was around Christmas. I remember the lights on the porch."

"You're right," he said, with a slow, abbreviated nod. "I remember them, too."

Cindy waited, suddenly breathless. The bag with her bagel remained on the bench between them, covering slowly with sprinkling snow.

Dan moved and abruptly slipped to one knee on the wooden floor as he had the night before. He took her hand. Cindy gaped at him, not sure what to expect. Certainly, not what the position usually implied. Last night, he'd used it to put on her shoes. She was wearing boots now, so it couldn't be that. She watched him, a trifle concerned.

"Cinderella," he said, with mock solemnity, "I'm no Prince Charming, but I've been wondering since the ball…"

Cindy fought down a laugh, even though the face he was making seemed designed to bring one on. "Yes?"

Squeezing her fingers, he kissed them, a small pressure from his warm lips. "Cinderella," he repeated, "would you like to give the 'making out' another try?"

They both burst out laughing. Cindy threw her arms around his neck. "You bet I would, Dan Hayes," she said, and kissed him with all the passion she'd acquired since that one time long ago. When they finally stopped for air, he leaned his forehead against hers.

"I think that was pretty perfect," he whispered.

So did she. "Still," she said anyway, "we might try it again, just to be sure?"

Dan blinked icy flakes from his lashes. "As frequently as your heart desires. I plan to always be there, if you'll let me."

Cindy kissed him again, lightly, smiling against his mouth. "Ditto," she said. "And no glass slipper required."

∽∽∽∽∽∽∽∽∽∽∽∽∽∽

More books in the
Connor Falls Christmas Series

Each novel and novella in the series is a standalone story, connected by a fictional small town called Connor Falls and the holiday season. They are stories filled with family relationships, friendships lost and found, loves old and new, and, of course, seasonal magic. There's no need to read the stories in order. New characters will intermingle with characters from other books, and no spoilers, I promise. Here's hoping you enjoy meeting them all.

Book One – *Hurry Home for Christmas*

Book Two – *I Knew in a Moment*

Book Three – *The Garland Ball*

When the Heart Brings You Home
A collection of three heartwarming novellas, which are also available separately in special print editions.

About The Author

Ms. Maderich is an author and artist who has been writing since she was seven years old, with her first published book, *Faith and Honor*, released by Warner Books in 1989. Since then, she has written romance (historical, contemporary, paranormal) for Kensington and various small press under several pen names. The publishing rights to *Once & Always* (historical romance as Alyssa Deane) were sold by Kensington to various publishers in other parts of the world, and the book was enjoyed in translation in Russia, France, Germany, and other countries.

Following her heart, the author's Connor Falls Christmas series is rich in themes that touch us all—family ties, friendship, love—and abounds with holiday texture in a smalltown setting.

She has also debuted her dark fantasy, young adult/crossover Shadow Journey series as Jo Allen Ash.

To learn more about her, please visit:

https://robinmaderich.blog
https://www.youtube.com/@robinmaderich6745
https://connorfallschristmas.wordpress.com
https://joallenash.com